STOLEN FAITH

'Read this book and cry and never forget.'

Anna Corrigan, Tuam victim and justice campaigner

D1407185

James McVeigh is a trade union activist from Belfast. He was born just off the Falls Road, where the story of *Stolen Faith* begins. Upon leaving school, he started studying to be an engineer, but after the hunger strikes and the death of Bobby Sands, he became involved in the conflict. He served sixteen years in prison before being released as part of the Good Friday Agreement. While in prison, James studied for a history degree, and when released, he went to Queens University and achieved a Masters in Human Rights. He has written two history books, *Executed* and *Goodbye Dearest Heart*, and this is his first novel.

As a young child, James stayed in Tuam as part of a church-organised break from the civil conflict in Belfast. When he returned decades later, he stumbled across the Tuam shrine and began to learn the tragic story of the mother and baby home and its secret burial chamber, a septic tank. This book is a tribute to all the women and children who died in or survived these terrible institutions.

A FORBIDDEN LOVE, A STOLEN CHILD,
A DIVIDED FAMILY

STOLEN
FAITH

A NOVEL

INSPIRED BY TRUE EVENTS

James McVeigh

First published 2022 by Brandon
An imprint of The O'Brien Press Ltd.
12 Terenure Road East, Rathgar, Dublin 6, D06 HD27, Ireland.
Tel: +353 1 4923333 Fax: +353 1 4922777
Email: books@obrien.ie
Website: obrien.ie
The O'Brien Press is a member of Publishing Ireland.

ISBN 978-1-78849-294-2

Printed in the UK by Clays Ltd, Elcograf S.p.A.
The paper in this book is produced using pulp from managed forests.

DISCLAIMER
This is a work of fiction. While drawing on the historical events of the Tuam mother and baby home and the Boston clerical abuse scandals, names, characters, businesses, places, events and incidents are either the products of the author's imagination or used in a fictitious manner. Any resemblance to actual persons, living or dead, or actual events is purely coincidental.

Published in

Dedication

This book is dedicated to my mother, Rosaleen.

'Tá grá agam duit.'

Disclaimer

CONTENTS

Acknowledgements

I would like to thank a number of people who helped bring this story to publication. First and foremost, I would like to thank Michael O'Brien and The O'Brien Press for believing in this story from day one. My friend and comrade Gerry A for his encouragement and inspiration. That wonderful actress Geraldine Hughes, who loved the book and invited me into her artistic world. Trisha Ziff for her support and encouragement. Jo Spain for her sage advice. My family for listening to me and my many ideas and plot lines. Tess Tattersall, my editor, for her invaluable guidance, Emma Byrne for her powerful cover design, and Nicola Reddy for her help in getting the book over the finish line.

And especially two wonderful women, Joan McDermott and Anna Corrigan, for their support and their contributions at the end of this book. I, like them, hope that this novel reminds us all that every single woman or child who survived or perished in these horrible institutions was a real person, who was loved. The victims and survivors deserve the truth and that the world know that truth.

Come away, O human child!

To the waters and the wild

With a faery, hand in hand,

For the world's more full of weeping than you can understand.

'The Stolen Child'

William Butler Yeats

PROLOGUE

The body was pale white, almost translucent. It was as if her skin was drawn tight, stretched against her slight skeletal frame. As one nun washed the blood from her cold naked skin with a wet rag, another stood watching, inspecting and waiting.

The bloodstained water gathered in the shallows of her emaciated body and then spilled from the metal trolley onto the floor, forming large pools. The floor resembled that of an abattoir. It was as if the young woman had been drained of every drop of blood.

The watching nun stood with her hands behind her back, rigid. She looked at the gruesome scene before her, dispassionately, calmly, like a butcher appraising the carcass before he makes the first cut. Having washed the body, the other nun dried her and lifted her easily from the trolley and placed her on a white bed sheet that was draped over a large table in the middle of the room.

At just five foot and five inches in height, she weighed hardly more than a small child. She had clearly starved or been starved. As she was placed on the sheet, her long raven black hair spread out behind her head, silhouetting her chalk-white face.

It was the face of a beautiful young woman. No, it was the face of a young woman who had once been very beautiful, not even death could disguise that. She was eighteen years of age. She stared at the ceiling above her through still green eyes and long dark lashes. Her high cheekbones protruded in her gaunt face.

The skin around her waist lay stretched and partly folded against her pubic bone. There were signs of stretchmarks across her stomach and hips. Her stomach appeared to be distended.

The two nuns now wrapped the body tightly in the white bed sheet and secured it with two lengths of baling twine. One nun then lifted her from the table, while the other lit an oil lamp. The nun with the lamp led the way followed by the other carrying the body. The scene resembled a macabre little funeral procession. The building was quiet, except that in the distance the faint cries of several children could be heard. The lamplight threw ghostly flickering shadows along the walls of the deserted corridor. They exited through a door onto open ground at the back of the building. The oil lamp gave them just enough light to navigate their way across the field to a secluded part of the grounds.

When they reached the corner of the large perimeter wall, the nun carrying the lamp swept loose leaves and grass from a square metal door beneath her foot. The area was an abandoned space, covered in high grass, brambles and wildflowers. The nun had navigated a small trodden path to the door. She had been here many times before. She removed a large key from her pocket, knelt and unlocked a heavy padlock that held the trap door secure and lifted the lid to expose a gaping hole that appeared blacker than coal.

Without a word the other nun leaned over the hole and dropped the small body into the darkness below. A second later there was a gentle thud and the sound of rats scurrying away. No prayers were said. There was only silence as the door was closed and locked once again. Before they left, one of the nuns kicked leaves and grass back across the metal door.

Elsewhere in the building a baby lay swaddled in a cot. She had a head of thick black hair and huge round dark eyes. Her features were very fine and symmetrical, and her skin was blemish free like a delicately painted porcelain doll. She was a very beautiful child. The image of her mother. It was obvious she was only a few hours old.

At a nearby table an elderly nun dipped the nib of a pen into a little inkwell and began to fill out death certificates for a young woman and a baby. She recorded the baby's name as Faith, the mother as recently deceased and the father unknown. She set the two death certificates to the side, dipped the nib of her pen into the ink again and began writing a new birth certificate.

CHAPTER 1

BELFAST, 1944

James McCann leaned out over the bow of the ship. So, this is where the doomed *Titanic* was built, Belfast, Ireland? A year ago, he had only heard of the country, imagined it, the land of his grandparents. A mystical green island full of comely *cailíní*, rebels, windswept mountains and mischievous fairies or 'little people', as his grandfather would call them. Now he was about to disembark here along with two thousand other US marines.

The scene before him looked very different. Industrial chimneys belched black smoke into the sky, huge coal stacks were being deposited from ships moored nearby, and dozens of khaki-painted trucks lined the harbour. Dockers, hard-looking men, shouted instructions to the crew as the ship, the *Angelique*, slowly edged closer to the grey concrete shore.

Their accents were very different to the softer Cork lilt of his grandfather and grandmother. They sounded deeper, harder somehow. A get-to-the-point type of accent. He recognised these faces, if not the accents. These were the same faces he saw down in Boston Port, his home city, and Charlestown Navy Yard, where he had worked before joining up and shipping out. Tough faces.

James could see thick ropes being thrown ashore as the *Angelique* pressed against a line of massive rubber tractor tyres strung along the side of the dock. Within minutes the ship had settled into a calm resting state and two large exit ramps were swung into position along her starboard side.

James's platoon was going to be one of the first to disembark. Their com-

pany sergeant yelled at the top of his lungs, "'A" COMPANY, MOOOOVE!'
The inevitable swear words that accompanied almost everything that Sergeant Lynch said were lost in a loud chorus of 'Yes, Sarge' that rolled along the side of the whole ship like a wave, as dozens of companies and hundreds of marines began to line up to leave.

The journey to the barracks was mercifully quick. The trucks raced through streets just awakening. Canvas covered the trucks as a downpour of rain lashed them and then suddenly stopped. James and everyone else strained to catch a glimpse of the city that would be their home for the next few weeks, or months maybe, who knew? This was the invasion of Europe for sure. Only the President and the generals knew where and when.

The streets were uniform rows of tiny red-brick houses with grey slate roofs. As the night began to lift, thin shafts of light appeared along the edges of some of the little square windows. Blackout curtains or old, black-painted newspapers curled away at the edges to release slivers of light. Smoke began to rise from numerous chimneys, a few at first and then dozens and when the trucks climbed towards the hills outside the city, they could see grey swirls rise in long lines above the streets. Not one apartment block or skyscraper. Now it was he who was landing in a strange new world.

Men hurried along the damp streets, collars up, cloth caps pulled down low across their faces and what seemed like thousands of women, thick high-heeled shoes and the hems of skirts showing below heavy coats and scarfs the only giveaway. Some of the guys closest to the back of the truck started shouting, 'Hey ladies?' 'Hey honey?' Others whistled.

They were not used to seeing so many women in one place at one time.

After months of isolated basic training and a long claustrophobic journey across the Atlantic, excitement filled the truck. For a second, they were no longer soldiers en route to battle but young men, boys on a college football trip, at a big baseball game or a rare day out to the fair. The smell of pretty girls and popcorn, of hot dogs and beer. James was swept up in the excitement.

* * *

It was a week before they were allowed off base and were able to explore Belfast. It was May, and the sun came out. Flowers bloomed and trees blossomed along the avenues and streets. They put a smile on the face of the city. James stood, hands in pockets, facing the grand, ornate City Hall. The huge central dome capped what looked to him like a white Italian palace. It was imposing – he was impressed.

Scaffolding climbed up one side of the building. The signs of a direct hit by the German Luftwaffe three years earlier were visible in the shrapnel that had perforated its façade. She was elegant still, but she now looked as if she had a bad case of acne.

Groups of office workers sat together on the front lawn of City Hall, eating lunch, chatting, laughing and flirting. The war seemed a million miles away. James had left the rest of the guys in a nearby hotel having tea and sandwiches with some local girls who worked on the base. He had decided to take his camera and explore the city. He hopped on a random tram, paid his fair and decided to go wherever it might take him.

On the tram he was met with smiles and nods. By now almost 120,000 GIs had passed through Belfast en route to some front or other. First North Africa and now probably France. The US Navy regularly docked in

Belfast and around the northwest coast, particularly in Derry City. The US Air Force flew regular sorties out across the Atlantic providing cover for convoys of troops and war material that travelled back and forth between the ports of New York and Boston and Britain. Thousands of US service-men had made Ireland and Belfast their temporary home for several years now.

The tram conductor chatted away, asked him where he was going. James explained, nowhere in particular, just somewhere, and they both laughed. The conductor winked conspiratorially and tapped his nose.

'A girl?' he asked and then quickly answered his own question. 'Say no more, young fella!'

James decided to jump off as they passed a pretty park. It was a good place to start his adventure. The conductor shook his hand, wished him well and told him that he would be on that route all day.

'Come back here later and we'll get you home to base safe and sound, son!'

The park was busy, like any park in any part of the world on a warm spring day. He could have been back in Charlestown, only the accents were different.

'Hey mister, got any gum?'

'Hey mister, got any chocolate?'

Kids swarmed around him, excited to see this exotic Yank in uniform. He reached into his pocket for the pack of gum.

'Right, guys, ready?'

Before tossing the open pack into the little crowd of boys and girls, he quickly made his escape out of the park before they decided to follow him hoping for more.

The road was busy. Another tram passed the park. He took a photo as it stopped to collect passengers and allowed others to get off. Busy little shops fronting Victorian two-storey houses lined the road: a grocery store, then what looked like a hardware store with the sign 'Hector's', above. Further along there was a butcher's, then a pharmacy, or chemist, as they called them here. Then a bar, always a bar. This one was called the Rock Bar. Further on down the road was another, this one called the Beehive. Great names.

Further on he stopped for a smoke. He leaned against the wall of what looked like a convent. He peered in through the ornate front gates to a small courtyard, where he read above the double doors 'The Little Church of Adoration to Our Lady'. Two nuns exited and passed him without greeting. They had stern middle-aged faces that seemed to give him a disapproving look as they went by. His 'Good morning, Sisters' was met with silence and suspicion.

He sat on a bench in the shade of the convent. He was lifting his camera to take a photo when he saw her. She was sitting on an upturned crate outside a store. The sign above the door read 'Seamus Rafferty's Hardware Shop'. She was beautiful, he could see that, even from this distance. She hadn't noticed him from the other side of the road. He took several photos of her as she talked unselfconsciously to another girl fixing odds and ends in crates outside the store. Their laughter carried across the road. She smiled and he caught his breath. Her smile was dazzling, even from where he sat. She laughed a loud deep infectious laugh at whatever had been said.

He studied her for minutes. She had long, jet-black hair parted in the middle. She did not wear it in the formal style of the day. It was loose, occasionally blowing across her face. There was a quality about her. He did not know how to describe her. She had a freedom about her, a something, a *je ne sais quoi*, as the French would say. Thick dark eyebrows and long lashes shaded green eyes, cat's eyes, a straight nose that sat between high cheekbones and above lush red lips. She did not look Irish, at least not in the popular understanding. She looked more like one of those Puerto Rican girls that went to nearby St Ann's back home.

He sat for another few minutes watching her and then decided, *What the hell, I'm going to go over and just say hello.* He walked across the road towards her. He was only a few yards away when she turned and looked straight at him.

He said, 'Hi,' and she smiled. He stumbled as he stepped up onto the sidewalk.

She laughed. 'You OK, soldier?'

His face reddened as he cursed to himself, *Shit.* He replied, 'Fine, Miss, thank you!' He said, 'Hi,' to the other girl, who looked a little older.

'You lost, soldier?' said the older girl.

'No, Mam, just exploring the city and taking some photographs.' He stepped forward and offered his hand. 'Private James McCann, US Marine Corps at your service, Mam.'

She looked at his hand, reluctantly shook it and muttered a 'Huh'.

He turned to the girl sitting, who stood up and held out her hand.

'Hello Private McCann, my name's Rose, Rose Rafferty.'

Her grip was firm, strong and she looked him straight in the eye.

'This is my big sister, Madge.'

With a mischievous smile on her face Rose curtsied slightly and Madge burst out laughing and shook her head.

'You're a terrible flirt. Stop it, Rose. Da will see us and we'll get in trouble.'

James blurted out nervously, 'I'm Irish!'

This time Rose burst out laughing and said, 'You don't sound Irish, Private, you sound A-mer-i-can,' in a very convincing East Coast accent. Both the girls laughed again.

James went even redder. 'I mean, my grandparents are Irish, from Cork.'

Madge straightened her dress and said, 'Rose, we've work to do, inside? Good day to you, Private!'

Rose smiled a broad warm smile and said, 'Bye, James, take care of yourself over there!'

Both disappeared inside the store. Never expecting to see him again.

* * *

The next few days James couldn't stop thinking and even dreaming about Rose Rafferty. He was counting the minutes, the hours, until his next furlough. He spoke to Captain Walsh, the photographer who was attached to the company, and asked him if he would develop his film. The next day he handed James the photographs and laughed.

'I can see why you wanted these ones developed. Quite a find, James. She's a gorgeous girl.'

James headed straight back to his company hut and his bunk. He took the photos out and quickly discarded every one except those of Rose. He pinned his favourite photo of her to the bottom of the bunk above him, put his hands behind his head and just stared. The rest of the guys drifted in a few at a time. There was the usual ruckus, some guys trying to wind others up, jokes, some funny, others hurtful. A bout of wrestling broke out in one corner of the hut that soon turned nasty.

Just as it was getting out of hand Sergeant Lynch slammed the door to the hut open and shouted at the top of his lungs, 'LIGHTS OUT, GIRLS! DE AUGUSTINO, MCEVOY, YOU BETTER BREAK IT UP AND GET INTO THOSE BUNKS, NOW!'

Within minutes everyone, including the wrestlers, had stripped down to their boxers and vests and got into their bunks. James stared at the photograph of Rose until the hut was plunged into blackness. He drifted off to sleep with her the very last thought on his mind.

Furlough finally arrived and James took the same tram that travelled past Rose's father's store. There was no sign of her outside as he passed, but when he got off a block ahead and started back towards the store she appeared. She carried a metal bucket in one hand and a brush in the other. Her hair was drawn into a ponytail and piled haphazardly on top of her head. Two or three loose strands hung down either side of her face, framing it. Even slightly dishevelled, wearing a plain white blouse and a wrinkled skirt, she still looked stunning. 'A real knockout gal' his dad would say.

'Hi Rose, remember me?'

She looked up and smiled. 'Well, Private McCann! Still with us, I see.'

She seemed pleased to see him and she had remembered his name – he was delighted.

'You're staying with us a little while longer then, Private?'

'Please, call me James, Rose? Yeah, I think we will be here for another few weeks at least. Maybe months. Sergeant Lynch says it will take a hell of a lot more ships to get us all to France.'

'OK, James McCann, what has you back in these parts? I see you've no camera with you this time!'

James reddened and said hesitantly, 'Do you mind that I came to see you again? Would you like to go on a date, Rose?'

Rose stopped her work. She leaned upon the brush, looked James straight in the eye and said, 'Hmm, is that so?'

Rose had had no shortage of potential suitors, both local lads as well as English and American servicemen. She knew they found her attractive – some had even called her beautiful, though she often laughed at the thought. She was just herself, Rose Rafferty. She didn't care what boys thought of her, or what anyone else thought for that matter. She had a mind of her own, her own thoughts and opinions. She didn't need anyone else to tell her what they were or what they should be.

Father Dillon, the parish priest, and Sister Celestine, who ran St Comgall's, her old school, had often chastised her, and occasionally punished her, for what they called her 'wilfulness'. To this day Father Dillon would cast her disapproving looks when she attended mass in nearby St Paul's. There were other times when she could feel his eyes on her, looking her up and down from head to toe, lingering on her chest. He made her skin crawl. When she did catch him staring at her, she would stare right back, until he would glance away in a mixture of embarrassment and obvious anger. She could just imagine him complaining to the sisters about 'that brazen little hussy, Rose Rafferty'. The thought always made her smile.

She looked into James's blue eyes and saw what she was sure was kindness there. He seemed shy and polite, not cocky or loud like some of the Yanks. He was neither in awe of her nor exhibited any sense of entitlement. He seemed genuinely humble. He was also quite handsome. She noticed for the first time, as she now examined his face, that he had a slightly crooked nose, broken probably. She decided it was cute. She liked this face. She would give this one a chance.

'OK, James, I'll meet you at the front of City Hall tomorrow at 12 noon. Does that suit you?'

'Yeah, of course, Rose.'

'Shoo, then, I've work to do.' She laughed before looking over her shoulder back into the store. 'B'fore m'Da sees us talking.'

The next few days and weeks flew by. They met every day James was off base and travelled to the north side of the city, away from 'prying eyes and nosey noses', as Rose would explain. One day, one moment that day, she reached out and took his hand. To her own amazement, it felt like the most natural thing in the world to do.

She fell in love first with his gentleness, with the way he looked at her. She would catch him smiling at her for no reason and he would simply shrug his shoulders, smile, a little embarrassed and say, 'I like the way you look; I like to look at your face, your smile. So, sue me!' She would laugh.

Then she fell in love with the way he talked about his family, the stories he would tell her about each of them. The love and respect he had for them showed on his face and in the words he used when he spoke about them. There was a tenderness in the way he expressed himself. She envied that closeness.

At home her father and her older brother, Frank, barked orders, gave instructions. Her father was a strict disciplinarian. Children were to be seen and not heard, especially girls. Daughters were to be strictly chaperoned and their virginity closely guarded until marriage. He seemed to her to be a hard and unyielding man. Her mother, Bernadette, was the opposite. She was a soft and kindly soul, who spent her time keeping the peace between father and daughter.

One afternoon, Rose and James sat on the grass at the zoo having lunch and he was telling her something about the other guys in his platoon. She looked across at his face and could see the depth of love there, even in his expression.

This boy is going to war, and is willing to die for his friends, and probably will. The thought terrified her. She suddenly realised, I'm falling in love with him.

She leaned over close to his face, gently held him in her two hands and kissed him tenderly. He drew back in surprise, but then kissed her in return.

* * *

Things back at base were getting busier. More ships and trucks were arriving each day with more troops. The number of troop ships in the harbour had almost doubled since James's arrival. Speculation, rumour and gossip about shipping out was rife. One thing they all agreed upon was that it was very close, probably days rather than weeks.

There was a big band dance night in the Floral Hall up beside the zoo on Saturday. All the guys were going and bringing their girlfriends, or at least those who had one. James asked Rose would she go and she said yes, and she would get Madge to come with her. There was a *céilí* that night in St Mary's Hall. They would tell her father they were going there. Father Dillon frequently attended the *céilí* to supervise and to make sure there was no inappropriate behaviour or contact between the boys and girls. They would be allowed to go if he believed Father Dillon would be there.

It was a glorious summer night. Two or three hundred boys, many of them in smart US uniforms, and girls wearing their finest dresses stretched back from the entrance to the Floral Hall. The brilliant white hall nestled among green trees and lush vegetation like a pearl. The long queue wrapped itself around the circular Art Deco building like a colourful sweet-scented garland. As James and his friends waited to get into the dance hall, it was impossible to see very far back or forward in the line. He could not make out any sign of Rose or Madge.

Eventually they reached the entrance and paid for their tickets. Once inside, their group dashed to secure themselves tables and chairs close to the dance floor and then staked their claim. No one would move until the hall was full and then only a few at a time. Standing groups would frequently occupy someone else's tables and chairs and occasionally a brawl would break out.

James stood anxiously watching the entrance for Rose. As the minutes passed, he became more and more worried that she might not turn up. He scanned the room, turning a full 360 degrees, thinking to himself, *Maybe I missed her coming in?* As he swung his attention back to the entrance, he stopped in his tracks. She stood there looking intently towards him. She was stunning. He almost ran around the hall to reach her and swept her up in his arms. They held each other in a tight grip and looked into each other's eyes. Everyone else disappeared as they kissed. It was Madge's voice that finally broke the spell.

'Rose, Rose, Jesus, stop that! Someone might know us here?!'

'Ah, for Christ's sake, Madge, would you calm down! No one will know us here; the place is full of Protestants. Let's sit down.'

James took Rose's hand and led her and Madge to their table, where he had closely guarded two seats for them.

'James, will you get me and Madge a drink? Two gins and tonics please!' She handed him a one-pound note and when James refused to take the money, she said firmly, 'I insist, James!'

'Jesus, Holy Mary and Joseph, Rose, you're going to get us both slaughtered when we get home,' said Madge.

Rose just laughed and smiled that smile back at her and said, 'Wise up, Madge. Let's enjoy ourselves. Tomorrow might never come.'

James and Rose danced most of the night and when they were not dancing, they held hands and talked and talked. Rose was a woman with ideas and James loved that.

'You know we make a great couple, James?'

He leaned closer, took her two hands in his and said, 'I love you, Rose Rafferty. If I survive this war, will you marry me and come home with me to Boston?'

'Yes, I will, James, in a heartbeat!' she replied, and then she hugged him until his bones cracked.

They talked and laughed and made crazy plans. He described Boston to her, the tall buildings and apartment blocks. The beautiful triple-deck houses with their open verandas. The game of baseball and the Red Sox. She told him she wanted to work, to earn her own money. He asked her what she wanted to do. Rose laughed and exclaimed, 'Anything, everything. What about movie star!'

At the end of the evening the crowd spilled out of the Floral Hall. They were greeted by a huge moon in the sky. Rose kicked her shoes off one by one and ran to the top of the hill. She pointed to the moon that sat on the horizon behind her, balanced it on the end of her finger and shouted, 'Come on, James. It's our moon tonight!'

Madge shouted, 'Rose, where are you going? We have to be getting home?'

As James ran up the hill after her, Rose shouted back, 'Tell Mum I'll be home soon.'

He followed her and they both disappeared into the trees.

She led him deeper into the trees until they found a clearing. James took off his jacket and laid it on the ground for them to sit on. They sat together in silence for a minute or two. Belfast Lough lay before them illuminated by the red moon.

'Do you know, Rose, that some Native American tribes called this moon the Rose moon? This is your moon, Rose!'

Her smile seemed to brighten the space between them. The moon was huge. Its reflection ran across the lough and lit up the whole mountain behind them.

'It's beautiful, isn't it?' said Rose.

'Beautiful! Did you know that some people say the mountain resembles Napoleon's nose?'

Rose giggled. 'You don't say, James McCann. And how might you know that?'

'Well, Miss Rafferty, you might be surprised at just how much I know about Belfast and Ireland. In fact, it so impressed one famous visitor, a Mr Jonathan Swift, who believed its silhouette resembled a sleeping giant, that it inspired him to write *Gulliver's Travels*.'

'Oh, so you're not just a pretty face, then?' And they both laughed.

Then for a few quiet moments they simply held hands and looked at the glorious moon.

'Some things are just meant to be, James. We are meant to be here together, this night, below this moon. It's a special night, don't you feel it? I can feel it.'

She pushed him onto his back and lay herself on top of him. She clasped his hands in hers, finger by finger, until they were locked and circled them around above his head in the grass. Before kissing him, she looked into his eyes and said, 'Tonight, James, I am yours, mind, body and soul, and you are mine. Forever!'

* * *

The next day all leave was cancelled at base and James's company was told to kit up and get ready to ship out within the next twenty-four to forty-eight hours. No one was getting on or off base unless they had orders to do so. James, along with every other GI who had a girl in town, was told to write her a letter and do it damn quick. He lay on his bunk, pen and paper in hand.

June 4, 1944

My darling Rose,

We are shipping out. I can tell you no more than that. I will not be allowed to see you before I leave. Last night was the most perfect night of my life. I love you with all my heart and all my soul.

If I survive this war, I will come back to Belfast and if you still want me, I will marry you. I'll take you back to Boston and my family will love you as much as I do. Boston is just about big enough for you, my love, and your big ideas, just about! I'm smiling here.

I will do my best to write to you every single day, circumstances permitting. I will post my letters where and when I get the opportunity.

You were always the one who believed, you were always the one who went on feelings, heart, instinct. Well, this time I believe. I believe in you, in us, in our life together.

I believe we met for a reason, and I believe because of you I will survive this war. Every time you see a full moon, especially a Rose moon, think of me, as I will think of you.

Your loving fiancé

James

PS I owe you a ring. x

Within a few hours, the mail was rounded up and the troops, including Private James McCann, were boarding ships on their way to England and France.

A few days later Seamus Rafferty was opening the store when the postman handed him a letter addressed to Rose. He stepped back inside and opened the letter. He went into a rage when he read it and muttered to himself, 'That little whore!'

He would kill her, he thought, as he rushed towards the stairs. Then he stopped. He knew she would simply defy him. He could beat her black and blue and she would still defy him. If she was pregnant and word got out, he would be shamed before the whole world. He would not be able to hold his head up in mass. People would pass the shop by and take their business elsewhere.

He sat down on a chair in the back parlour and stared at last night's embers in the hearth. After a few minutes he stood up and approached the fire. He took the letter from his pocket and tossed it in. The letter smouldered before eventually bursting into flames.

The next morning he waited outside the store to catch the postman. He handed him a twenty-pound note, a considerable sum of money, and said, 'Any letter addressed to our Rose is to be returned to sender, understand?'

'Of course, Mr Rafferty, of course.'

'Good morning to yah.' He tipped his head towards the road as if to say 'On your way' and turned back into the store.

'Good morning, Mr Rafferty,' said the postman, as he scurried away, tucking the twenty-pound note deep into his pocket.

CHAPTER 2

BELFAST, 1944

Rose watched and waited for a letter every day, but none came. Each day she walked to the docks and watched the ships depart, hoping to catch a glimpse of James. She knew there could be any number of reasons why she had not received a letter yet. But she was sure she would. She continued to wait and to hope. She missed her period. She was normally as regular as clockwork. She knew her body well. She was pregnant. *This baby is a blessing*, she said to herself. She did not give a damn what anyone would think or say. James would return from France; they would marry and move to Boston. They would have a fantastic life together. Theirs would be a family and a home full of love.

Weeks passed and still no letter came. The child began to grow inside her and she grew bigger. She began to worry that someone else might notice. When she examined her tummy at night, it appeared huge to her, though rationally she realised it couldn't be, not in such a few short months. She thought she detected a new sullenness about her father. Was she simply imagining things? Whatever the case, she knew she would have to tell her parents sometime, but when?

One week later they were sitting having dinner together in a dining room off the back parlour. Her father stared at her malevolently. At that moment, she knew he knew. It was written across his face. Rose looked straight at him and said, 'I'm having a baby!'

There was a shocked silence before her father sprung to his feet in a rage, tipping the table and its contents everywhere. He lifted his hand to strike her.

'You dare, just you dare!' Rose stood facing him with her fists clenched at her side. 'I swear, I swear to God, if you hurt me or hurt this child, I will kill you. As God is my witness, I will kill you.'

Her mother was pale and shaking as she stepped between the two of them.

'Please, Seamus, please don't hit her. She's having a baby. It's not right, Seamus!'

Her father stood glaring at her for a few moments before he stormed out of the room.

* * *

Seamus grabbed his jacket from the end of the staircase and left. He walked across the road to the public house, stood at the bar and ordered a whiskey. His presence caused some surprise and quite a few of the regulars glanced in his direction and whispered. Seamus Rafferty had long frowned upon alcohol and such establishments. He was a Catholic Pioneer and wore his abstinence pin with pride. In all his years living just across the road, he had never once set foot in there.

'A whiskey, Mr Rafferty,' said the barman and sat the glass on the counter in front of him.

Seamus gulped it down, slammed the glass on the counter and threw a handful of coins beside it before turning and walking out. He strode up the road, brimming with anger, until he came to the parochial house. He rang the bell and waited.

The housekeeper answered the door and in a surprised tone said, 'Why,

Mr Rafferty, is something wrong?'

'I'd like to speak to Father Dillon, if he is at home?'

'He is, indeed, Mr Rafferty. Let me tell him you have called.'

He was led into a sitting room where he was joined by Father Dillon. They shook hands.

'Sit down, Seamus. Are you OK? You seem upset?'

'Father, I'm ashamed to tell you, deeply ashamed, but my youngest daughter Rose is having a baby. A bastard!' He spat the word as if there were a nasty vile taste in his mouth. 'I don't know what to do, Father. What shall I do?'

Father Dillon rose and crossed the room, and he placed his hand on Seamus's shoulder.

'She has shamed you deeply, and she has sinned against God and the Holy Church, but hers is the sin, not yours. We must send her away before she shames you in front of the whole parish.

'The sisters have a mother and baby home in Tuam, Galway. Far away from here. We can send her there to have the child. That way you and your family can avoid any shame, Seamus. No one need know!'

'Yes, Father, of course.'

'Have her ready to travel the day after tomorrow at 8am with her belongings. I will arrange for one of the sisters to travel with her to Tuam.'

As they walked towards the door of the parochial house, Father Dillon stopped, leaned closer and said, 'You know, Seamus, she cannot be allowed to keep the child. It must be put up for adoption. She cannot return here with a bastard, to shame you in front of the whole parish.'

'No, of course not, Father, and I can't thank you enough.'

'We will make sure no one knows about this, Seamus; you have my solemn word on that.'

When Father Dillon returned to his sitting room, he poured himself a glass of Jameson's whiskey and sat in his favourite chair. He looked at the glass, swirled the whiskey and smiled.

The next day Seamus explained the situation to Rose in very blunt terms: she was to pack her bag and leave or be thrown out onto the street with nowhere to go and no money to look after herself and the baby. She was eighteen, with no job – she had worked in the shop all her life – and she had little or no money and nowhere else to turn. She packed her bag.

That evening Father Dillon called to the house along with an elderly nun, Sister Theresa, who would travel with Rose by train the next day, first to Dublin, then to Galway. As he left the house Father Dillon was handed an envelope by Seamus with one hundred pounds inside.

'Thank you, Father, for all your help. It's a small donation to help towards her keep.'

Father Dillon quickly pocketed the money and left.

* * *

Rose had still received no word from James. She was worried, anxious. Had he been wounded? Had he been killed? If he lived, she had no doubt that he would eventually come and find her. That night she wrote a letter to him and left it with Madge in case he arrived back in Belfast searching for her.

Father Dillon had given her a short handwritten note and said, 'Present this to the Mother Superior when you arrive and you will be admitted.' She had opened it and read it.

Children's Home, Tuam, County Galway
Please admit Rose Rafferty, eighteen years of age, of St Paul's parish, Belfast.
She expects to be confined immediately upon arrival.
Signed: Father C. Dillon
St Paul's parish priest, Belfast

Admitted? Imprisoned more like, she thought.

Rose woke early the next morning, washed and dressed. Madge brought her tea and toast in her room. When she had finished, Madge carried her small case down the stairs in front of her in tears. Her mother handed her a packed lunch for the journey and slipped some money into her hand. The three of them hugged and cried. The nun waited quietly.

'Take care, my love, and we will see you soon,' said her mother.

Madge sobbed, 'I'm going to miss you so much, Rose.'

'I'll be grand, don't you worry. I'll be back before you know it and on my way to Boston. Just you wait and see.'

Her father and her older brother were nowhere to be seen. *Da was a cold bastard and Frank was no better*, she thought. She and the nun crossed the road and boarded a tram to the city centre and to Dublin.

They travelled all day and arrived in Tuam late into the night. They were collected at the train station and taken by taxi to the home. The nun accompanying her knocked on a large heavy door. Another nun greeted them warmly and beckoned them in. Rose handed her the note from Father Dillon. Having read the note, the nun led Rose down a long corridor to the mothers' sleeping quarters.

It was a large dormitory with a dozen single beds along both sides of the room. She could see they were occupied but nothing more. She could hear the sound of breathing, of snoring. The room smelled of sweat, damp and disinfectant.

She was shown to her bed. A shaky metal bed with a skinny mattress and thin blankets. The autumn cold was beginning to bite already, and the room felt chilly and damp. There was no sign of a fire, a fireplace or heating of any sort. She undressed quickly and got into bed, hugged her tummy, thought of James and eventually drifted into a restless sleep.

* * *

At 6am they were woken by the nuns. Rose could see other women emerge from below the dark blankets. This would become a daily routine for her and dozens of other girls – there were no exceptions and no excuses accepted. Some of the other young mothers in the dormitory left to look after their babies, who slept elsewhere. Rose was told by a young nun, Sister Bridget, that she should come with her to see the Head Sister. She was chatty, and she lifted Rose's spirits as they walked along. It was a relief to see a friendly face. She hoped there were more like her. Sister Bridget opened the door and informed the Head Sister that Rose Rafferty was here. She winked at Rose as if to say good luck as she left her waiting.

Rose stood there alone for at least ten minutes before hearing a voice within.

'Come in, Miss Rafferty.'

She entered a spacious office. It was spartan and austere, like the woman before her, seated behind a very large, ornate mahogany desk. It was hard to define her exact age. The nuns' black and white habits hid much and made them all seem older than they were. Rose guessed she was in her early fifties. She had thin eyebrows and lips that seemed to be set in a permanent frown. Round tortoiseshell spectacles rested on a sharp nose. She stared unblinking at Rose for what seemed to be ages before speaking.

'My name is Sister Marie; I am the head of the Bon Secours order here in Tuam and the sister in charge of this home. It is very important, Miss Rafferty, that you understand our rules here. They are applied strictly, with no exceptions.' She paused.

'We rise at 6am. You will be expected to assist with the feeding of our children. At 8.30am each day mass is said, which you are expected to attend. Following mass, you will assist with cleaning, laundry duties and cooking or whatever other duties are allocated to you. You will have no idle time. "Idle hands are the Devil's playthings" and we tolerate no Devil's play here.

'You will be sheltered, you will be fed, but we expect you to work hard and to contemplate the grave sin that has brought you here.

'This is not a social club or a place to make friends. During mealtimes and when nursing children we have a strict "no talking" rule. Should you break any of our rules, you will be punished, severely!

'Respect these rules, Miss Rafferty, and be grateful for the generosity and mercy of the Holy Church. You may leave now and prepare for mass.'

Sister Bridget had returned and was waiting outside the office to escort Rose back to the dormitory. Rose was shown the laundry, the kitchen and the nursery wings. She was almost overwhelmed by the strong smell of urine and faeces as she entered the nursery wings. Sister Bridget seemed oblivious or perhaps conditioned to the smells and the noise of the dozens of hysterical children standing in their cots.

Rose was told that after mass each morning she would assist in the laundry, help in the kitchen after lunch and then help with the children in the late afternoon. Sister Bridget also explained that everyone was expected to take turns helping with night feeds on a regular and rotating basis. Rose was immediately set to work and work she did.

After only a few days, she was exhausted. The food was horrible, often cold, always bland and completely lacking in any sustenance. In the first week alone, she lost several pounds in weight. The mothers wore a harassed and weary look on their faces and all of them were themselves pale and thin. This was hell, not a home.

The worst was yet to come. She learned that there were 271 children staying in the home and only sixty-one mothers to take care of them. Over two hundred of the children were very small, from newborn babies to toddlers, squeezed into several rooms in two large wings. The children were neglected, malnourished and, in many cases, skeletal figures with sunken eyes and cheeks.

The place was absolute bedlam. Even with the best will in the world, it was impossible to give the number of children there the care they needed. Fresh clothes, nappies and bed sheets were in short supply. Many children were left to lie or stand in urine-soaked clothes and bedding and dirty nappies for days on end. It was a scene of horror. Diet was poor, conditions were unhygienic, and disease was rampant.

Rose tried to do everything that she could for the poor children, but there were just too few women to change every child, to wash every child, to feed every child, to nurse every crying child. Some of the sisters were kind and compassionate women who did their very best, like Sister Bridget. But there were others who were cold and indifferent to the suffering surrounding them. One nun seemed to take a perverse pleasure in the hardships the young mothers were forced to endure, Sister Carmel. She shared the Church's teaching that these women were 'fallen' and these children were the unwanted detritus of a grave mortal sin. Every time Rose left the children, she felt exhausted and broken-hearted.

* * *

A couple of weeks later the home received a visit from the council Inspection Board. Sister Marie had been forewarned about the inspection. Every effort had been made to tidy the home up, to present the mothers and children in the best possible light. She had set mothers and nuns to feverishly clean the nursery units. The inspector, a man, randomly inspected just a few of the nursery rooms. In his report he recorded that most of the children that he saw 'were healthy in appearance'.

Following his brief inspection, he was invited to lunch with Sister Marie and enjoyed a very rare three-course meal of broth, chicken and country vegetables as the main, and a delicious rhubarb crumble with custard for dessert. He thanked the Head Sister profusely and commented that he had not enjoyed such a fine meal since 1939, before the Emergency.

Rose was desperate that things might improve following the inspection, but absolutely nothing changed.

Late one night while she was on night-feed duty, a young child was found dead in its cot. No doctor was sent for. Rose watched in horror as the tiny frail body was wrapped in a shroud made from cloth cut from a stained bed sheet. A priest arrived and performed a short ceremony and then promptly departed. Rose was left to watch over the remains as the duty sister went to inform Sister Marie of the death.

Rose approached the cot. She gently lifted the child in her arms and whispered, 'Shush, my darling, my little angel.'

Her body convulsed as tears streamed down her face and soaked the cloth that held the child. She began to sob uncontrollably for this child, for its mother, indeed for herself and for her own child.

She was lost in her grief when she felt hands try to take the child away from her. She opened her eyes and saw Sister Marie standing in the doorway. She heard her say to three other nuns who had entered the room, 'Take the child from her and dispose of it.'

Rose backed away with the child tight her arms.

'No, no, no,' she repeated over and over. 'You will not take this child; you will not take this child.' One of the nuns grabbed for the child and Rose screamed, 'You will not take this poor child.'

The two other nuns held her arms, while the first one tried to wrestle the child away from her. Rose screamed and screamed, she fought and kicked, until the child was ripped from her embrace. She lay on the floor in a state of madness and despair. She heard Sister Marie comment to another nun, 'The girl is obviously mentally deranged in some way. Keep a close eye on her and make sure she is made to work hard. "Idle hands are the Devil's playthings", Sister, remember that!'

Rose was eventually lifted and led to a small room. Sister Bridget came and gently undressed her and helped her into bed. She dipped a small hand cloth into a basin of water on a table in the room and tenderly washed her face. Her own tears ran down her face and onto Rose. She left quietly but locked the door behind her, as Sister Marie had instructed her to do.

As Rose fell into an exhausted sleep, two nuns carried the child's remains to the back of the grounds of the home and to the old septic tank that lay buried there. The child was unceremoniously dropped into the tank. Before they left, Sister Carmel kicked the weeds and grass back across the square metal door. It was as if this place had never existed, this child had never been born.

Rose was allowed to return to the dormitory and to work. To her shock and surprise, nothing more was said about the death of the child. Sister Marie had decided to pretend that absolutely nothing had happened. Better to give the 'unseemly' event no more attention than it deserved.

But Rose knew it did happen and would never forget it as long as she lived.

* * *

After a month at the home, Rose had already lost considerable weight and now had that pale haunted look that had greeted her when she had first arrived. She swore to herself that once her baby was born, she would leave. She would take her child to a place of safety, home to her mother and sister. They would take her back no matter what her father thought or said. Each night she fell into bed and prayed that James would come soon and save her from this nightmare. But time passed with still no word.

After another month the full force of winter blew through the home. If any fires were lit, they were not for the mothers or the children. Christmas came and went like any other day. The children received no presents or toys. They would not have known what to do with them. Not a single toy or play area was to be found in the entire home. The children, it seemed, were there to be punished for the 'sins' of their mothers.

Rose got bigger and thinner at the same time. The relentless routine of work and virtual starvation had worn her down physically but not dampened her spirit. She continued to hope and pray for James's safe return. They received little news of the war in Europe except that which a few of the nuns were prepared to tell them. The conflict raged on, but the Germans were in retreat on two fronts, from the west in France and from the east in Russia. While her stay in the home seemed like an eternity, she knew it would be some time before the war would end and James could return. In the meantime, she would try to survive.

Her due date, 10 March, came and went. She was now very weak and tired. The expectant mothers received no professional medical care. No doctor ever visited the home. She understood that childbirth could be a brutal experience; it could even be a death sentence. Mothers worked right up until they went into labour. No pain relief was ever offered no matter the complications. Mortality rates among mothers and babies were extremely high. No effort was made to instruct the mothers about what to expect or to reassure them in any way. Despite her very best efforts to hide the fact, Rose was terrified.

A couple of weeks later, as she worked in the laundry, she felt a sudden rush of hot liquid between her legs. The water pooled around her feet as she stared at it in shock. She searched the room for Sister Bridget and called out to her. One of the other girls folding sheets beside her furtively leaned over and said, 'Don't worry. Your waters have broken – it's perfectly natural. You're having your baby.'

That was as much as she would dare say before turning her attention back to ironing and folding the worn and stained sheets. The nuns' fresh bedding was washed, ironed and folded crisp white separately at another table.

Sister Bridget hurried to Rose, but Sister Carmel reached her first.

'Right, Miss Rafferty, you're about to have your baby. Follow me! Stay here, Sister Bridget, and make sure the work carries on in my absence.'

Rose followed her, embarrassed and in a state of shock. She was led to a private room. It contained a simple bed with a metal basin and jug resting on wooden locker beside a small curtainless window. In the middle of the room was a large wooden table. Sister Carmel told her to lie down on the bed and remove her underwear. Rose was left to lie in her damp clothes alone while the nun went to seek assistance. She had left the room without uttering a single word of explanation or comfort.

Rose began to experience severe cramps in her stomach. She lifted her hand to her mouth and moaned. All the girls had been warned repeatedly since arrival in the home that they were to give birth quietly and without disturbing everyone else. If there was any pain, well, it was sent from God himself for the mortal sin they had committed. They must bear it quietly as a just punishment.

It was almost an hour before Sister Carmel returned with another woman. She was a few years older than Rose, only a young girl herself, but she had been in the home much longer. She was dressed in rough and dirty clothing covered in mud. She had just been called from the allotment where she and another woman had been gathering potatoes.

'Hello,' she said. 'And what's your name?'

Sister Carmel replied, 'Rafferty!' at the same time that Rose replied, 'Rose.'

Rose asked, 'Where's the doctor?'

Sister Carmel barked, 'You don't need a doctor, Miss Rafferty.'

The other woman gave her hands a thorough wash before drying them on her mud-covered dress.

She laid a cool damp hand on Rose's brow, smiled a kindly smile and said, 'Rose, you are having your baby right now. Everything that you are feeling is perfectly natural and normal. I know that you are hurtin', darlin', but I want you to believe me when I tell you that you and your baby are going to be just fine. I'm going to help you have this baby.' She grasped Rose's hand tightly, smiled calmly to her and said, 'OK?'

'OK,' said Rose.

The woman then explained to Rose that she was going to examine her, and not to be embarrassed. After examining her, she told her that it would not be very long until she had her baby.

'The cramps in your body are telling you, darlin', that the baby is almost ready for this world, so they will get a little bit worse. Remember: the worse they get, the sooner your baby will be here, and all this pain will be over.'

The pain did get worse, much worse. Rose did her best not to scream and instead gritted her teeth and groaned whenever it intensified. Minutes turned into an hour and a single hour into several hours. Rose was too tired and in too much pain to notice the strain and worry that had begun to show on the other woman's face.

It was well into the early hours of the morning and sometimes she was simply lost in the pain. She felt the sweat run down her forehead and cheeks. No matter how hard she tried to turn her attention to what was happening around her, to what she was being told, another wave of pain would radiate through her entire body. She closed her eyes and clenched her teeth to prevent herself from screaming at the top of her voice.

Occasionally, she would catch whispered words or comments, but they were only fragments. She was mostly oblivious to the tension and fear in the eyes of the woman attending her.

*　*　*

The woman knew that the baby was too big, and Rose's young, small body was struggling. Again, she pleaded quietly with Sister Carmel to send for a doctor. This time the nun replied that she would go and speak to Sister Marie and left.

The woman turned to Rose and tried to reassure her, but deep down she knew the situation had now become grave.

She whispered into Rose's ear, 'Now that that bitch is gone, Rose, my name is Kathleen, Kathleen O'Rawe. I know this is agony, love, but for your baby's sake I need you to keep tryin'. Don't give up, darlin'. Don't give up on this wee baby of yours.' Kathleen had been forbidden by the nuns from giving her name to the women giving birth.

She leaned over Rose and gently kissed her forehead.

'This baby is going to be beautiful, just like its mam.'

Sister Carmel returned and beckoned Kathleen out into the corridor.

'Sister Marie has agreed that the doctor may be sent for first thing in the morning, at a respectable hour, if he is still required.'

Kathleen began to protest and explain that this young woman could – no, would – die if a doctor was not sent for now.

'Just get on with it and do as you're told,' replied Sister Carmel.

Kathleen returned to the room and to Rose, while Sister Carmel looked on dispassionately from the doorway. She stood ramrod straight with her hands clasped behind her back.

'Right, my love. This is it. This baby wants to be born. I know you're sore and I know you're tired, but if you don't push this baby out now, it might not live.' She looked directly into Rose's eyes. 'Do you understand me, Rose? You need to fight for this baby!'

Rose looked back at her, nodded and screamed as she pushed the baby out.

Kathleen quickly cut the cord with a pair of large fabric scissors she kept in her pocket. A heavy flow of blood was already beginning to stream from Rose's body. Kathleen wiped the baby as clean as she could, as quickly as she could, before lifting her onto Rose's heaving chest.

'You have a beautiful daughter, Rose.' She lifted the little girl's hand to rest it on Rose's face.

Rose stared at the child in wonderment. The pain had now receded, and she simply felt exhausted. 'Hello my beautiful girl,' she whispered. The child stared at her face and seemed to recognise her voice. Rose felt her eyelids grow heavier with every passing second. She smiled weakly at the child and said in a quiet voice, 'I love you, my darling.'

In the meantime, Kathleen rapidly began to press towels tightly between Rose's legs to try to reduce the flow of blood. She was haemorrhaging badly, and a large amount of blood had already begun to pool between her legs.

She turned and strode towards the nun at the door.

'If you do not send for a doctor right this minute, this young woman, this child, will die,' she shouted into her face. 'You callous bitch!'

As Sister Carmel left the room, Kathleen turned her attention back to Rose and her daughter. She feared that Rose was losing too much blood too quickly already. She had seen this once before. If the right drugs were not administered fast enough and the haemorrhaging not stopped, the mother would die. By refusing to send for a doctor much sooner, these nuns had killed this girl as surely as any cold-blooded murderer.

Sister Bridget entered the room. She sat on the side of the bed and smiled at Rose.

'Isn't she beautiful, Sister Bridget, my beautiful baby?'

'The image of her mother, Rose, the most beautiful baby I have ever seen.'

Sister Bridget struggled to maintain her composure as her voice shook and the tears began to stream down her cheeks.

Kathleen asked, 'What will you call this gorgeous child, Rose?'

'Faith! Her name is Faith and her father is Private James McCann, from Boston, Massachusetts.'

Rose's voice was barely a whisper as she grew weaker. Bridget leaned closer and kissed her forehead.

'Sister Bridget, promise me, before God, that you will write to James and tell him about Faith?'

Sister Bridget nodded in agreement.

'No, swear it before almighty God. Swear it!'

'I swear before almighty God, Rose. I do!'

The doctor arrived two and a half hours later. By that time Rose Rafferty had died of what he described in the death certificate as 'postpartum haemorrhage' brought on by a tear in the uterus.

Sometime later Sister Bridget wrote a letter to Private James McCann but was too terrified to post it.

CHAPTER 3

BOSTON, PRESENT DAY

There was a very large crowd at the funeral in Forest Hills Cemetery, Boston. Some of her father's old Second World War army buddies shook her hand and said, 'Sorry for your loss, Maggie. Your dad was a great guy.'

There was only a handful of them left. They were now old men in their eighties. Some of the union guys were there as well. Her dad had been a longshoreman in Boston docks for most of his adult life.

Maggie sat down a dozen seats away from her brother Conor and his family. They had hardly exchanged more than a few polite but strained pleasantries since she had arrived back home for their dad's funeral.

She felt numb, hollow. She had cried herself dry and now wore a pair of large dark sunglasses to hide her red and puffed eyelids. Her mother had died when she was just a young child and it was her dad who had raised her and Conor. They had been a tight family growing up. Her dad had been a wonderful father. Tender, affectionate – hugs and kisses were compulsory in the McCann household. 'Love you' closed every conversation.

Family had been so important to her dad, and it had broken his heart that she and Conor had grown so far apart. What would happen now that the one person who had held the family together, even tenuously, was gone? She felt detached, as if her roots had been ripped from the ground and thrown into strong winds. She desperately wanted to grab hold of something, someone, before she was carried away.

She pretended to listen to Bishop Timothy O'Rourke's sermon, or was it another one of his outdated and frequently offensive morality lectures? Twenty-first century fire and brimstone. *No wonder people are leaving the Church in droves, you asshole,* she thought to herself and not for the first time.

'Jimmy McCann and his dear departed wife, Margaret, were good Catholic parents. No, folks, let me rephrase that – they were *great* Catholic parents, who raised two wonderful children, Conor and Maggie. Superintendent Conor McCann, who has become one of our city's most respected and decorated police officers ...'

He beamed a glowing smile towards her brother Conor and began to rhyme off a long list of his many achievements and his meteoric rise through the Boston Police Department. Not least his central role in apprehending the young Tsarnaev brothers, who were responsible for the Boston Marathon bombing. From behind her sunglasses, she cast a glance at Conor, half expecting him to genuflect and kiss the bishop's ring.

'And of course, little Maggie ...'

Screw you too, you patronising creep, she almost said out loud. She gave him the most cynical smile she could muster. It never failed to amaze her that these conservative old men continued to oversee one of the most powerful institutions in the world. It was an empire of misogyny.

During the emerging scandal about child sex abuse within the Catholic Church, O'Rourke had been one of the strongest supporters of Cardinal Law, who had knowingly and consciously moved paedophile priests around different parishes in Boston, leaving them free to continue abusing chil-

dren. An arch conservative, he had managed to avoid being directly impli-
cated in the attempts to cover up the horrific abuse of children by Catholic
priests exposed by the Boston *Globe* team in 2002.

That didn't mean he wasn't guilty as hell. She was damn sure he was.

Maggie had started working for the *New York Times* then and had written a detailed piece on the failure of the Catholic Church to punish Law
and others following these revelations. As far as she was concerned, the
Church hierarchy that covered up the abuse had effectively gotten away
scot-free.

She had also heavily criticised the Boston PD for its failure to pursue not
just the abusers but those like Law, who had covered it up. As she saw it,
many Irish-American Catholic cops, like her own brother, were complicit
in the abuse because they had either failed to believe victims or deliberately
chose to ignore the evidence of child abuse by priests in order to protect the
Church. She and Conor had hardly spoken since.

She had loved her father dearly, but her strong criticism of the Catholic
Church and the Boston PD had put a strain on their relationship in recent
years. Her dad had been an old-fashioned Irish-American Catholic and a
stalwart of his local church, St Thomas Aquinas. They had grown up just a
few blocks away.

Maggie said her goodbyes to Conor and the family and headed back
home. Home, for the moment at least, was the family house on South
Street. She had taken extended leave from work. She had built up so much
unused leave, she knew she could never use it all, but she had decided to
take a few months before heading back to New York. There were a lot of
arrangements to make, loose ends to be tied up. Not least the house – it
would need to be cleared out and they'd have to decide what to do with it.

It was one of those old triple-decked Boston houses. Pretty as hell. Her dad had bought it for a song in the 1950s when Jamaica Plain was a community in decline, but the community had fought back. By the time her father had died, the old properties had become fashionable again and were being bought up and turned into multiple luxury condominiums. Their childhood home was now worth over $1 million.

Maggie let herself into the house. Her father's coats still hung on the wall. Mail addressed to him had piled up on the sideboard just inside the door. Months of it. Her father had spent the last six months of his life in nearby Laurel Ridge Rehabilitation Centre recuperating from a stroke.

She looked at herself in the hall mirror and thought, *Shit, who is that?* Her wavy hair was still dark, but only courtesy of Vidal Sassoon and her monthly trip to the hair salon, and she wore it shorter now. Where had the years gone? She used to brush her very long hair in this mirror before heading out to school, then college, then discos and clubs, and eventually protests and demonstrations. Twenty years later, all she could see were visible – all too visible – lines and wrinkles. She was in her mid-forties but felt like she was sliding very fast down a slippery slope towards her fifties.

Mom and Dad were dead, and she had hardly spoken a civil word to her brother in over a decade. Fuck! She needed a drink. She lifted the pile of mail and carried it to the kitchen. She put it on the dining table and lifted a bottle of Sam Adams from the fridge. She sat down, twisted the lid, looked at the bottle and laughed to herself. The old man only ever drank Sam Adams.

'Buy Boston, buy American,' he would always say. Cars, cigarettes and especially beer. The brewery was still there on Germania Street in Jamaica Plain, providing local people with jobs.

'Here's to you, Dad.'

She began to work her way through the mail and the beers in the fridge. Advertisements, more advertisements, insurance, credit cards, loans, whatever you wanted. It was the age of buy now, pay later – or never pay at all.

She lifted an envelope. This one had elegant handwriting on it, a rarity in these days of emails and social media. It also had several stamps on it, from Ireland, and it was franked with various Boston postmarks, as if it had been passed around the city. She tore it open and began to read.

Mrs Maureen Kane

120 University Terrace

Galway City

Ireland

Dear Mr McCann,

I hope this letter finds you and finds you alive and in good health. We have no forwarding address, other than Boston, Massachusetts. You will find enclosed a letter written by an aunt of mine, a nun, Sister Bridget Kane. Sister Bridget recently passed away and while going through her possessions we found this old letter addressed to yourself.

I apologise for opening and reading the letter because it contains information that may well cause you a great deal of hurt and pain, even so many years after the fact. The letter speaks for itself, and I will say no more.

If I can be of assistance in any way, you can contact me at my address or at the phone number below.

Yours,

Maureen Kane

Maggie found a second letter in the envelope and opened it. It was so old and faded she couldn't make out the date.

Bon Secours Mother and Baby Home

Tuam

Galway

Dear James McCann,

We have never met but I have heard your name more times than I can count. I am a nun in the Bon Secours Mother and Baby Home in Tuam, County Galway. This letter and what I am about to tell you will come as a grave shock to you and I am struggling to find the kindest words to soften it in some way. But there are no words, there is no way to tell you without breaking your heart, as mine has been. And so, I must simply and plainly tell you that on 24 March 1945 at 4.13am, Rose Rafferty gave birth to your daughter, Faith, here in Tuam. Shortly thereafter, your beautiful Rose died due to complications during the birth. She is buried in an unmarked grave in the grounds of this home, though I do not know exactly where. This is a place of horror, not charity.

Rose and I had become close friends during her stay, and she spoke of you constantly. I know that you were to be married upon your return from the war. Rose arrived here from Belfast a few months after you were shipped out.

She never once lost hope – or should I say, Faith – that you would return to her after the war. God in his infinite wisdom had other plans for Rose Rafferty.

Your beautiful daughter, who looked just like her mother, was adopted by a family from Boston. I do not know their name or their address, only that they reside in Boston.

My most fervent prayer is that one day you will be united with your daughter, Faith, and that you know the depth of the love that Rose had for you and for your daughter.

Yours,

Sister Bridget Kane

Maggie dropped the letter on the table in shock.

'My God.'

She was stunned. Her hands trembled as she lifted the page to read it again and again. Is this some sort of sick joke? she thought. She sat staring at the letter for ages. She looked at her watch. It was 3.15pm Boston time. That would make it, what? 8.15pm or 9.15pm in Ireland? She googled the time difference on her phone. Yeah, they were five hours ahead, 8.15pm.

She lifted the first letter and dialled the number at the bottom. She hoped it was some sort of prank. It rang!

A woman with an Irish accent answered, 'Hello?'

'Can I speak to a Mrs Maureen Kane, please?'

'Yes, speaking. Can I help you?'

Maggie paused to compose herself.

'Mrs Kane, my name is Maggie McCann. I'm ringing from Boston, the US.'

There was a brief silence at the other end of the line.

'Mrs Kane, my father was James McCann.'

'I'm very sorry, Miss McCann, but we were never sure your father was alive or that he would receive the letter. You have received my letter, then?'

'Mrs Kane or whoever your name is, is this some sort of joke? Or maybe it's a mistake? The wrong James McCann?'

'Miss McCann, all I can tell you is that hours before she died, my aunt Bridget begged me to find that letter and send it to a Private James McCann, from Boston, Massachusetts. I can't say for certain that it's your father – how could I? Look, I'm very sorry. Maybe I shouldn't have posted it. I – I just didn't know what else to do.'

For once in her life Maggie did not know what to say – she was lost for words. This was a bombshell.

'OK! OK! Jesus Christ! What am I supposed to do with this? We just buried my father today.'

'Oh my God! I'm very sorry, Miss McCann. I'm so sorry that I sent that letter at all now. After all these years it could do no good, but my aunt begged me to send it. She said she had made a solemn promise before God and Rose all those years ago and it had tortured her soul ever since. I really didn't know what else to do. God forgive me and her!'

Maggie thanked the lady but cursed her inwardly and then hung up. She walked to the fridge and got another beer, sat down and lit a cigarette. *What t'hell am I going to do with this?* she wondered.

She lifted her phone again and rang Conor.

'Maggie? Is something wrong?'

'Conor, you need to get over here now. I've found something.'

'What have you found, Maggie?'

'Just get over here – you gotta see it!'

* * *

It took Conor just over a half an hour to drive over. As soon as he could afford it, he had moved out of Jamaica Plain and bought a house in afflu-ent West Roxbury. He and Brenda, his ambitious wife, had it all mapped out. Before they had even had any kids, they had picked the schools they wanted to send them to and the careers they would follow. Both of their children were now attending two of the best Catholic schools in Boston, St Theresa of Avila and Catholic Memorial School. They were great kids.

As he opened the front door and stepped into the hall, Maggie appeared.

'So what is it, Maggie?'

She handed him the letter and a fresh beer.

'Read that and drink that – you're going to need it!'

After a few minutes Conor said, 'Is this some sort of joke?'

'It was in the pile of mail on Dad's sideboard in the hall. Must have been there months. Conor, it looks legit. I rang the lady who sent it from Ireland. She swears it's real. Is it Dad? Have we a half-sister we didn't know about? You tell me?'

'Oh, for Christ's sake, Maggie, of course it's not real, or if it is it's got nothing to do with Dad. There must be thousands of McCanns in Boston, all over the East Coast.'

'Look, maybe you're right. I hope to hell you are right. It might not be Dad. Did Dad ever tell you anything about his time in Ireland before being shipped out to France?'

'Maggie, don't go there. It's a load of crap, OK!'

'Where did Dad keep all his war stuff? Is it in the loft? Didn't he keep it in an old chest?'

Conor took a long slug from his beer.

'I suppose you ain't gonna drop this until you know for a fact that it's a crock of shit?'

He stood up, walked next-door to their father's study and emerged holding out a key.

'Knock yourself out, Sherlock!'

Maggie took the key from him and bounded up the stairs two at a time, Conor following slowly behind her.

When they got into the loft, he had to dig his way through all sorts of stuff. Christmas decorations, old furniture, old toys. His dad had kept just about everything they had ever played with, wore, made in school. He was that kind of dad – a great one.

There it was tucked away in the back corner. One of those large old travel chests that no one used anymore, except as tables in hip coffee shops or cocktail bars. Maggie cleared a space around it and opened it with the key Conor had given her.

Inside they found their father's dress uniform folded neatly on top, his service medals and his battered helmet. To the side was his old camera. Conor had forgotten that his dad had taken hundreds of photographs during the war. He had stopped taking pictures at the end of the war for some unspoken reason. He supposed his dad had seen horrible things or photographed events he just wanted to forget when he got home again. There were odds and ends, eclectic mementos of his time in Europe. A bottle of French wine. A pretty Christmas snow globe made in Berlin. Old French, German and English newspapers detailing the war.

They shuffled through all the photos and found some that had been taken in Ireland, but none of them with any girls. Just their dad and some of his friends, in smart uniforms, standing outside what looked like a grand government building.

There were boxes and boxes and Maggie insisted they search every one of them. Nothing.

'Right, Maggie, satisfied? Nothing. Now put the stuff away and let's go.'

'Just hold on, will you? Where's Dad's service gun? You remember his old .45 and holster? Where is it?'

Maggie returned to the chest and began lifting everything out and setting it in a pile on the floor.

'Oh, for fuck's sake, Maggie!'

When the chest was empty, he watched her run her fingers around the bottom. She caught the lip or the edge of something. She was able to pinch the edge of the bottom of the chest on two sides and lift it clear. There was a space below. Conor could see Maggie's excitement at the find. He was apprehensive.

They found their father's service weapon, an old .45 and holster. There was also a Luger pistol and some German military paraphernalia, an ornate SS knife and some military decorations. Conor wondered where his dad had gotten them or whom he had taken them off. And there was a large pile of black and white photos and old letters tied neatly together with ribbon. Tied into the bow of the ribbon was a diamond ring. Both of them recognised their father's handwriting on the last envelope.

Miss Rose Rafferty

Rafferty's Hardware Store

49 Falls Road

Belfast

Northern Ireland

Maggie untied the bundle and handed Conor the photographs. There were dozens of letters, all addressed in the same way and stamped 'return to sender'.

Conor thumbed through a handful of black and white photos. There was a beautiful young girl in all of them and, in one, their dad in uniform and the girl standing in front of a circular white Art Deco building. They were holding hands, she was smiling at the camera and he was smiling at her, adoringly. He handed the photo to Maggie and lifted one of the unopened letters. She nodded to him to open it.

My Dearest Rose,

I can't tell you anything about where I am or what has happened along the way, you know there's strict censorship. I'm alive and that's what counts. I have the little Our Lady medal you gave me, and I believe she, with the help of your prayers, my love, is protecting me.

I cannot tell you how much I miss you, sweetheart, except to say you are in my thoughts almost every waking moment of the day and night. You even visit me in my dreams. I have your photo close to my heart. It's getting pretty worn already. I take it out and stare at it constantly. I look at your beautiful face, that smile, and I just smile from ear to ear. Remember you used to catch me staring at you and I'd say, 'I like the way you look; I like to look at your face, your smile. So, sue me!'

The guys are ribbing me because of it and it's your fault. But I don't give a damn. You will laugh at this, love. Some of the guys who don't have a sweetheart say to me occasionally, 'Hey Jimmy, let's see that doll of yours? She's like a movie star.'

I just tell them we are getting married as soon as I get back to Belfast and we are moving straight back to God's own country, Boston, the first chance.

I love you with all my heart, Rose. Give Madge my regards. I am keeping watch for that Rose moon. Be sure to do the same, my darling. When I get to

Paris, I'm going to get you that ring, the biggest diamond ring I can find.

Your adoring fiancé,

James

Conor handed Maggie the letter. He felt the blood drain from his face. She read it herself and after a stunned silence she said, 'Conor, we have a big sister, Faith, somewhere in this city, and we need to find her.'

CHAPTER 4

BOSTON,
PRESENT DAY

Maggie spent that night and the next morning researching and taking note of what was already known about the Bon Secours mother and baby home in Ireland. What she found shocked even her.

The home operated between 1925 and 1961 in Tuam, County Galway. Unmarried pregnant women were sent there to have their 'illegitimate' children. These were 'children of the Devil', as one local man recalled being taught in a nearby school. The new Southern Irish Free State had been founded in 1921 following a guerrilla war for independence from Britain. It was a deeply conservative Catholic and patriarchal state. Unmarried mothers were often shunned and ostracised within their own families and communities. The Catholic hierarchy, parish priests and the religious orders exercised an oppressive control over the flock they administered to, not to mention the government.

A local historian and campaigner, Catherine Corless, had uncovered a truly horrific story of abuse and cruelty within the Galway home. She was able to establish through a meticulous search of death records that 796 children there had died of what were recorded as 'congenital debility', 'marasmus' (malnutrition) and infectious diseases. But there was no record of burials and no burial sites either on the grounds of the home or in the surrounding area. So where were these poor children's remains? After extensive research, Corless claimed that the children had been buried in an unmarked grave on the site.

Following the closure of the home, it was finally demolished in 1972. In 1975 two twelve-year-old children playing on the site of the old home uncovered a chamber 'filled to the brim' with children's skeletons. The hole was resealed after a local priest said some prayers at the site. The authorities, including the local Gardaí, claimed the remains most likely dated from the Famine period, but Corless could find no record of any Famine grave in the vicinity of the home.

Some local people had erected a small makeshift religious shrine in the corner of a field that had been part of the grounds. Rumours persisted that children who had died prematurely at the home had been secretly buried there. When Corless had examined the old site plans, she discovered that the location of the shrine corresponded with the location of an old underground septic tank.

Corless first published her allegations in 2012, but it was 2015 before local and international pressure, including extensive foreign press coverage, forced the Irish government to establish a Commission of Investigation into the allegations.

But it was a newspaper article that caught Maggie's attention. In 2015, an Irish newspaper claimed that the Health Service Executive had raised concerns three years before that as many as one thousand children may have been 'trafficked' from the home to the United States. The report mentioned the possibility that death certificates were falsified so that children could be 'brokered for adoption'. This matter had arisen when a senior social worker responsible for adoption services discovered what she described as 'a large archive of photographs, documentation and correspondence relating to children sent for adoption to the USA'.

Maggie sat back and said out loud, 'Jesus Christ!'

There were eighteen such homes in just the twenty-six counties of Ireland under investigation for the same practices. A similar investigation in the North of Ireland hadn't even begun.

My God, there could be thousands of children who were trafficked to the US for adoption, she thought to herself. *'Trafficked' – wasn't that just another way of saying 'stolen' or 'sold'?*

When she came across another newspaper article, 'The Stolen Children of Ireland', she could hardly believe it – it was by her colleague Michael O'Malley at the *New York Times*. She lifted the phone and rang him.

'Hi Mike, it's Maggie here.'

'Hi Maggie. Listen, sorry to hear about your dad. Thought you were on leave – what's up?'

'Thanks, Mike. I am but I'm doing a bit of work on something I think you can help with.'

'Fire away.'

'"The Stolen Children of Ireland" – what can you tell me about the kids that survived and were adopted here in the US?'

'Do I need to know why you're asking?'

'It's a long story, but I'm digging into something about the kids who were adopted stateside. If it develops into anything, I'll give you a mention. So, what do you know?'

'It's been a few years since I did the piece. I'll pull out anything that I think might be relevant and get it sent to you in the next few days, OK? I spent three weeks over there researching it.'

'You remember anything about the adoptions?'

'Sure do, couldn't forget even if I tried. They were organised on a huge scale by the Catholic Church, I remember that much. I came across records of chartered flights out of Shannon airport into New York, with – and get this – on at least one flight, five hundred children on board for adoption. Five hundred, Maggie! This was organised on an industrial scale by the Church. Thousands of birth certificates were falsified. Most kids didn't even have passports. Thousands of kids must have literally been shipped to the States.'

'Anything else, Mike?'

'I'd check out large donations to the Catholic Church here stateside during that period. Follow the money. One last thing, Maggie. A couple of years ago an Irish civil servant found boxes of old files on the adoptions, photographs of kids, copies of birth certificates, lots of material. You should try to get access to those records.'

* * *

Maggie had arranged to meet Conor for lunch to discuss where they went from here. Conor had suggested The Oceanaire Seafood Room downtown. Maggie suggested the Brendan Behan pub on Centre Street in the old neighbourhood. When she saw the expression on his face she said, 'Relax, Conor, you ain't gotta buy a round or anything!'

The two of them smiled at the joke, the first thing they had smiled at together in a long time.

'You always were a tight bastard, Conor!'

'Yeah, yeah, you sound just like Dad.' He said it with a hint of affection that made her smile.

Maggie was already in the bar when Conor arrived. He slid into the booth opposite her. She had a freshly pulled pint of Guinness sitting in front of her.

'You fancy a beer?'

'No thanks, Maggie, I'm on the job.'

'Fair enough.'

'You order any food yet?'

Maggie said not yet.

'Hey, kid? Two dogs and fries over here. And a still water for me. You want another Guinness?'

'No thanks.'

She told him all she had learned about the home and some of the leads she intended to pursue.

'Conor, this place was a major shithole. They think they've found 796 kids' bodies buried in a cesspit at the back of the home and a dozen adult female remains.'

'Yeah, I think I remember reading something about it. Gruesome.'

'There's a colleague of mine at the *Times* did a piece on it a few years ago. He's gonna pull out anything that he thinks might help us find Faith.'

She opened her notepad.

'There's a Commission of Investigation looking at this stuff back in Ireland right now. And get this, as many as a thousand kids may have been illegally adopted from this home alone. Our problem is that most of these kids were stolen from their single mothers and had their birth certificates altered to cover the Church's tracks. Faith may have just disappeared off the face of the earth in 1945.'

Conor shook his head and said, 'Now, Maggie, let's not turn this into another Church conspiracy or a witch hunt, OK? Lots of kids were adopted from Ireland back then. It was a pretty poor country. Some single parents there couldn't afford to raise their kids, and some people here could. It's a tough world, tougher then.'

'Jesus Christ, Conor, are you for real?'

'Look, Maggie, let's keep this simple, OK? We are looking for a kid called Faith Rafferty who was adopted by a family here in Boston. I will make an appointment to talk to Bishop O'Rourke. There's bound to be a record of the kids who were adopted and they've no reason to hide that information.'

Maggie shook her head and said, 'OK, Conor, let's do it your way for now. Talk to the bishop. Let's see how easy it is to find Faith Rafferty.'

* * *

After lunch, Conor returned to his office in Boston PD Headquarters in Roxbury. At the age of fifty-three, he was the youngest head of the Bureau of Investigative Services in the history of the Boston PD. Tall and athletic, he was a fitness junkie who rose religiously at 6am and went training for an hour before heading to the office. He had a thick head of hair, going grey, cut closely to his head. He was handsome rather than good-looking. A slightly crooked nose gave him a hard look. Conor appeared to be a tough guy who would take no shit and that is exactly what he was. The BIS was responsible for the Homicide Unit, the Drug Control Unit, Family Justice, Sexual Crimes and the Forensic Science Division. He was already being talked about as a possible future Commissioner of Police.

After college he followed his dad into the Marines and had served as a lieutenant during the Gulf War. He had been awarded a Silver Star for extraordinary heroism. On his discharge from the army, he had joined the

Boston PD and had served with distinction, first in the Drug Unit in East Boston and Mattapan and then in City Homicide, before being appointed superintendent and the Head of BIS. He was extremely intelligent, ambitious and driven.

Before the Gulf War Conor had been what he himself would have described as a practical Catholic. He attended mass and respected the Church, just as his mom and dad had taught him to. However, the experience of the war had changed his attitude to Catholicism. When he joined the Boston PD, he had witnessed some of the worst kinds of crime, child homicide, gang violence and only recently, Islamic terrorism. During the chaos of the desert operation and his police work in East Boston and Mattapan he had found in the Church a necessary comfort.

Yeah, he was ambitious. He knew how to play the game of politics. It helped to have the support of the bishop and the Church. But he did not wear his faith on his sleeve or try to ram it down anyone else's throat. People assumed that he was trying to climb the career ladder, Commissioner of Police, Mayor, Governor, who knew? But what most people missed, including his kid sister Maggie, was that more than anything, more than politics and ambition, he now had a deep personal faith.

Maggie just wanted to tear everything down, the government, corporate America and of course the Catholic Church. She was angry at just about everything and everybody, including him. Conor knew the Church was far from perfect. He knew that priests had abused children. He knew the hierarchy did not handle the situation very well. *Hell, none of us knew how to deal with these cases back then*, he thought. Even the Boston PD was learning, had fucked up and made mistakes. Was it any wonder the Church also made mistakes? But that is exactly what they were – there was no conspiracy, just ordinary people making mistakes.

Conor rang the bishop's residence and spoke to his personal assistant. She was able to offer him an appointment for the next day.

He arrived early. He had been there several times before at the personal invitation of the bishop. O'Rourke made it his business to help any influential Irish-American Catholic politician or public servant who was supportive of the Church. Though there seemed to be fewer and fewer of them with each passing year.

The very grand, nineteenth-century building was located at the end of a tree-lined driveway. The new Cardinal of Boston who had replaced Cardinal Law had moved out of Law's palatial residence into a much more modest house. He wanted to convey a message more in keeping with the poor origins of Christ and the early Church. Not everyone, it seemed, had got the message, including O'Rourke. He clearly enjoyed the finer things in life. Conor was shown into his office.

'The bishop will be with you shortly, Conor.'

'Thanks, Dolores.'

Bishop O'Rourke entered the room and Conor rose to shake his hand. Up close, Conor could see that he was immaculately dressed. His clothes were tailored, not bought off the rack. He was cleanshaven and his hair was perfectly trimmed. Conor noted that he wore designer glasses. He was clearly a man who took a great deal of care with his appearance.

'Bishop O'Rourke, thank you for taking the time to meet me.'

'Of course, Conor, it's always a pleasure to do whatever I can for the Boston Police Department, not to mention one of the Church's own sons. So, what can I do for you?'

When the bishop sat down, he slowly reclined in his chair and placed his two outstretched arms on his desk. Conor couldn't help but notice the bishop's generous waistline.

He knew O'Rourke expected him to raise a matter of police business. When Conor began to explain the reason for his visit, the warm smile quickly disappeared from the bishop's face. Conor withheld the parts of the story that indicated that the Church might have acted illegally in the way these children were adopted or the allegations that unmarried mothers were mistreated in the homes. He concluded by saying, 'Bishop O'Rourke, my only concern is to trace the whereabouts of my sister Faith. We have no desire to rake over the past or to cause the Church any unnecessary embarrassment.'

The bishop paused for some moments before replying. He leaned forward to rest his elbows on the desk and joined his hands as if in prayer, a look of concern now showing on his face.

'Well, I must say that that is a sad and tragic tale, indeed. I think you will appreciate that this was a very long time ago and I have no idea whether records were kept. But I can assure you, Conor, that I will do *everything* I can to help.'

* * *

Later that week Conor and Maggie had an appointment with their father's attorney. The reading of the will. Maggie was dreading it. She didn't want to have to think about a will, the house, the money, her dad's personal things, his clothes, his books. It was too soon. She just wanted to leave everything exactly as it was. As if he were still here. Yes, it was too soon. On the drive over to the lawyer's office, she wondered what Conor was likely to say, what he would want to do. They had both put off having the conversation about their dad's house and his belongings. She didn't know what to expect.

When Maggie arrived in the office Conor was already there, sitting chatting to the attorney. *Oh very cosy*, she thought. Another one of his pals, no doubt. She felt her hackles rise.

'Hi.'

'Hi.'

It was all the two of them could muster.

'Please, take a seat, Maggie,' said the attorney. 'We were just chatting about your dad and his Irish whiskey collection. He knew his Irish whiskey, no one better. It's really quite a valuable collection. Let's get started, shall we?'

He handed Maggie and Conor copies of their father's will and began to take them through it. Everything – the house, his savings, his investments, his whiskey – now belonged equally to them both. His savings and investments were substantial. 'Your dad was a very smart investor. It would have been much more substantial before 9/11,' the attorney explained. 'You would have been millionaires, well, just over one million each.' His investments had been hit badly following 9/11 and had never fully recovered. 'Still, there is a substantial six-figure sum for each of you. So, guys, the money is the easy piece. I will divide your dad's savings equally and have the money transferred to your accounts. It will take a little bit longer to cash in his investments, but you should have that within three to four weeks. The big question is what do you want to do with the house?'

At exactly the same moment both replied.

'Sell it,' said Conor.

'Keep it,' said Maggie.

They turned and glared at one another. Before they could speak, the attorney judiciously intervened.

'Look, there's absolutely no need to decide now. Take some time, discuss it and when you have *both* agreed, just give me a call and we can make whatever arrangements are necessary. One last item. Your dad has left instructions that some money, a substantial sum of money, actually, be donated to two charities. The first is the Boston Longshoremen's Benevolent Fund, fifty thousand dollars. I know your dad was a passionate union member all his working life. The second is the Catholic Charities of America, fifty thousand dollars.'

Maggie almost spat the words, 'You have got to be kidding!' She turned to look at Conor, who simply shrugged his shoulders in response. *Over my dead body, they will!* she said to herself. These bishops already had too much money. Some North American bishops had invested huge sums of Church money in purchasing or extending what could only be described as opulent residences with amenities that any dictator or up-and coming 'Gangsta' rapper would have been proud of.

Even Pope Francis had lambasted what he described as 'airport bishops' who spent most of their time jet-setting rather than administering to their flock. A CNN investigation had found that ten out of the thirty-four archbishops in the US lived in Church-owned residences worth more than $1 million. Chicago's Cardinal lived in a mansion worth $14.3 million located in one of the city's most affluent neighbourhoods. The Archbishop of Miami lived in a six-bed, six-bathroom house with a pool, overlooking picturesque Biscayne Bay. The Archbishop of Newark, New Jersey, had added a $500,000 wing onto his already substantial residence, which included an indoor exercise pool, a hot tub and a library.

'I'm afraid, Maggie, those were your dad's explicit instructions. As the executor of his will, I must respect his wishes. The Catholic Charities of America will receive a tax-free donation of fifty thousand dollars from your dad's estate.'

CHAPTER 5

BOSTON, 1946

Soon after Rose died, a death certificate was falsified to say that Faith Rafferty had died with her mother. Faith was given a new birth certificate and a new name. The Archbishop of Massachusetts had written to the head of the Bon Secours order in Ireland on behalf of a wealthy Boston family, seeking, as a personal favour to him, a young Catholic girl for adoption. The order was only too happy to oblige. Several pretty little girls in the Tuam home were washed, especially dressed and photographed and a catalogue was sent to the archbishop. The family could pick their favourite child and within a few months, she would be despatched to Boston. No questions were asked about the prospective parents or their suitability to adopt. The archbishop's recommendation was more than enough. They picked a beautiful dark-haired toddler – they picked Faith.

In the month of November that year the Catholic Charities of America made the arrangements for Faith and dozens of other children to be flown to the US for adoption. There were many such flights before and after to Boston, New York and California. Earlier that year the Catholic Charities of America had chartered an entire plane to fly hundreds of children to the US for adoption throughout the States. Barely a quarter of them were legal and had passports issued by the Irish State.

The head of the Catholic Charities of America took the time to write personally to Faith's adoptive parents to thank them for their donation. This family had been particularly generous.

Dear Sir,

We at the Catholic Charities are extremely grateful for your generosity and thoughtfulness. It is only through the fees we receive from our adoptive couples that we are able to carry on our important work here in Boston.

Faith and two dozen other children had flown into New York and been taken by train to Boston. By the time they arrived, they were exhausted, disorientated, frightened and tearful. Faith was taken to the archbishop's residence to meet her new parents; the rest were taken to St Michael's parish hall to be collected by their new families.

CHAPTER 6

BOSTON,
PRESENT DAY

Maggie had no illusions. There was not a chance in heaven or hell that O'Rourke would help Conor find Faith. The Church had too much to lose and someone like O'Rourke would always put the interests of the Church above anyone else's. Conor would just have to find out for himself. There was no way she was going to wait.

She made herself a strong coffee in the kitchen and sat down in front of her Mac to do a little digging. She began with some research on Catholic adoption charities and found there was a historic connection to Ireland. The Catholic Charities of America, formed in 1910 from a collection of local charities spread across North America, had been headed from 1920 to 1960 by Monsignor John O'Grady, an Irish priest from County Clare. O'Grady was a social reformer within the Church and a strong advocate of immigration to the US and the practice of adoption from Catholic countries, including his own.

She decided to narrow down her search for information specifically to her own city and found the local branch of the Catholic Charities of America, the organisation that had been responsible for arranging adoptions after the war.

'Shit,' she muttered out loud. Even here she could not avoid O'Rourke, as the charity was directly responsible to the bishop.

In 2006 the Boston branch of the Catholic Charities of America had announced that they would no longer be providing adoption services, citing the new state law that spelt out that homosexuals must be allowed to adopt. O'Rourke had made a statement to the media explaining the decision to cease operations.

'The Vatican under Pope Benedict XVI has called homosexual adoption "gravely immoral", in part because it deprives our Catholic children of "experience of either fatherhood or motherhood". We, I' – he emphasised the 'I' – 'wholeheartedly agree with the Holy Father.'

'What an asshole,' she mumbled to herself. This guy was a real piece of work.

O'Rourke had previously met with Governor Mitt Romney to make a case for an exemption from the law, but Romney was unable to help. The decision ended over one hundred years of adoption activity by the charity. When Cardinal Law had resigned and was replaced, the new cardinal had resumed adoption activities, allowing same-sex couples the opportunity to adopt. O'Rourke had strongly objected but had been ordered by the new cardinal to implement the policy.

Maggie rang the Catholic Charities of America and asked to speak to the person in charge of the adoption programme. She was put through to a female voice.

'Hi, my name is Maggie McCann. I'm a journalist with the *New York Times*. I was wondering if I could arrange a meeting with you?'

'Can I ask what it is in relation to, Miss McCann?'

'Sure. I'm writing a piece on historic adoptions from Ireland after the Second World War, and I was hoping you could help me. Call me Maggie, please, everyone does.'

There was a moment's pause at the other end of the line.

'I'm afraid we will not be able to help, Miss McCann. As you can appreciate, the information we hold is strictly private. Perhaps you could put your request in writing to our chief executive explaining what it is exactly you are seeking, then we might be able to help?'

Maggie knew she was getting the brush-off.

'Certainly, I'll do that. Thank you for your assistance.'

Some chance of that, she thought. Where next? She rang the Department of Children and Families, the state adoption agency. It was one of those automated services, with endless questions and options that seemed to take forever and lead nowhere. After almost twenty minutes she hung up.

'Shit,' she said again in frustration. She decided to visit their office the next day. She knew it wasn't going to be that easy.

She spent another frustrating day being sent from one office to another. Nothing. The individuals she did speak to were polite but uninterested in her enquiries.

'Sorry we can't help. Why not try ...'

That evening she retired to the Brendan Behan to plan her next steps with a few well-earned beers. She got her mobile out and scrolled down her contacts list, wondering who might be able to help. Who worked in local government?

She stopped at 'Sarah' and remembered she was a social worker in Boston – well, she had been when they had last spoken, what was it, two, three years ago? Nothing ventured, nothing gained. She hit the number.

'Hello?'

'Hi Sarah, it's Maggie McCann here.'

'Well, hey stranger. How you doin', Maggie? You still in New York?'

'No, I'm back home for a while, Sarah. My dad died a few weeks ago.'

'Oh Maggie, I'm so sorry.'

'Yeah, thank you, Sarah. I'm still shellshocked. Listen, before I start crying again, I need to ask you a favour.'

'Fire away.'

'Do you know anyone who works in the Department of Children and Families, specifically in relation to adoptions?'

'Yeah, I do actually. We work very closely with them, as you might expect. A lot of the families we support, well, we have to take some of the children into care. Ultimately, some of them end up being placed for adoption. I've a good friend works there, Carole McKenna. She's a senior caseworker.'

'Do you think you could arrange for me to meet her?'

'Of course. I'll call her now.'

* * *

The next day Maggie arrived at the Department of Children and Families office just in time for her appointment. She reported to reception and within minutes Carole McKenna appeared.

'Hi, Maggie? We spoke on the phone yesterday. Carole, nice to meet you.' She gave Maggie a warm smile, shook her hand firmly and said, 'Follow me. I was just about to grab myself a strong coffee – you like one?'

'Yeah, sure, why not? Lots of milk, lots of coffee, if you've got it? No sugar,' replied Maggie.

Carole showed Maggie into a small office before saying, 'I'll be right back with those coffees.'

Carole was in her late forties. She was tall and good-looking, with long cornrows and a big smile. She was in great shape.

Maggie looked at her reflection in the window. *What was wrong with these people? Couldn't they be like the rest of us ordinary human beings?* she thought, sucking her mildly flabby stomach in for a few seconds before quickly releasing it.

She looked around the office. On the wall was a large, framed image of Nelson Mandela with an emboldened title, 'The Long Walk to Freedom'. There was a small collection of books on a shelf below the image. She ran her finger across them, Toni Morrison – *Beloved*, Flannery O'Connor – *Wise Blood*, Cormac Ó Gráda – *Black '47 and Beyond: The Great Irish Famine in History, Economy, and Memory*, and *Soul Thieves: The Appropriation and Misrepresentation of African American Popular Culture*, edited by Brown and Kopano. The rest were a mixture of family law and reference books.

Hmmm. Interesting, thought Maggie. She was surprised to see the Irish literature and the O'Connor novel tucked in between Mandela and Morrison and *Black '47*. Maggie had read O'Connor's work, Southern Gothic in style, when she was studying for her degree, a century ago, it felt like. She had been drawn to the flawed characters in her novels and short stories, perhaps glimpsed her older self in them. Though a practising Catholic, O'Connor often dealt with the difficult questions the Church faced, faith and fidelity. O'Connor had died of lupus at the young age of thirty-nine. She had been a great writer, could have become one of the greatest had she lived.

Maggie pulled out *Black '47*. She had not read the book, but she knew the subject in great detail, the so-called Irish 'famine' of 1847. Of course, Maggie preferred to describe this cataclysmic event in Irish history as the Irish Genocide or, if she had a few beers and an English audience, the English genocide of the Irish.

Over a million Irish had died of starvation and another million had been forced to make the perilous journey to North America, not simply because the potato crop had been destroyed by a blight but primarily because the English, the landlords and the greedy ambitious Irish middle class had exported tons and tons of food to England to feed the workers of the English Industrial Revolution. Their profits had been made upon the stinking remains of a million emaciated Irish corpses.

Carole came back into the office carrying two mugs.

'Aha, I see you've found my *Black '47*. My husband's Irish, in case you're wondering. We've a boy and a girl. I always say Black/Irish, the best of both.'

She handed Maggie her coffee, lifted a photo frame from her desk and passed it to her.

'That's Danny, my husband, our daughter Molly and Danny Jr, our son.'

'Beautiful family! Cute husband.'

They both laughed.

'Yeah, he is, isn't he?!' said Carole. 'He teaches in Boston College – guess what? Modern Irish history. Between Danny and the kids, I'm an expert on Irish history.'

'Is that so? Well, what do you know about the Tuam mother and baby home in Galway?' asked Maggie.

'Not much. I remember Danny talking about it a few years ago.'

'I'll be honest with you, Carole. I really need your help!'

Maggie spent the rest of the morning explaining their father's story and the search to find Faith.

'Wow!' said Carole when Maggie had finished talking.

'Will you help me?'

'Goddamn right I'll help! Say, what are you doing tonight?'

'Nothing, why?'

'You're coming to my home for dinner – and we are going to work out how we find Faith.'

* * *

Carole McKenna and her family lived in South End, north of Jamaica Plain. Maggie picked up a bottle of white wine and hailed a cab. She had been to South End quite a few times over the years. In fact, before moving to New York she had lived there for a year. She still had a few friends in the neighbourhood. It was one of those districts that people fell in love with, moved to and stayed. It was a young vibrant community with a big heart and loads of history and character.

The cab pulled up outside a lovely Georgian-style house. The road and the house had an old European charm about them. Two rows of majestic trees lined the street. Maggie paid the cab and mounted the steps to the door. Either side of her an ornate steel fence embedded with leaves and flowers rolled up to the front of the building like curling bougainvillea. The house itself was one in a row of very old and very elegant red-brick houses. It was like stepping back in time to a bygone era.

Maggie rang the bell on the enormous red wooden door and after a few seconds the light in the hall came on and the door was opened. Carole McKenna greeted her with a huge smile.

'Hi Maggie, come on in. Give me your coat and I'll hang it up for you.'

'I brought some wine. I wasn't sure if you were a wine or beer person?' said Maggie.

'Both,' Carole replied and laughed. 'But I prefer beer, to be honest.

Danny will drink the wine!'

'Good,' said Maggie and laughed along. 'We grew up around the corner from the Sam Adams plant in Jamaica Plain. Mother's milk and all that.'

'A woman after my own heart!'

Carole led her into a large living room and introduced her to her husband. Danny was a tall guy, fit looking with steel-grey hair and a beard cut closely to his face. He wore a pair of brown horn-rimmed glasses. Maggie shook the hand he held out, a strong firm handshake. Her dad used to say the mark of a man was his handshake. 'If a man cannot look you in the eye and give you a firm handshake, he can't be trusted.'

'Hi Maggie, *céad míle fáilte!*'

Carole intervened. 'He said, "a hundred thousand welcomes"! Maggie, meet Danny. Danny, meet Maggie.'

'*Go raibh maith agat*, Danny,' said Maggie, thanking him in halting Irish.

'Ah, good on yah!' he replied and beamed a big smile back at her.

'That's as much as I know now. Don't be thinking I can actually speak Irish.'

'Maggie, a very wise man once taught me, "*Is fearr Gaeilge bhriste, ná Béarla cliste.*" And do you know what that translates as?'

Maggie shook her head.

'It means poor Irish or even a little Irish is far better than clever English. You deserve a decent drink for that effort. What'll ya have? Wine or beer?'

'A beer please, Danny.'

When her husband was away getting the drinks, Carole explained that he was from Belfast in the North of Ireland and that he came from an Irish-speaking family.

'He loves the Irish language, and now he'll think you are simply the best.'

The two women laughed.

Maggie felt right at home. They seemed to be a great couple, with 'no airs and graces'. Another one of her dad's phrases, which meant they were down to earth. She had noticed more and more how things that her dad used to say were creeping into her own thoughts. Maybe they were always there, and she just never noticed until he had passed away. She missed him terribly.

Danny came back into the room with two Sam Adams beers for Maggie and his wife and a glass of white wine for himself.

'I hope you like chilli, Maggie? My turn to cook tonight so nothing fancy, I'm afraid.'

'I love chilli, suits me fine,' she replied.

They chatted over dinner. Maggie told them both more about what had happened recently, about Faith and her father.

'That is an incredible story. Beautiful and tragic at the same time. It makes my blood boil when I think about what went on in Tuam, but not just Tuam – lots of other homes scattered throughout my country!' said Danny.

'I'm glad my dad didn't live to find out about Rose and his daughter Faith. It would have broken his heart.'

'I'd like to help if I can?' said Danny. 'You know, I've visited the grave site in Tuam?'

'No way!'

'Yeah, it was a long time ago. I was only a kid. Belfast had literally burst into flames in 1969 following a civil rights campaign, similar to your own one here, as pro-British mobs ran amok across the city, burning Irish Catholic homes and businesses to the ground. The old police force stood by and watched as sectarian gangs swept through our district setting fire to whole streets. Our home was destroyed, and we found ourselves sleeping in the local parish hall.

'A few months later myself and hundreds of other kids were sent to Tuam, you know, to take us out of the war zone? We stayed in the mother and baby home for about a fortnight.'

'Danny, you have got to be kidding me!' exclaimed Maggie.

'I'm deadly serious. It's a small island. It wasn't being run as a mother and baby home then. I think the place had closed at that stage. Of course, we knew nothing about the history of it. We were just kids.

'Years later, when I was studying modern Irish history in Galway University I returned to the site. During the Civil War, the place was used as a military barracks by Irish troops in favour of the Anglo-Irish Treaty. In 1922 several anti-Treaty IRA guerrillas who had been captured were executed within the grounds. A piece of the wall was left standing, and it retains the strike marks from the firing squad that carried out the executions.

'As I studied the bullet holes on the wall and read a plaque that told of the executions, I noticed a small shrine to Our Lady in the far corner of a nearby field. I walked across to it and asked the guy who was with me what the shrine was for. All he could tell me was that it was believed that the remains of children, perhaps "illegitimate" children who had died in the home, had been buried there.

'Of course, few really knew what had happened. It was maybe twenty-five years later that the full story, the full horror of what had taken place there, broke.'

'Jesus Christ! I can't believe that I'm sitting here telling you about Rose and Faith and you have actually stood on the grounds where Rose is most probably buried at the place where my sister was born.' Maggie choked up and let out a shudder of breath.

Carole got up and put her arms around Maggie. There was silence in the room for a few moments before Maggie took a deep breath and spoke.

'How do we find Faith and how can we hold the bastards who stole her to account?'

Carole explained the normal process of searching for birth parents or adopted children. Either party would apply to the Catholic charity for the file to be opened and information provided. The problem in this case was that neither the birth parents nor the adopted child was making an application for disclosure of information.

'Hell, we don't even know Faith's adopted name. So, what do we do, Carole?' asked Maggie.

'First thing tomorrow morning you call to my office, and I'll help you fill in a form requesting information. We might not know her name or the name of her adoptive parents, but we know the year she was born and where she was adopted from. It's a good place to start.'

'Are you likely to find anything?' asked Danny.

'That's one thing about the Catholic Church – they kept meticulous records of their activities. The challenge here is to persuade the Catholic charity and the bishop to open up the files they hold.'

'I didn't realise it was going to be this easy. *Sláinte*, you two!' said Maggie with a grin.

They raised their glasses in unison.

'*Sláinte*,' they said in a determined chorus as the glasses clinked.

CHAPTER 7

BOSTON, 1956

Michael Finnegan had applied through the Catholic Charities of America to adopt a young boy from Ireland. He had applied several times to the Boston City adoption board but had been rejected as 'unsuitable'.

Micky was a tall man, strong as a bull. Someone had once described him as a 'gregarious' fellow, and he would sometimes use the word to describe his personality. He liked how it sounded, 'gregarious', he would say, as if it meant special. What Micky would call gregarious, others would have called loud and aggressive.

He and his wife, who was a rather slight, quiet woman, had moved to Charlestown four years earlier. They had moved around the city frequently over the years, never quite settling down anywhere. While Micky had made himself widely known within the community, his wife kept to herself and rarely ventured out of their apartment, except to shop for groceries or attend mass with her husband on a Sunday. Even then she rarely spoke and seemed timid and withdrawn. Micky was known to take a drink and to lift his fists frequently, perhaps even to his petite wife. But then again, so did many of the men in Charlestown. It was nobody's business, and no one made it their business, certainly not the Church.

Micky was also a friend of the local parish priest and often volunteered to help in the church and parish hall. He coached the parish children's baseball team along with Father Timothy O'Rourke and often accompanied them on trips across the city and beyond. He was well liked by the children's parents, who appreciated the time he volunteered to look after the kids. Most Catholic families in Charlestown were big with six, seven, eight or more children. The parents were glad to have some of them taken off their hands for a few hours each week.

The parish priest was only too happy to recommend Micky Finnegan to the Catholic Charities when he raised the matter of adoption. Micky had asked Father O'Rourke if it would be possible to adopt a boy between the ages of five and ten, explaining that they would not have to worry about night feeds and dirty nappies, and it would be a great age to get the kid involved in the parish baseball team.

'Of course.' The parish priest had laughed and replied saying, 'Maybe he'll be blessed with a million-dollar arm, eh, Micky?'

'Too right, Faatha,' Micky had replied.

Micky and his wife were sent a black and white photo of five-year-old Peter Kavanagh, the boy they would adopt. Unlike wealthy couples, they did not get to pick or to consider a selection of candidates.

Peter was a slight boy, with thick dark curly hair and an angelic face. He looked a bit uncomfortable in the photo, the smile forced. Peter was dressed in his Sunday best and was holding a teddy bear under one arm and a small suitcase in the other. It was the only time he had been dressed so well or held a teddy bear. After the photo had been taken, it was promptly taken from him and the good clothes returned to the closet, to be held for another boy and another photo.

Micky collected little Peter Kavanagh and took him home. A week later, maybe even less, Micky returned home drunk. He ordered his wife to go to bed, which she did promptly without a word. She immediately switched the lights out, closed her eyes tight and wrapped the pillow around her head. Micky let himself into Peter's room and locked the door behind him.

* * *

As his new parents had formally adopted Peter Kavanagh after he had arrived in Boston, his name was changed to Peter Finnegan. Soon, he was well and truly a Boston kid. A few years later he started Charlestown High School in Medford Street. He enjoyed his classes and joined the school baseball team, where he excelled. He was a quiet kid who kept to himself.

As the years progressed, Peter withdrew further into his shell. His teachers had put his initial quietness down to his shy personality and thought that, like many new students, he would take time to settle down and make friends. But he didn't. He at least seemed to be enjoying the newfound freedom the time at school and baseball practice gave him. He would frequently volunteer for extracurricular activities and was keen to help in any way he could, even if it meant staying on after school hours.

Peter always arrived at school early. His teacher, Mr Baker, had asked if he would set up the assembly hall for morning prayers and he had said he would be happy to. Every morning while the other boys were playing in the yard, Peter would unstack the chairs and line them out in rows. He would lay out a dozen chairs on the stage for the teachers and for the parish priest, who would lead the school in prayers each morning.

Father Timothy O'Rourke was tall and well built. Though young, he had a confidence about him. Some of the teachers thought him arrogant. Every morning, like a giant, he strode the corridors of the school joking with the boys, wrestling occasionally with one or two. He was an enthusiastic patron of sports in the school and was regularly found in the sports hall and on the sports field watching the action. In between games he would be in the changing rooms giving the boys a pep talk. Win or lose, he would be there to greet the boys after they returned.

Father O'Rourke had taken a liking to Peter. Peter was delighted with the praise and the attention he received. It was very different from the type of attention he received at home. Father O'Rourke would shout from the sidelines when Peter batted, 'Knock it out of the park, Peter!'

When he did, Peter loved the congratulations from his teammates, the praise from the coach and from Father O'Rourke. For the first time in his young life, he had found love and support. He felt he belonged somewhere.

After one of the games, which they had won, Father O'Rourke had hugged Peter. He had laid his arm across Peter's shoulder and asked him if he would like to become an altar boy.

'Yes, Father, please!'

Peter was thrilled. He had watched the older altar boys help Father O'Rourke during mass and had been envious. The mass seemed a magical ceremony to him and to be given the opportunity to help with the Sacraments in front of the whole parish, well, he was just so proud. The boys themselves looked beautiful in their gowns and lace vestments. To be close to Jesus in such a way would be very special. He could not wait. He knew his dad would be pleased; he was a friend of Father O'Rourke's.

Later that week he had attended a practice session in the church. Father O'Rourke had been there to help, along with another altar boy who would be assisting with mass that Sunday. Peter was excited and nervous in equal measure.

At the end of the session Father O'Rourke had brought him to a small changing room, where he would change for mass, and allocated him a little locker. At the very end Peter had been given the vestments that he would wear. Father O'Rourke had shown him how to dress.

First, he slipped his arms into a large maroon smock that buttoned down the front and that now hung just above his ankles. Then he pulled on a white outer smock. Its neck, cuffs and edging were adorned with about 5 inches of intricate lace. He buttoned a crisp white dog collar around his neck. There was a large mirror in the corner of the changing room and Father O'Rourke stood Peter in front of it and told him to join his hands in front of himself.

'You will be the most beautiful altar boy in St Michael's, Peter, a little angel!'

Father O'Rourke rested his hands on Peter's shoulders and hugged him tightly. Peter was overwhelmed with emotion when he saw himself in the mirror and had to choke back tears.

'Thank you very much, Father,' said Peter with all the sincerity he could convey.

Father O'Rourke turned Peter around, removed a handkerchief from his pocket and gently dried his tears. He took Peter's face in both his hands and kissed him on the lips.

'Everything will be just perfect on Sunday, Peter, just perfect.'

That Sunday Peter rose early and got ready. He really took his time washing and dressing. He had polished his shoes until they gleamed, and he had brushed his hair until it shone. He would be helping with his first mass, and he wanted to look his very best.

The church was full as mass began. Peter followed every move of the lead altar boy. He watched Father O'Rourke adoringly as he said mass. On more than one occasion Father O'Rourke had looked straight at him and smiled approvingly. Peter had thought his heart would burst with love and pride. He stared at the crucified Jesus looking down upon the altar and prayed. He had never felt closer to God. He sensed his worries and the pain he hid deep inside begin to dissolve.

After mass, the altar boys returned to the changing rooms. Father O'Rourke praised them both for how well they had done. He asked Peter to follow him to his own changing room, to help him remove his vestments. The other altar boys changed and left.

Father O'Rourke removed his stole, folded it neatly and placed it in a drawer. He bent forward and asked Peter to pull the outer smock over his head. He was able to unbutton the inner smock himself before putting both on a hanger and placing them in a cupboard. He told Peter to sit down on the old wooden bench that lay along one side of the room. Peter looked up at the large portrait that hung on the wall facing him. 'St Nicholas, the Patron St of Children', it read. Father O'Rourke walked across the room and locked the door. He turned and walked back to Peter, towering over the child.

'Your father tells me you are a good boy, Peter!'

He placed his left hand on Peter's shoulder and unzipped the fly of his trousers.

CHAPTER 8

BOSTON, PRESENT DAY

Conor had rung the bishop's residence several times and each time he was informed that the bishop was either out on Church business or in a meeting. After the fourth phone call in as many days, he knew they were giving him the run-around.

He had told the bishop he had no axe to grind with the Church – he just wanted to find Faith. Why could O'Rourke not have just done the decent thing and helped him find her? There was only one rational explanation: the bishop was hiding something. He was either protecting himself or the Church, maybe both.

That night after the children had been put to bed, Conor decided to tell Brenda everything and seek her advice on what to do next. She listened to Conor's story about Rose, his father, baby Faith and what Maggie had found out. He explained that his gut feeling was that Bishop O'Rourke was trying to hide something.

'Brenda, it looks like the Church acted illegally and shipped thousands of children from Ireland to cities like Boston. In most cases the nuns changed their names and falsified new identities. These kids were effectively sold to wealthy Irish American families who wanted to adopt.'

Brenda was horrified at the thought of those 796 babies dumped in a septic tank. It sent a visible shiver down her spine.

'So, what are you going to do?' she asked.

'I can't let it go, Brenda. Even apart from finding Faith, there are thousands of people out there who don't even know who they really are. They deserve to know who their real mothers were and how they were treated. It's clear now that O'Rourke won't co-operate. I'm going to have to find a good reason to seize and examine the Church files. We have to seriously consider prosecuting anyone in the Church hierarchy who conspired to cover this shit up.'

Brenda was silent for a few moments before she asked, 'Conor, are you sure you want to do this?'

'What do you mean?' he replied.

'You've worked so hard to get here – we both have – and we've talked about this, worked towards this, the youngest Commissioner of Police in the history of the Boston PD? We are so close. You can't afford to make powerful enemies.'

'What do you want me to do, Brenda, walk away? Tell Maggie I don't give a damn about Faith? I'm a cop, Brenda, and this is my sister. These kids were stolen by the Church.'

'And this is the Catholic Church we are talking about, Conor. Bishop O'Rourke is a powerful figure in this city. Can you really afford to make him an enemy? All I'm asking you to do is to take some time to think about this, love. Don't make any hasty decisions.'

Brenda put her arms around Conor's neck and hugged him.

'Please, honey, all I'm asking is that you think about this a little longer.'

Conor decided to go for a run and changed into his sweats. When he was stressed or anxious, he would go for a late-night run, clear his mind. He closed the front door behind him, descended the steps from the porch onto Lagrange Street and began to jog. The street was quiet, with 'hardly a sinner about', one of his dad's old phrases.

He struck a strong pace straight away along the deserted sidewalk. Within a few minutes he was breathing heavily, and the sweat had already begun to bead on his forehead. As he turned left onto Centre Street, he was lost in the rhythm of his own breathing and pumping legs. He felt his worries evaporate.

Before he knew it, he was passing St Theresa-Avila Catholic church. He slowed his run and stopped outside. Though it was late, the front doors were open and the lights were on inside. He checked his watch, 11.20pm, and remembered that tonight there was a midnight mass. He walked in, blessed himself with holy water from the font and took a seat in the back pew.

The church was empty except for an elderly man who walked slowly across the top altar lighting candles. He moved with a slow fluid grace, touching the flickering flame he held in his hand to each of the large candles. Conor watched him and wondered who he was, how long he had performed this function in the church. Ten years, twenty, thirty or more? He walked across the altar carefully, with a delicate reverence, navigating his way between the collection of ornate standing candlesticks, statues and the stone altar table itself. There was something wonderfully peaceful about the quiet, something reassuring about the presence of the old man.

Conor closed his eyes and prayed. He only ever prayed to Our Lady. When he had been stationed in Kuwait during Desert Storm, he had 'Queen of Heaven' tattooed across his chest above his heart. He never fully understood why he felt this connection to the mother of Jesus. His own mother had died when he was barely a teenager. He supposed in some way they were one and the same together, mothers. Whenever he contemplated

God, he often thought of a feminine figure rather than a male one, loving, compassionate, forgiving, like a mother. It seemed to make more sense to him.

He began to pray softly to himself, 'Hail Mary full of Grace, the Lord is with Thee, blessed art thou amongst women, blessed is the fruit of thy womb Jesus ...' He closed his eyes and tried to conjure an image of his own mother before the cancer had wreaked its cruel havoc upon her body, before it had robbed her of her vibrancy. He asked her, as he always did at difficult times, what should he do? He asked her to guide him and to watch over him. No, not just him, him and Maggie. They were in this together now. He hadn't included Maggie in his prayers in a long time. She'd been a right pain in the ass in recent years and instead of trying to make up anymore, he'd just pushed her away. It was easier not to communicate at all. They disagreed on just about everything, politics, religion, the Church. But maybe she hadn't been so wrong about O'Rourke and the Church after all? He realised he had been too quick to dismiss her instincts. He knew what his mom and dad would wish for, what they'd want him to do. To build a bridge back to Maggie. He promised them he would try.

After a while he became aware of people beginning to enter the church to attend midnight mass. He got up and quietly left to resume his run, a plan already forming in his mind.

*   *   *

The next morning Conor called two of his detectives from the Sexual Crimes Unit into his office, Stacey Washington and Sam Goldberg. Stacey was an African-American Baptist and Sam was an agnostic Jew.

'Take a seat. I want you to put any cases you have right now on hold. If there is anything urgent, let me know and we will reallocate it. I want the both of you to get all the files we have on sexual abuse within the Catholic Church in Boston and review them.'

'What's this about, Chief?' asked Detective Washington.

'I want you to look for any reference to children adopted from Ireland, and I want you to look for any reference to the role of senior members of the Catholic hierarchy in covering up abuse, particularly Bishop Timothy O'Rourke, or Father or Monsignor O'Rourke, as he was before he became a bishop. Start cross-checking that name O'Rourke in any of the files.'

'How far do you want us to go back, Chief?' said Detective Washington.

'To the end of the Second World War, guys,' said Conor.

Detective Goldberg let out an audible groan. 'That's a lot of paperwork, Chief!'

'Clear your desks. I'm making this a priority. We know kids were abused, but I want to know who covered up the abuse, and whether O'Rourke was involved. There were fewer checks and balances in those days. I want to know if known sexual predators were allowed to adopt any of these kids and who knew about it. We have gone after the priests who abused children; this time we are going after the people at the top who knew what was happening and covered it up. You OK with that?' He looked directly at both detectives.

Detectives Goldberg and Washington glanced at each other, and Washington replied for them both.

'Totally!'

'And Detectives, this is a sensitive investigation. I don't want Bishop O'Rourke's name mentioned outside of my office, OK? This needs to stay tight, for now!'

'Understood, Chief!' they replied in unison.

After they'd left, Conor lifted the phone and rang Maggie.

'Hi sis, how you doin'? We gotta talk. Why don't we sit down and catch up?'

'Sure, I'm making spaghetti tonight – why don't you drop by after work for a bite of supper?'

'Great! I'll drop by around 7pm, OK?'

'Perfect. Conor, stop at a packie and pick up a few beers, would ya?'

Conor smiled to himself. Some of the old slang was slipping back into Maggie's vocabulary already. *You can take the girl out of the Hub but never the Hub out of the girl*, he thought. *No matter where we went or ended up, Boston would always be the centre of the universe.*

'Sure. And Maggie?'

'Yeah?'

'It's good to have you home, kid!'

* * *

Later that night Conor picked up a dozen beers on his way over to his dad's house. He let himself in. As he closed the front door behind him, he could smell the spaghetti sauce from down the hall. He could hear Ed Sheeran's 'Galway Girl' coming from the radio in the kitchen and Maggie singing along. She sounded just like their mother. He stopped for a moment and closed his eyes.

The hall was in darkness. In truth the front hall still looked almost exactly as it had when he was a boy. The same mirror, the same old worn banister they would hang their coats on. His dad had kept the house much the same after his mother had died. Conor stood in silence and took in the smells and the sounds. The memories wrapped themselves around him in a soothing embrace.

Maggie was standing by the cooker when he entered the kitchen. She turned and said, 'I thought I heard you coming in.'

Conor sat the beer on the kitchen table, walked over to where she stood and embraced her. Maggie was a little shocked and didn't know what to do, but then she put her arms around his waist and hugged him back. She felt tears well up in her eyes. They just stood there for a minute, maybe longer, eyes closed, and held each other. Afterwards they sat, ate and reminisced about growing up. They talked about Mom and Dad, about Rose and then Faith. They laughed and remembered and the distance between them narrowed.

When they were kids, they had been super close. They had been the cliché: he was the protective older brother and she was the kid sister who adored her big brother. When he was serving in Kuwait, Maggie had decided to study journalism in college.

Growing up she had been a bit of a rebel without a cause. By the time he had returned home from service and joined the Boston PD, she had become a rebel *with* a cause. It just wasn't his cause. From that point on they had steadily grown apart. They had argued, things were said, and they had ended up on opposite sides of the police barricades. Maggie had gotten herself a job with the *New York Times* and had moved to the Big Apple. Over the years she had built herself a reputation as a hard-hitting investigative journalist, critical of the establishment, particularly corporate America, the police, including the Boston PD, and the Catholic Church. He hoped that this time they could be on the same side.

CHAPTER 9

BOSTON, 1969

The two young men had bought a bottle of cheap bourbon from a local store in downtown Dorchester. While one paid for the liquor and distracted the guy behind the counter, the other stole a twelve pack of beer. They hurried down the block and jumped into the car they had stolen earlier. An hour later they were both mean drunk and looking for trouble.

'Head over to South End.'

'What t'fuck for? You looking to get yourself one of those Southie queers?'

'Fuck you!'

They both laughed.

They headed to South End, one of the original melting pots of Boston. It was made up of lots of different communities, Irish Catholic, Jewish, African American, Puerto Rican, Chinese and Greek. The district had become a blues and jazz Mecca, with famous clubs such as the Royal Palms, Eddie Levine's, the Hi-Hat, The Cave and many more, attracting people from all over the city. In the 1940s the area began to attract a new type of immigrant, gay men and women.

They drove down Massachusetts Avenue and turned into Tremont Street. It was a warm summer Saturday night, and the place was buzzing.

'Pull over, pull over. Let's hit the bars.'

'What with? We're busted! I spent the last dollar we had on the bourbon.'

'Shit!' the young passenger exclaimed. 'I ain't drivin' round in this fuckin kaa all night.'

They turned a corner into a side street. It was quieter with just a few restaurants. At the end of the road, they turned onto Beacon Street. A few minutes later they passed the Hotel Fensgate. The Fensgate hosted a ball every weekend and was one of only a few venues in the city that could be described as gay friendly.

Thelma and Marilyn left the hotel just as the car passed. Thelma and Marilyn were their drag queen names. During the week they were just ordinary Charles Stewart and Michael Jones. They linked one another as they turned back towards Tremont Street. They liked to cruise Tremont and Washington Streets hoping to pick up guys.

'Holy Mother, did you see those queer fuckers?' the driver almost shouted.

'Yeah, I did. Turn the kaa around,' said the passenger in a sudden rage.

As the driver turned the car, the passenger, Peter Finnegan, bent forward, reached under the seat and gripped a revolver that was sitting there. It was a heavy gunmetal grey, a .38 Smith & Wesson police revolver. He had stolen it from a home they had broken into a few days earlier. He jammed it into the waistband of his jeans and pulled his shirt over it.

Peter had already spent a year in juvenile detention for grievous bodily harm. Despite a promising academic record in his early years, he had left school without any qualifications. He dropped the baseball team in his second year, and church activities and began hanging out with a tough crowd. It was then that he started to get involved in his first fights with other boys at school. Within two years he had gone from being a sweet quiet kid to a delinquent.

No one quite knew why. His dad was a mean drunk who was known to lift his fists to his wife. Maybe it was something to do with that? Maybe he took a beating at home? Maybe he was just plain mean like his dad? The teachers had tried their best to steer him off the course he was on, but they were unable to reach him. He steadily lost interest in his studies and became increasingly detached. He was prone to bursts of anger and violence and no amount of discipline would stop him. By the time he was sixteen, he was just another teenager hustling for a living on the streets of Boston. No one knew his story and as far as Peter himself was concerned, no one really gave a damn either.

Peter approached Thelma and Marilyn from behind. As he drew parallel with them, he pulled the revolver from his waistband and pointed the weapon straight at both women.

'Give me your fuckin' money!' he screamed at the two of them.

Thelma immediately froze and the blood drained from her face. She seemed to fall against Marilyn's shoulder. Marilyn stepped between Thelma and the young man, as if to protect her.

'Hey kid, just take it easy. You can take anything that we have.' She took a step towards the young man and raised her right hand. She held a small clutch bag and reached out to pass it to him.

He fired a single shot. Marilyn collapsed backwards. Thelma began to scream hysterically.

Peter leaned over Marilyn and snatched the bag from her hand. Before turning away, he swung a kick at her as she lay on the ground, the toe of his boot catching her on the side of the head, dislodging her wig. He exploded in fury, viciously kicking her again and again. Afterwards Thelma would describe Peter Finnegan to the police. She would never forget the look of sheer rage on his face.

That night in hospital Marilyn, Michael Jones, died of her injuries. It was now a murder enquiry. Some of the cops who attended the crime scene and had then escorted Thelma to the precinct thought it was funny. There was little or no sympathy for Thelma or Marilyn. Some of the cops at the precinct thought they deserved it. 'Fucking queers!' one cop had mumbled within earshot of Thelma.

The next morning Peter was arrested, not in relation to the murder of Marilyn – no one was in any hurry to solve that homicide – but for breaking and entering. Peter was apprehended in a stolen car with the cop's stolen police issue revolver hidden under the front passenger seat. When the investigating officers examined the weapon, it was obvious it had been fired recently. There was a single spent round in one of the chambers. It was only at this point that the detectives linked the two cases and had no choice but to question Peter in relation to the murder of Marilyn.

Two cops from Homicide interviewed Peter. As far as they were concerned, he was just another little punk. When he refused to co-operate, he got a severe beating, the first of several over the course of the day. That night he confessed to a string of offences and to Marilyn's murder. Once he began to talk, he couldn't stop, the floodgates opened and he eventually told the detectives why he hated 'queers'.

The two detectives who took his statement were incredulous. Peter Finnegan told them of how he had been sexually molested by his adopted father. While an altar boy in St Michael's church in Charlestown, he claimed he had been violently raped countless times by his parish priest, Father Timothy O'Rourke. After the first time, Father O'Rourke had given him a gold crucifix and chain to wear. He had explained that it was a special cross because he was a special boy, and he must never take it off.

Only later did Peter realise that the cross and chain was a symbol, a brand that other child molesters would recognise. O'Rourke had passed him around a circle of priests, including more than one on occasion.

He had run away from home and ended up on the streets. One small crime led to another more serious and another more serious again. Initially, it was a case of steal or starve. But the streets were cruel, and he had learned to be just as cruel to survive. His sweet childish nature had been crushed a little piece at a time and what was left was mean and twisted. If he had been a dog, it might have been more humane to have had him put to sleep.

Later, locked up in his cell, Peter chose to end his own agony and save the state the expense of a costly trial and execution. In the dead of night, tormented and alone, he hung himself.

The lead detective on the case had typed up his report on the murder. He had also typed up the kid's statement with the allegations of sexual abuse and he took it to his superior officer, Captain O'Flynn. The captain was a devout Catholic and a senior member of various religious confraternities in Boston. He told him to destroy it and forget about it. The detective did eventually forget about the case, but for some reason he didn't destroy the statement. Instead, he buried the file at the back of his filing cabinet. After his retirement, the files, along with thousands of others in the building, were moved to the basement.

CHAPTER 10

BOSTON, PRESENT DAY

Within a week of writing to the Catholic Charities of America seeking information in relation to Faith, Maggie had received a letter informing her that the charity was unable to help. Only the birth parents or the adoptee themselves could access that information. With Carole's help, Maggie then applied to the Massachusetts Probate and Family Court Department seeking a ruling that the charity be directed to open the relevant files to her family. A hearing was scheduled for later that month, 23 September, at 10am in the Boston Municipal Court. The case was set to be heard before the Honourable Judge Siobhan Coogan.

Early that morning Conor dropped Maggie and Carole off at the courthouse. They had agreed that it would be better if he kept a low profile in relation to the case. He would work away behind the scenes for now. 'Good luck!' he shouted before driving away.

She remembered a time when Conor would take her everywhere with him. When he returned home from school and college he would shout, 'Where's my little sticking plaster?' She would run down the stairs or along the hall and into his arms. Her dad had described her as Conor's little sticking plaster because she followed him everywhere. The search for Faith had thrown them together once again, in fact had forced them to work together.

She realised now that what they had learned about the Church and about O'Rourke had shaken his own personal faith. She hadn't really understood how he felt until recently, until that night in the kitchen when they had talked, really talked, for the first time in years.

He was pissed and angry. He felt betrayed by O'Rourke. *That makes two of us, bro.*

Maggie waved and watched the car disappear into heavy traffic.

She and Carole headed into the courthouse. There were armed police guards searching people in the foyer. Everyone entering the building passed through a metal-detecting arch, while their bags and briefcases were scanned for weapons and explosives. Before the Marathon bombings no one had dreamed that Boston would be a target for Islamic terrorists. Now the city was on permanent alert.

Once through security, Maggie and Carole checked the court notices to see where the case was to be heard – courtroom two. Maggie had decided to represent herself, rather than hire a lawyer. The case was relatively straight-forward, though by no means guaranteed to succeed. Carole had explained that it was common for individuals to represent themselves in such cases. The hearings were usually quite informal and relaxed.

When they entered courtroom two, Maggie gave her name to the court clerk, and he told them to take a seat on the benches at the back. He explained that the court would begin sitting at 10am. That when the judge entered the room, they must stand until she was seated. He couldn't tell them when they would be called or in what order the cases would be heard.

'Don't worry. When your name is called out, just make your way to the table on the left in front of the judge.'

There were already quite a few people seated there, chatting nervously among themselves. As a probate and family court, there was a mixture of different types of people and cases to be heard. Divorcees either ignoring or staring venomously at each other. Estranged and embittered siblings contesting a will, sitting at opposite ends of the courtroom. As Carole put it, if looks could kill, they would both have been casualties caught in the crossfire, causing Maggie to burst out laughing.

'Don't be laughing!' mumbled Carole as she elbowed Maggie in the ribs.

There was a large group of lawyers gathered in an area to the right of the courtroom. Some of them broke away and came over to consult with their clients in the public gallery. They were an unremarkable bunch. Most of them were either quite young or quite old. Starting out or just about ready to check out by the look of some of the older faces. Some of the young lawyers looked nervous and were overcompensating by trying to project a confidence or experience they clearly lacked. The older lawyers wore either a cynical smile or no smile at all. They were running on empty and counting the days and the dollars until they could afford to retire to the golf course or to Florida.

At 9.50am three more lawyers entered the courtroom. These looked and behaved very differently to the rest. All three were very smartly dressed. Their suits were finely tailored, expensive and stylish without being ostentatious. They moved in a V formation, like geese in flight. The other lawyers quickly made space for the newcomers. It was as if legal royalty had entered the court. They were met with a chorus of greetings from some of the lawyers present, especially the younger more ambitious ones.

It was obvious that the three lawyers were headed by the female in the group. She led the way and the two younger men followed, one carrying a briefcase and the other carrying a large bundle of legal papers. Carole leaned closer to Maggie and said, 'I don't know who they are representing but if it's the Church, this thing just got damn serious pretty quickly. You know who she is?'

'No. Who is she?' replied Maggie.

'Her name is Barbara Clarke, and she works for one of the most prestigious law firms here in Boston. Seriously, Maggie, what on earth is going on?'

'Well, I'm not surprised at all. I told you that asshole O'Rourke would fight this all the way.'

'These guys bill a thousand dollars an hour, Maggie. They're heavy hitters.'

'Who gives a shit.'

Maggie had a big grin on her face. Carole reached over and squeezed her hand and said, 'Let's do this.'

'All rise! The Right Honourable Judge Coogan presiding.'

'Please take your seats,' said the judge as she sat down.

It was over two hours before Maggie was called by the clerk.

'Miss Margaret McCann, please step forward and address the judge.'

'Good morning, Miss McCann. These proceedings are quite informal, as you can see. Are you representing yourself today?' asked the judge.

'Yes, Your Honour,' replied Maggie. Her heart was thumping in her chest.

'And you, Miss Clarke, I take it are representing Bishop O'Rourke for the Catholic Diocese of Massachusetts?'

'Yes, Your Honour, I am.'

'OK, let's get started. Miss McCann, would you present your case?' The judge smiled at Maggie and added, 'Just relax, Miss McCann. Take your time.'

Maggie outlined her request that the court order the Catholic Diocese to open its adoption records for 1945 and 1946. She then told the judge of having received an old letter from a recently deceased nun in Ireland informing her father that, unknown to him, he had a daughter who had been born in Ireland in 1945 and then adopted in Boston.

Maggie handed Sister Bridget's letter to the clerk, who passed it up to the judge.

'Your Honour, I don't know if you are aware of the background to our case? I have a copy of a piece that was printed in the *New York Times* entitled "The Stolen Children of Ireland", and with your permission I'd like to present it to you?' Maggie could feel her breathing slow. She was getting into her rhythm.

'Yes, Miss McCann, hand it to the clerk.'

'It outlines in some detail the cruel nature of these mother and baby homes in Ireland and just as importantly it describes how many thousands of children were trafficked from Ireland to the US for adoption. It also describes how in many of these cases the adoptions were illegal and in fact in very many cases the nuns falsified both death and birth certificates. Both those words, Your Honour, "trafficked" and "illegal", are used in an official Irish government report into these adoptions. That report is referenced in the *Times* piece.

'Your Honour, the only means we have of identifying my sister Faith is through Church records. I am convinced that if Faith were here and she was asked, *Do you want to know who your parents were? Do you want to know your real identity? Do you wish to know that you have a brother and a sister here in Boston?* she would answer, *Yes! Yes, I do!*

'I think it is very clear, Your Honour, that were my father or Faith's mother Rose alive today, both would want Faith to know who she really is. There would be no question of either the birth parents or the adoptee herself seeking to have this information kept secret.

'Thank you, Your Honour. That is all I have to say,' Maggie concluded.

'Thank you, Miss McCann. You may take your seat for the moment,' replied the judge.

Maggie sat down beside Carole, who whispered, 'Well done!'

'Miss Clarke, would you like to present the case for the Diocese?'

'Thank you, Your Honour.' Barbara Clarke showed absolutely no sign of nerves. She moved and spoke with clarity and confidence. Maggie understood now why she was in charge.

'Your Honour, Massachusetts state law in this matter is very clear. Placement agencies like the Catholic Charities of America can only release identifying information to one of three groups: the adopted person himself or herself, the adoptive parent or a biological parent. In this case, Miss McCann is none of the above. There is no provision within the state of Massachusetts for siblings to access this type of sensitive and confidential information.

'If it pleases Your Honour, I would like to draw your attention to both state and federal case law in respect of this matter?'

'Yes, carry on, Miss Clarke.'

'Your Honour, in *Fineburg versus Suffolk,* it was found that any of the three groups identified, including the adopted child, I quote "does not have an automatic right to access" identifying information about the biological parents and can only access that information, and again I quote, "upon a showing of good cause".

'It is our contention, Your Honour, that Miss McCann has clearly failed to demonstrate "good cause". There is no evidence, other than this letter, which could simply be a work of fiction, that Miss McCann is in any way related to the individual she seeks to identify.

'Moreover, Your Honour, Miss McCann has asked for access to private information in relation to the adoption of not just one individual but all those, of which there may well be a number, placed for adoption in Boston by the Catholic Charities of America during the course of the years 1945 and 1946.

'Your Honour, this would not only be a breach of Massachusetts state law but would force the Diocese to breach its legal and moral obligations to protect the right to privacy of those families party to these adoptions under the Constitution. Rights that were further reinforced in the case *Almy Society Inc. versus Mellon.*

'If it would please Your Honour, both cases are referenced in our written submission to the court. My colleague will provide the clerk with a copy for your attention.

'Thank you, Your Honour,' she finished.

'Thank You, Miss Clarke, and thank you, Miss McCann.' The judge looked at the clock and noted the time, 1.10pm.

'Given the time, I am going to break for lunch. I will consider the case over lunch and will issue a determination when the court resumes at 2.15pm. I expect both parties will be present?'

'Yes, Your Honour,' replied Maggie and Barbara Clarke simultaneously.

Barbara Clarke smiled at the judge, turned and sauntered out of the court as if she had already won the case. She looked cocky as hell, too cocky, Maggie thought. She whispered to Carole, 'I'd love to see that smile wiped off her face, the smug bitch!'

* * *

Maggie and Carole grabbed a quick sandwich in a nearby deli and Maggie called Conor to let him know what was happening. She told him she'd call straight after the verdict.

When they returned to the courtroom there seemed to be a larger number of people present. The case had generated some interest among the lawyers in the building and a few of them had made their way into court to listen to Judge Coogan's verdict.

'All rise. Please stand for the Right Honourable Judge Siobhan Coogan,' called the clerk of the court.

After the judge took her seat, she addressed Maggie and Barbara Clarke.

'Thank you both for your submissions. Miss Clarke, you have presented a very compelling argument in relation to the issue of privacy in this case.'

Maggie's heart sank as Barbara Clarke smiled back at the judge, who continued her speech.

'You are absolutely right that all of the adopting families and indeed the potential adoptees themselves are entitled to their privacy and it would be inconceivable that the court would simply order these files opened to Miss McCann.

'However, I have read Miss McCann's supporting evidence and it is clear that there is a compelling argument that both the Catholic Church in Ireland and the Catholic Charities of America did act illegally and did falsify both death certificates and birth certificates when children were "trafficked" from Ireland. This is no flight of fancy on Miss McCann's part.'

Sensing victory, Maggie turned to glance at Carole. She could see the smile disappear from Barbara Clarke's face.

'Given that in many of these adoptions, the Church acted illegally, falsified documents and withheld that information from the birth mothers, the adopting parents and, most importantly of all, the adopted children themselves here in Boston, I feel obliged to find a solution that protects the privacy of those families and individuals but also provides them with this information and empowers them to make a decision themselves.

'Therefore, I will be instructing an independent third party to examine those files, to identify the adoptees, to inform them of the circumstances, including Miss McCann's desire to meet with them, and to allow them to make the decision as to whether they wish to pursue this matter further.

'Miss McCann, it will be up to the adoptees themselves to decide whether they wish to meet with you!'

CHAPTER 11

BOSTON,
PRESENT DAY

Conor checked in with Detectives Washington and Goldberg every few days. There was a huge number of files to be read. Boston PD had moved into its new modern headquarters in Roxbury in 1997. All the old paper files were stored in the basement of the building, thousands of them. The place was big certainly enough – Number 1 Schroeder Plaza occupied an entire city block.

Whenever Conor had any spare time he would join Washington and Goldberg digging their way through the mountain of files. Sometimes he would work through the night, alone. There was no other way to do it except to read every file. What made the search even more difficult was that the old files were organised by year and by precinct, rather than by the type of crime. There was no simple way of narrowing the search down. This time there were no computers, no search engines to pinpoint and cross-reference information. This was old-fashioned detective work. They were looking for several needles buried in a very large haystack.

Conor could tell that both detectives were pissed off with the drudgery of the search. File after file, day after day. They had been searching for several weeks now with no success. He was beginning to consider changing strategy. Maybe they weren't going to find anything here.

Though they were surprised that the Chief was assisting in the search, the detectives were glad of his help. It was obvious to both of them that this was personal in some way. They just weren't sure how.

Conor joined Washington and Goldberg just after lunch.

'Hi guys, brought you coffee. How we doin'?'

'Nothing of any significance yet, Chief,' replied Washington.

They spent the rest of the afternoon and early evening reading through the files. They had started their search with 1945 and day by day had worked their way through each year. They were now on the 1960s.

Each of them sat at a large rectangular table with a stack of files piled beside them. Conor sipped his black coffee as he flicked through another file, which included a dense collection of paper sheets, old, typed statements, handwritten notes and a small number of black and white crime-scene photographs. Nothing again!

Across the table Washington looked up from the file she was reading and exclaimed, 'Jackpot! Take a look at this, Chief!'

She stood up and pushed a thin, dull-red cardboard file across the table to him. It had no identifying lettering or markings on the cover other than the date, 12 July 1969. He opened it and read the first page.

Statement of Peter Finnegan, Address Formerly 22 Eden Street, Charlestown, Boston, currently of no fixed address. Dated 12 July 1969

Signed: Detective John Casey, Jr.

At 19.45pm in custody Room 6, I took a statement from the above suspect Mr Peter Finnegan. During our interview Mr Finnegan made several allegations of a sexual nature against his father, Mr Michael Finnegan, the local

parish priest, Father Timothy O'Rourke, and other unidentified individuals, including several other Catholic
priests.

At the end of the interview, I asked Mr Finnegan if
he was willing to make a written statement in relation
to these allegations and to sign it and he said he was.
During the interview and while writing the statement
Mr Finnegan was visibly upset and broke down in tears
on several occasions.

The following statement was witnessed by myself and
my colleague Detective Joseph McAuley:

I was adopted from Ireland when I was about five. I
don't remember very much about arriving in Boston or
moving into my new home, I was only a kid. But I do
remember being raped. I don't really know exactly how to
describe what happened to me, but the man who adopted
me, Michael Finnegan, raped me in my bedroom just a few
days after I arrived in Boston. It makes me want to puke
at the thought of what he did to me. I was only a kid and
he raped me.

From that first night I went to bed terrified, every
single night. I still can't sleep because of what Finnegan
did to me. I cried myself to sleep every night and prayed
that someone would come and save me, but they never did.
That's why I ran away.

But he wasn't the worst. The worst was the parish
priest, Father Timothy O'Rourke, from St Michael's parish

where I lived. When I became a little older, O'Rourke asked me if I wanted to become an altar boy and I said yes. Straight after saying my first mass, O'Rourke raped me in the sacristy.

O'Rourke was an animal, a real nasty piece of work. He would bite me while he raped me. He would leave bite marks on me, deliberately. For years I wouldn't undress unless I was alone because that animal would bite me when he raped me. He left me with scars. He enjoyed hurting me. I remember he was always laughing, enjoying it. When I cried, he seemed to enjoy it more. He was pure evil.

I remember there was a special mass with more than one priest. I don't know their names, but after the mass, O'Rourke and the two other priests raped me. They took turns. After they were done, O'Rourke kept saying I was 'special', that the other priests knew I was special too, that one day I could become a priest, but I had to keep what they did to me a secret. A secret between us and God.

After that I was raped on a regular basis by different priests. After mass, after baseball games, even at home. The cross and chain that O'Rourke had put around my neck the first time he did it was like a sign that they had hung on me saying, 'Rape me whenever you want'.

They destroyed my life. I ran away from home the first chance I got when I was about fourteen. There was no safe place for me, not at home, not at school, not in church. I started drinking and fighting and ended up in juvenile detention a few years later.

I can still see their faces. I can still smell their breath. I have never told anyone about this. To begin with, I was too afraid and then later I was too ashamed. For so long I thought it was my fault. At the start, they told me I was special, then when I started saying no, fighting back, they told me I was messed up. But it was Michael Finnegan and Father Timothy O'Rourke who messed me up. That's why I'm here. They stole everything from me, everything, even my faith in God.

I'm sorry I shot the queer guy, I really am.

Signed: Peter Finnegan

Conor sat back in his chair after he had read the statement. He read it again. He was stunned. He had suspected O'Rourke had been trying to protect the Church, but this? Never! This guy had been a close family friend. He had officiated at both his children's First Holy Communions. Conor was reeling. But then he felt a cold anger rise through his body as he stared at the file. He felt his jaw harden and his fists tighten. Then he leaned forward, slowly pushed the file across the table to Detective Washington and stood up.

'Find out what happened to this kid. I want to know all there is about this scumbag Michael Finnegan if he's still alive. In the meantime, keep digging. We've nearly got this piece of shit O'Rourke.'

The next day Detectives Washington and Goldberg were able to inform Conor that Michael Finnegan was still alive and was living alone in Mattapan. He was luckier than his victim. Washington explained how young Peter Finnegan had taken his own life in a custody cell the night he had made his statement.

Finding the statement was a breakthrough, but the three of them knew it wasn't enough. Such statements were admissible in court as evidence because they constituted the last words of a dying person. The legal rationale was that someone who was either dying or believed their death to be imminent would have less of a reason to lie or fabricate a statement. But in the absence of any other supporting evidence, Conor knew that if they moved too soon against O'Rourke he would walk.

Conor knew Mattapan all too well, as it had some of the highest crime rates in Boston. Despite the fact that Mattapan's population was less than 5 percent of the city's total, over a quarter of all crime that happened in Boston occurred there. Ironically, the district's original Native American name meant 'a good place to be'. Some people outside the district had started calling the area 'Murderpan', and it had stuck.

Despite its bad reputation, crime in Mattapan was significantly down, but it still had its dark corners. Poverty had helped make drugs prevalent and once hard narcotics got their grip on a community, it was like Japanese knotweed – it rotted the very foundations and violent crime always followed.

Conor had seen the worst of it, including the most horrific child homicides and abuse when he worked in the Drug Control Unit. Who needed the Devil when human beings were themselves capable of such horror? He knew some sexual predators like O'Rourke hid in the open behind a façade of respectability and preyed upon their victims in living rooms, church sacristies and behind classroom doors. But it was in the dark corners that other predators like Michael Finnegan scurried.

Finnegan lived just a block away from Almont Park and its new children's adventure play area. There were two schools and a kindergarten within a square kilometre of his house. *Just a coincidence?* wondered Conor. It rarely was. Paedophiles were often the most devious, calculating and methodical of all the human predators. They were devoid of empathy and were capable of the most horrible acts of depravity against children without experiencing even a scintilla of remorse or regret.

Conor asked Detective Goldberg to run a check on Finnegan. An hour later he knocked on Conor's office door.

'Chief, this old guy Finnegan lives alone. As far as I can ascertain his wife died of cancer some twenty years ago. Apart from Peter Finnegan, they had just one other child, another boy they adopted, Francis. Michael Finnegan has retired now, but he used to work as a gardener in schools right across the city.'

'Find out what you can about this other son Francis. If he molested one child, he probably did the same to the other. Look up where he is living now. We need to talk to him. And start checking to see if there is a record of any children either being molested, going missing or murdered around Almont Park.'

'Sure, Chief. How far do you want me to go back?'

'Start with the last ten years and keep going! And tell Stacey to meet me in the car park in fifteen minutes. We're gonna go speak to Mr Finnegan, Sr.'

* * *

Half an hour later Conor and Detective Washinton pulled up near Michael Finnegan's home. It was a big house at the end of the block.

It had a double garage and was surrounded by high bushes and mature trees that hid a large garden at the back. The house itself was well kept but looked dated. The windows had off-white lace curtains rather than modern blinds. There was an old-model Ford Transit van parked in the driveway, alongside a battered trailer.

'Not bad for a retired gardener!' remarked Conor. 'Take a discreet look round back. Wait until I knock on the door and be careful, OK.'

Conor mounted the steps to the front door, knocked and nodded to Washington. She disappeared around the side of the garage. He held his detective badge in his left hand and slipped his right hand into the side of his jacket and unclipped his weapon. He wasn't about to take any chances.

After a minute Michael Finnegan opened the door.

Finnegan was a tall man, 6'2" or maybe 6'3". He had broad angular shoulders. He must have been very tall when he was younger. Despite his age, he still carried himself well. There was nothing frail about him. He was wearing a pair of washed-out jeans and a black turtleneck sweater under a checked shirt that lay open at the front. His thinning hair was pure white, and he wore a tightly trimmed beard that was the same. He had a square jaw that protruded a little, and a wide nose that looked as if it had been punched a few times, a brawler's nose. His tanned skin was lined with age and probably the weather.

'Mr Michael Finnegan?'

'Yes?'

Conor lifted his badge and said, 'Detective Conor McCann, Boston PD. Mr Finnegan, do you think I could come in? There is a matter that we are investigating, and we think you might be able to help.'

Conor watched Finnegan closely to gauge his response. There was a brief look of surprise in his expression, and he hesitated before replying.

'What's it about, Detective?'

'Your son, Mr Finnegan.'

'My son?' He paused and turned his head as if to glance back into the house for a moment. 'Well, I guess you otta come into the pahlah,' he replied hesitantly.

Finnegan turned and led Conor into a sitting room on the right. It was clean and tidy. The wallpaper was dated, very dated, and there was an old portrait of John F. Kennedy on the wall. It sat beside another portrait of Pope John Paul II. In between the two hung a large crucifix.

Conor looked around the room. It struck him that there were no family photographs, no paintings, no decorative ornaments of any sort, just the two portraits, a crucifix, a large mirror above the fireplace, a worn armchair and a couch. The place felt like it had been caught in a time trap. It looked and smelled old. It reminded him of something, he wasn't quite sure what. It would come to him.

'Sit down, Detective,' said Finnegan, pointing to the couch. 'How can I help? You mentioned my son, Francis. Is something wrong?'

Conor sat down on the couch while Finnegan took the armchair across from him.

'No, Mr Finnegan, it's not just about your son Francis. I'd like to ask you a few questions about your son Peter.'

'Petah?' A look of shock passed over Finnegan's face, his polite smile disappeared, his pupils enlarged and Conor could hear a quick inhalation of breath. In less than a few heartbeats, Finnegan had regained his composure. He was a cool character, confident. Too composed in the circumstances. But Conor had seen it, even for that brief moment – a look of fear.

'My son Petah died over fifty years ago, Detective. Of what possible interest could that be to the Boston Police Department now?' There was a sharp, even arrogant tone to his voice.

'We are investigating the illegal trafficking of children from Ireland to Boston by the Catholic Church. I believe you adopted both your sons, Peter and Francis, from Ireland. Is that correct?'

'It is, yes. My late wife was unable to have children, so we adopted the two boys.'

'I believe your first son, Peter, took his own life in police custody while being held as a murder suspect back in 1969?'

'Yeah, we did our best to raise him right, but he was just bad, plain bad. It was probably our fault, my fault really. I spoiled him, you see, Detective. We couldn't control him. Drinking, fighting, stealing. He broke my heart, and he broke my poor wife's heart.'

Conor thought it was odd that Finnegan immediately placed the blame squarely at Peter's feet. He made no attempt to excuse him, no words of compassion or regret. Nor did he express any affection for the boy. Cold.

'And Francis?'

'He lives outside the city now, in Cambridge. I don't get to see him and the grandchildren as much as I'd like to.'

'Can you remember how the adoptions were arranged, who arranged them? Was it the Catholic Charities of America or your parish priest?'

'Detective, it was a very long time ago. I really can't remember.'

'Would you have any documentation relating to either adoption?'

'I will certainly have a look and see if my wife kept any of the paperwork. She tended to look after those things. If I find anything, Detective, I'll be sure to be in touch. I'd like to help if I can.'

Finnegan stood as if to say this conversation is over. As Conor followed him out to the hall, he asked, 'Who did you say your parish priest was when you adopted the boys?'

Finnegan hesitated and managed to say, 'Detective, I honestly can't remember. I wasn't much for mass back then or the Church. We moved around the city a lot looking for work.'

Conor knew instinctively that he was being evasive.

They shook hands at the door. 'Thank you, Mr Finnegan. If you remember any information about the adoptions or find any documents, please contact me.' Conor handed him his business card.

'I will of course, Detective.'

Washington was waiting for him in the car. As they drove off, Conor remembered what the living room reminded him of – a priest's residence.

CHAPTER 12

BOSTON, PRESENT DAY

Within a few weeks the court-appointed investigators were examining the Church's records of adoptions from Ireland. Over the course of 1945 and 1946 they found there were thirty-seven children flown into the US and adopted by families in the Boston area. Of those thirty-seven, fourteen were girls and five of them had been born in March 1945 and so would fit the potential profile of Faith Rafferty. None of them was named either Faith or Rafferty. That name had disappeared from the records.

The court had contacted Maggie to inform her that two of the possible candidates had passed away. Maggie's heart sank when she heard. What if one of them was Faith? She rang Conor to tell him the bad news.

'Surely after all this she can't be dead?' she almost pleaded with Conor.

'No way, Maggie! Put that out of your mind. She's alive. We were meant to find her.'

Despite his words, Maggie could tell from the sound of his voice that he was deflated. *Is this really the end of the line?* she wondered. She shook herself. There were three good chances it wasn't.

* * *

The three women still alive were all living in Boston. Judge Coogan drafted a letter for each of the adoptees explaining the circumstances of the case and enquiring whether they wished to meet with Miss Maggie McCann, who was searching for her sister. Two of the women contacted by the court indicated that they were willing to meet. But one declined. Just over three weeks after the court hearing, Maggie was provided with the names and contact details of the two women. She was surprised when Judge Coogan rang her directly to inform her and again wished her well in her search.

Maggie rang Conor straight away as she was excited to share the news.

'Hi bro, I've some good news and bad, I'm afraid. Can you drop over later? I'd rather tell you face to face.'

'Of course. I'll be there in an hour, sis.'

Maggie could hear the eagerness in his voice.

'Conor, would you mind if I invited Carole over too?'

'No, not all. She deserves to be part of this. See you soon.'

* * *

Carole arrived at Maggie's shortly after Conor. As she pulled up outside, she thought, *What a beautiful old house!*

She stood and stared and couldn't help but think that this should have been Rose and Faith's home. But the Catholic Church had stolen that opportunity from them. The house reminded her of why she loved Boston. When she had arrived in the city as a mature student, the people and the place had charmed her.

Carole was African American and had been born and raised in the city of Tulsa, Oklahoma. Tulsa was a city with racism in its DNA. In 1921 one of the most infamous race riots in American history occurred there, the Tulsa Race Massacre, or the Greenwood Massacre, named after the black district that was attacked by white racist mobs. The mobs, many of whom were deputised and armed by the Tulsa police, swept through Greenwood like a devil's tornado, burning and looting property. More than thirty-five blocks of properties, including many businesses and homes, were destroyed in the pogrom. Hundreds were murdered and thousands were left homeless.

Wealth and privilege were no protection from racist attack, not if your skin was black. Greenwood was commonly called the 'Black Wall Street' and was without doubt the wealthiest black community in the US at the time. Racist attitudes mixed with a generous dose of good old-fashioned envy combined to create a deadly explosion of race hatred.

Decades later Carole had been on the receiving end of the same racism, from people who were most likely the direct descendants of those who were responsible for the massacre. Her home had been firebombed in a random racist attack by a group of drunken white teenagers. The following year, Carole's four-year-old daughter had been abducted from their front garden. Two days later the child's naked body had been found close to a nearby wood. She had been raped and strangled. The child's murder had nearly destroyed her. She had clung to life by a thread. Only her determination to see the killer caught had stopped her from taking her own life.

She sometimes wondered whether very much had actually changed. Black lives hadn't mattered very much in 1921; she wasn't sure they did now either. When the opportunity arose for her to get out, she grasped it with both hands.

In 2003 Carole was lucky enough to be offered a college scholarship. Some three hundred such scholarships were offered by the state legislature to the descendants of the original Greenwood residents as part of an attempt by government to promote reconciliation and as an act of official remorse for the role that the police and government had played in those horrible events. Carole's great-grandparents had owned a successful business on Greenwood Avenue, which like many others had been destroyed during the massacre. Many of her relatives, including her great-grandfather, had perished in the conflagration.

She had moved to New York to study psychology in Columbia University and then to Boston University to complete her PhD on prejudice, racism and clinical depression in the black community. It was here that she met Danny, fell in love and got married. On one of their first dates, they had told each other their story, where they had come from and where they wanted to go. She was mesmerised by his first-hand account of the Belfast anti-Catholic pogroms that had left him and his family homeless in Ireland in 1969. After all, this was now her history too. They were both refugees, wanderers looking for a place to call home. They had found that in each other.

After university she was drawn to the area of social work, and child protection in particular. So many children fell through the huge gaps in the child welfare protection system and ended up the victims of horrible physical and sexual abuse. Every day she got up and went to work, not for the paycheque but because she was determined to make a difference. She hadn't been able to save her firstborn daughter, but she would spend the rest of her life protecting and saving the lives of other children. When Maggie had contacted her, Carole had determined to do whatever she could to help her find Faith.

* * *

Maggie answered the door and showed Carole into the living room where Conor was already sitting.

'I'm going to grab a beer. Would you like one?' he asked.

'Yeah, sure,' they both replied almost simultaneously with a chuckle of laughter.

After a minute Conor returned with the beers. 'Here you go, ladies. *Sláinte!* Maggie, you start. Fill me in on what's happened and then I'll bring you both up to date on my end.'

Maggie was excited and nervous. 'Conor, Judge Coogan herself rang me today to tell me that the court has tracked down three of the women identified as having been adopted from Ireland that match Faith's profile. Two of them have agreed to meet with us but one has refused, point blank.

'Here's the incredible part! One woman is a retired high school principal named Aisling O'Sullivan and the second woman, and this is going to blow your minds, guys, wait for it …' – Maggie paused and shook her head from side to side in apparent disbelief – '… is the District Attorney for Boston, Karan O'Loughlin.'

There was a stunned silence for a few moments as Conor and Carole just looked at Maggie in shock.

Conor laughed out loud and said, 'You've got to be kidding! The District Attorney, our District Attorney?'

'Wow,' was all that Carole could say before she to burst out laughing and said very slowly, 'Get-to-fu–'

'She might not be Faith, but it's a one in three chance that she is. I say I ring both of them tomorrow and make an appointment for us to meet. What do you think?' asked Maggie.

'Yeah, agreed. I'll arrange the DNA tests straight away,' replied Conor.

Conor had explained that ultimately a DNA test was the only way to establish beyond doubt who or which one was Faith. They would need to ask each of the women if they were willing to take a test.

'How does that actually work?' asked Carole.

'We take a generous saliva sample, have its DNA tested and compared with ours. It's a pretty simple process these days.'

'How long before we know the results?' asked Maggie.

Conor replied with a smile, 'For me? A day! An hour if I can help it.'

'OK, what's been happening at your end?'

Conor took a slow deep breath before he spoke. 'We made a break-through in our search, a huge breakthrough. We found an old file in our records from 1969 that contained a statement from a young man named Peter Finnegan, who had been adopted from Ireland. In it he alleges that his father started sexually abusing him just days after he arrived in Boston.'

Conor paused and looked straight at Maggie. 'But not only that, he alleged that the local parish priest also abused him. He named Father Timothy O'Rourke!'

'I fucking knew it!' exclaimed Maggie, but her voice trembled with emotion.

'Yes, you were right, Maggie. He did have something to hide, and not just the illegal adoptions. O'Rourke is a child abuser!

'It gets worse,' Conor continued. 'In his statement Finnegan also alleges he was raped by a number of different priests across Boston, sometimes separately and sometimes together. It's conceivable that we might have a paedophile ring, which includes O'Rourke, on our hands.

'Unfortunately, young Peter Finnegan killed himself in police custody just hours after making the statement and it lay buried among thousands of old paper files for over five decades. We are going to have to find additional corroborating evidence if we are to have any hope of putting O'Rourke behind bars.

'But here's the twist in the tale. Peter's father, Michael Finnegan, adopted a second child from Ireland some years later, Francis, and he is alive and well and living in Cambridge. My money says that Finnegan abused this kid as well, maybe even O'Rourke did.

'This low-life Michael Finnegan is alive and living a comfortable life as a retired gardener. And guess where he worked? In schools.'

* * *

The next day Maggie rang both of the women and made an appointment to meet with them. The two were eager to meet, though clearly a little bit apprehensive about what they might find out. Whether they were Faith or not, the knowledge that they might not be who they thought they were and the very thought that they might have been stolen from their birth mothers was horrendous.

The District Attorney Karan O'Loughlin asked if they could call to her office the following morning and Maggie had agreed. Conor picked Maggie up and drove them to downtown Boston. Neither said very much on the journey there. They were both lost in their own thoughts. They both knew exactly what they were going to tell her – that was the easy part, the story of Rose and their father James and Faith. But what should they do? How should they act? How should they greet one another? What questions should they ask? How would Karan herself react? Conor was nervous, but it was he who finally broke the silence as they parked.

'Maggie, is this Faith we are meeting, our sister?'

Maggie could see he was choking up.

'Don't you dare start me off, Conor McCann!'

She lifted her shoulder bag and took out an envelope with several black and white photos inside. Photos of their dad and Rose together and a few of Rose on her own. She handed them to him.

'Conor, look at those photos and look at these of Karan O'Loughlin I downloaded onto my phone last night.'

She opened her phone, brought up several images she'd screenshotted and passed it to him.

'Look at her college photos and look at Rose. You tell me? Tell me I'm simply not imagining things. Tell me I'm not just seeing what I want to see?'

Conor stared at two photos of Rose and Karan.

'My God!' was all he could say at first. 'They look like sisters, Maggie!'

This time Maggie broke down.

'Right, let's get our shit together. I believe it's her, Conor, but let science do its job.'

Conor reached over and squeezed her hand.

'Let's meet our sister!'

*   *   *

Karan O'Loughlin was an impressive lady. She was the daughter of a wealthy Boston family. Her father had been a Boston judge who had served on the state Supreme Court. Her mother had been an Ivy League professor who had taught economics, first in New York and then in Boston.

She had graduated from Harvard with a first-class degree in Law. Even at a young age, she was considered a brilliant student with huge potential. She could have had her pick of the law firms. While many of her friends and colleagues had expected her to be recruited by one of the large corporates in the city, she chose instead to join a smaller practice that specialised in immigration law. Few would have guessed it, but she had a streak of independence and a penchant for siding with the underdog that she followed throughout her career, both in law and in politics.

She very quickly earned herself a reputation for determined litigation and an incisive courtroom style. She had an encyclopaedic legal memory and a killer delivery. When in court she took no prisoners, so to speak. She was one of only a few female lawyers in the whole country to be appointed Assistant District Attorney in the 1970s.

She had run for and been elected to the Senate for the Democratic Party in the 1980s but had declined to stand for a second term having been somewhat disillusioned by the state of stasis and conservatism that gripped the Capitol under Ronald Reagan. She had returned to private practice in Boston before becoming the first female to be appointed District Attorney for Boston, Chelsea, Revere and Winthrop. This was her second term.

Maggie and Conor were greeted at her office by her personal assistant. He shook both their hands.

'Hi folks, my name is Tony. You find us, OK? Follow me, just through here. She's waiting on you both.'

He opened the door to her office and motioned them in.

Karan was now in her late seventies, but she looked like a woman ten, maybe fifteen years younger. Her hair was unfashionably white, which she wore short and in a casual, slightly dishevelled style. She had an intangible presence about her, style and substance. When she entered a room, people turned to look. When she spoke, people listened.

She had piercing green eyes – cat's eyes – and eyebrows that were on point. Conor and Maggie had been thrown by the short white hair and the paler complexion. When she was younger and darker, she had often been mistaken for a Puerto Rican or Latino instead of an Irish American. They could both see the similarity to Rose now.

'Hi, come in.'

Karan came around her desk and greeted them with a broad smile and a warm handshake. She grasped Maggie's hand and then Conor's with both hers and squeezed them tightly. All three were battling the urge to reach out and embrace one another.

'It's truly lovely to meet the both of you. Please sit down and make yourselves comfortable.'

When she was sitting down herself, she continued, 'I don't mind telling you that this is the most nervous I've been in a long time, either inside or outside a courtroom. I don't know about you two, but I didn't know whether to shake your hands or hug you both. We might be brother and sisters, but maybe not. It's really hard to know how to behave in these peculiar circumstances.'

She smiled broadly at them. Her comments immediately put Maggie and Conor at ease, which clearly had been her intention. She didn't appear the least bit nervous.

'Yeah, it really is, isn't it?' replied Maggie. 'Let me tell you about Faith, about Rose and our father, and then we have something we want to show you. If that's OK with you?' she added.

'Yes, please do!'

Maggie told the complete story. Of Tuam and the horrors that young women and children endured there. Of receiving the letters from Ireland, then finding their father's letters along with photos of him and Rose hidden in their attic. And their search to find Faith and how that had led them to her.

Conor handed Karan the letter from Sister Bridget and watched her as she read it. She was good at hiding her emotions; she had had plenty of practice over the years. Then Maggie passed her the old photos of Rose and their father together. Both wondered if she would see her own youthful self in Rose just as they had. It was obvious from the expression on her face that she did.

She stood up with the photograph of Rose and James in her right hand and turned to look out across the city skyline. For no more than thirty seconds or so, but what seemed an age, she just stood quietly with her back to them both. No one said a word. Karan lifted her left hand to her face and brushed away tears that had risen unbidden from somewhere deep inside.

Maggie could see her shoulders rise and fall as Karan struggled to control her emotions. Maggie wanted to reach out and embrace her. She wanted to tell her that her mother had loved her deeply and that her father would have loved her and wanted her.

She stood up and walked to the window, stood next to her quietly and took her hand. Karan had stopped breathing involuntarily at the sight of the photographs and then suddenly struggled to draw her breath. The tears now rolled off her lower lashes and streamed down her cheeks. Maggie could see her struggle to gain control, but her breathing eventually began to slow and return to normal. Maggie handed her a tissue, which she took with a grateful smile and wiped the tears away.

'Thank you,' she said gently. 'Thank you, both!' she said as she turned and hugged Maggie and then walked over to hug Conor.

They all sat down again and then Karan asked, 'So, what do we do now? How do we get this DNA test done and how long will it take to get the results back?'

Conor smiled and said, 'I'll take a swab of your saliva and a swab of Maggie's, and I'll send them off to the forensic laboratory. We'll have the results back this afternoon. I'll be able to call you both as soon as I know.

'We saw what you saw in those photos, Karan, but we need this test done to confirm what we are all thinking. You're our sister – you're Faith!'

Within a few hours they had the results. The tests confirmed that Maggie and Karan were related.

CHAPTER 13

DUBLIN, 1959

Mary Keenan had been a very bright and inquisitive student with a real appetite for learning. She would have loved to have finished secondary school, but her family couldn't afford to pay the fees. Instead, Mary was sent home to prepare for marriage and motherhood. In the meantime, she was expected to help her mother look after her father, her older brother and the five younger children.

Her brother Tom was just one year older than her and had found work in the Dublin docks as a stevedore, loading and unloading goods from the ships that docked there. Whenever work was available most boys moved seamlessly from school to employment. Girls, particularly working-class girls, were offered no such opportunities. Their 'place' was still very much in the home.

Mary yearned to escape the oppressive confines of her home. She had dreamed of attending university and pursuing a career, but she was trapped in a place and a time where she felt she did not belong.

The family lived in Mount Pleasant Buildings, between the Ranelagh and Rathmines districts of Dublin. They had been moved there – or rather had been dumped there – by Dublin Corporation when they had fallen behind in rent they owed. Mary, her six siblings and their parents were now squeezed into a dilapidated, damp, rat-infested, two-bedroom flat with no toilet, bathroom or hot running water. Tenants were forced to share filthy communal toilets and washing facilities.

Next door to the Keenans was a family of nine, and further down the corridor was a family of twelve. The Church's teaching on the imperative of procreation and its implacable opposition to birth control led to exceptionally large Catholic families, who were often squeezed into small, terraced houses or multi-occupancy tenement blocks, which were totally unsuited to the number of inhabitants. Three or four to a bed was common and, in some of the larger families, a veritable luxury.

The four blocks of flats had been built in the 1930s, but by the late 1940s the Corporation had begun to use the flats as a social dumping ground. If you couldn't pay your rent, that's where you were sent. Inevitably, some families with a record of antisocial behaviour in other parts of Dublin were moved there as well. Together poverty, crime, vandalism and local government neglect had combined to create a modern slum.

It was a bleak and depressing place to live, though the young children there scarcely realised it. They played among the squalor and the rubbish as if it were the most exciting place imaginable. Old furniture that had been discarded, broken prams and later burnt-out cars became their castles and forts, horses and stagecoaches. Dangerous and deadly abandoned buildings, empty factories and shops became their adventure playgrounds.

If Mount Pleasant Buildings was a slum, Mount Pleasant Square, just a few hundred metres away as the crow flies, was its complete opposite, an oasis, an urban Shangri-La. It was one of the earliest Georgian squares built in Dublin and housed, for the most part, wealthy businessmen, doctors and solicitors and their families. Along with its own little park in the centre, there was the exclusive Mount Pleasant Lawn Tennis Club, with its private tennis and squash courts. Stepping into the Square was like stepping into a Jane Austen novel, with its grand, three-storey houses, its servants and its gentry.

Here indeed was a true tale of two cities, the Dublin of the wretched and the Dublin of the blessed. The Gardaí made sure that the inhabitants of both rarely met. The residents of the Square paid their taxes and expected to be shielded from the intrusion of their 'uncouth' and 'dangerous' neighbours.

Mary's mother Peggy had managed to find a job cleaning one of the grand houses twice a week and she often brought Mary with her to help. Her father Eoin had been out of work for a period and spent most of his time and their scarce money drinking in the shebeens of working-class Dublin.

Despite their many problems, their fights, and their fallouts, despite the conveyor belt of pregnancies and children and the depression that often followed, Peggy and Eoin were obedient Catholics. Contraception and divorce were unthinkable. Every night Peggy would lead the family in saying a decade of the Rosary. Every Sunday, the whole family would clean up and put on their Sunday best – Peggy pressing Eoin's suit and Mary applying spit and polish to his well-worn black leather brogues – to attend mass in nearby St Mary's Pro Cathedral. This was the one place, a sort of no-man's land between the social classes, where the two groups would mix for one hour each week. During mass, the residents of Mount Pleasant Buildings were allowed to share a pew with their wealthy neighbours from Mount Pleasant Square. Perhaps Christ, too, donned his threadbare suit and worn brogues and sat among the families, wondering at the absurdity.

* * *

The big house on Mount Pleasant Square was owned by a young doctor in his thirties and his family. Every time Mary accompanied her mother to clean the house, she would bump into him. He was always friendly, and occasionally charming. He was also incredibly handsome. She had never met anyone like him before and was completely in awe. Mary fell in love for the first time.

More and more Mary took over the cleaning duties at the big house, while her mother was forced to stay at home with one or other of her sick siblings. She increasingly found herself alone with the young doctor. He would frequently return home during the day, while Mary was there working. The politeness soon turned to compliments, the compliments to flirtation, the flirting to a first kiss, and before she had time to think he had swept her up and carried her to a bedroom where they had sex. She was too overwhelmed with these new feelings, of awe, of deference, of love and sexual attraction, to stop and think twice or say no.

For a month or so she was wrapped up in this heady environment, this bubble that seemed to float somewhere between heaven and earth, until one day she arrived for work as usual to be greeted by the lady of the house. She was abruptly handed an envelope with her wages and told her services were no longer needed. She never saw the doctor again and a month later realised she was pregnant. She was dumbfounded. She knew how it happened … but to her? She was terrified of how her parents would react.

She held off telling them for as long as she possibly could, but when she confessed, pregnant or not, her father took his belt to her and beat her viciously as she cowered between the bed and the wardrobe in the bedroom for protection. Before she knew it, she had been vigorously chastised, called a 'sinful girl' by the parish priest and swiftly dispatched to a Catholic mother and baby home in Tuam to give birth to the child.

After just one week she realised she had landed not in a home or a place of compassion but in a place of unremitting cruelty, a house of horrors where young pregnant mothers were starved, frequently beaten, constantly threatened and overworked to the point of physical collapse.

Later that year Mary gave birth to a healthy baby boy whom she named Francis. Much to her own surprise, she fell instantly in love with him and when not working she spent every possible minute attending to his needs. She didn't fully comprehend where this love had sprung from, but it was powerful and sublime. Her bond with the baby grew stronger by the day. Some of the nuns had started talking to her about giving him up for adoption. According to them, it was in the child's best interests, and she could get back to her old life, find a husband and start a 'legitimate' family, a good Catholic family. 'As God himself intended it to be!' She simply ignored them. She felt a steely resolve grow quietly within her. She had absolutely no intention whatsoever of being separated from Francis.

One day she was told to report to the Head Sister, Sister Carmel. She stood outside the office waiting to be called in. Sister Carmel had spent over twenty years at the home. She was an imposing physical character, tall and rigid in her bearing. It seemed to match her personality, which was dry and intimidating.

Both the other nuns and the mothers were terrified of her. Over the years she had occasionally struck some of the young mothers in full view of other residents and indeed had dragged several others through the corridors of the building by the hair.

Sister Carmel seemed to resent the young women in her care. She rarely spoke a kind word to any of them. In fact, no one could remember a single occasion when she had exhibited kindness or compassion to a mother or a child.

'Come in, Miss Keenan!'

Mary was trembling as she entered the office. Sister Carmel sat ramrod straight behind her desk. She beckoned Mary to stand in front of her. No chair was available or was offered.

'Miss Keenan, it is time for you to return home. I wanted to take this one last opportunity to offer you some spiritual guidance before you leave us.

'It was sin that brought you here, a grave sin, the sin of lust. The basest of emotions.' With a visible look of disgust upon her face, Sister Carmel continued. 'To copulate outside of marriage, like the beasts of the field, is vile behaviour and contrary to the teachings of the Church.

'I hope that you have learned a valuable lesson from your time here. You now have an opportunity to return to your family and to start again. You have an opportunity to redeem yourself in the eyes of Jesus Christ Our Saviour.

'Find yourself a good Catholic boy, marry him and raise a large, pious Catholic family within the sanctity of holy marriage.

'I have already spoken to your parents, and they have agreed that your son should be placed for adoption with a decent Catholic family. You can be assured that he will be well cared for. You need have no concern in that regard. I'm sure you will agree that this is in the best interests of the child.

'Your parents will be arriving here tomorrow afternoon to escort you home. You can leave now and gather your belongings in preparation for your departure.'

Sister Carmel looked down towards some paperwork on her desk. Mary stood exactly where she was and waited for the nun to notice. Her heart skipped a beat and she held her breath. It was a few seconds before Sister Carmel realised that Mary had made no attempt to turn and leave the office. When she looked up, Mary said in a clear and determined voice, 'No, Sister. Francis is my child. I am his mother. When I leave, he will be leaving with me.'

The next day Mary was dragged from the building by her father while her mother repeatedly told her to forget about the child, that this was what was best for the boy. Mary had refused to leave willingly and had screamed at them and the nuns who accompanied them.

'I want my baby!' she repeated over and over until she was hoarse. Despite her protestations, her parents forced Mary to come back to Dublin with them.

Within a week, Mary stole some money that her mother kept hidden in an empty tea tin in the flat and took the first bus straight back to Tuam.

When she arrived, night had fallen, and it had begun to rain heavily. Mary walked from the town centre to the gates of the home. By the time she got there she was soaked through. The place was in darkness.

It was early the next day when some of the nuns saw a young woman standing in front of the building. At first no one paid any attention to the lonely figure, but after a few hours, more of the nuns and residents began to take notice of the woman who remained standing, silently, outside the gates, in the pouring rain.

By late afternoon, the solitary figure was the talk of the home. Who was she? What was she doing out there in the rain? It was early evening before one of the nuns decided to inform Sister Carmel that a young woman had been standing in the same place, directly outside the gates, staring at the home for most of the day.

Sister Carmel made her way to the reception, accompanied by the nun who had informed her of the presence of the young woman. She opened one of the large double doors and stepped out into the lashing rain. She crossed the twenty or so metres between the entrance and the gates of the home. She was almost at the gates when she recognised the rain-soaked figure who stood there.

'I want my baby!' said Mary Keenan.

CHAPTER 14

BOSTON, PRESENT DAY

Conor was on his way to see Francis Finnegan. He headed north, crossed the Charles River into Cambridge and headed for its most famous landmark and biggest employer, Harvard University. Francis worked there as a bio-tech researcher.

Conor knew the city well. When he was at college, he and his friends would drive out at the weekends. There were some great clubs and bars. They'd hang out at Shay's pub on JFK Street before heading to a club. Of course, the main reason they took the trip almost every weekend was because of the college girls. Between undergraduate and postgraduate students there were about 15,000 of them attending Harvard.

The city had a really cool vibe. When Conor and Brenda had been planning to move out of Jamaica Plain, they had seriously looked at Cambridge before finally deciding upon West Roxbury. But it had been a close call. As he drove through the city centre, he remembered why he had loved Cambridge. The place was immaculate, stylish and had a great buzz going on.

The Harvard campus was huge. He'd rung ahead and learned that Francis was based at the Richard A. and Susan F. Smith Campus Centre, just off Massachusetts Avenue. He didn't want to cold call the guy and scare him off. Instead, he had decided to come see him face to face. He had no intention of just rocking up and asking him if Michael Finnegan had molested him. He would tell him they were investigating illegal adoptions from Ireland, which was partly true, and see how he reacted to the subject of his father.

When Conor reached the Campus Centre, he found the office easily and rapped on the door.

'Yeah? Come on in.'

Conor barely heard the reply from the other side of the door. The voice spoke softly, almost timidly.

The man sitting behind the desk was in his early sixties or thereabouts. He had light brown hair worn short at the sides. It was thinning naturally on top. He wore square gold-rimmed glasses that sat above a slightly pink nose, as if he had been out in the sun for too long. *The curse of the Irish*, Conor thought to himself.

Francis Finnegan smiled and asked, 'Can I help you?'

Conor flashed his badge and introduced himself. 'I'm looking for Mr Francis Finnegan?'

'You've found him.'

'Would you mind if I sat down, Mr Finnegan?'

'No, not at all, Detective, please,' he said, as he gestured to the chair on the other side of the desk. He smiled warmly. 'How can I help, Detective?'

Whatever he thought the reason for Conor's visit was, it wasn't going to be this. Conor knew what he was about to say would bring back a lot of horrible memories. This was a part of the job that he hated.

'I'm part of a task force that is investigating illegal adoptions from Ireland that were arranged by the Catholic Church here in Boston. According to the files we have, you were adopted by your family here in Boston in 1964?'

Francis almost physically recoiled. The blood drained from his face, leaving him a chalk-white colour. He was clearly in shock and took a few moments to reply. The warm smile had disappeared.

Shit! Conor thought to himself. Francis's reaction told him what he already suspected. Finnegan had abused this kid too. There was no record of any complaints from Francis about his father, though Conor knew that meant nothing. Most kids were too afraid to say anything and besides, who would he have complained to – the parish priest? *What a fucking joke!* he thought. *The cops?* He knew now that Maggie had been right. The Boston Police with its predominant Irish-Catholic culture had turned a blind eye to what was going on within families and what many priests themselves were doing to kids. The Church hierarchy had said *stay out of our business* and the Boston PD had dutifully complied.

'That's right. I was adopted from Ireland in late 1964. But why on earth is that relevant now almost sixty years later?'

Conor decided to tell him all that he knew about the mother and baby homes and the Church's practice of forcibly separating children from their mothers and sending them illegally to the US and Boston in particular.

'So, what are you saying, Detective? Are you telling me that I was stolen from my mother back in Ireland?'

'Possibly, yes. Probably, actually,' Conor replied bluntly.

Francis shook his head in disbelief.

'It's likely that your mother was given no choice in the matter of your adoption. It's also very possible that your name was changed, and you were issued with a new birth certificate and a new name.

'There is considerable documented evidence that the falsification of birth certificates was common practice in many of these homes.'

In a shaking voice Francis asked the question again. 'Let me get this right, Detective. Are you telling me that my mother did not want to give me up for adoption?'

'I can't tell you that for certain, Mr Finnegan, but it is a very real possibility, yes!'

Francis drew a shudder of breath, lowered his head and his eyes began to well up. He stood up abruptly, walked around his desk and out the door. As he left the room, he managed to say, 'Please excuse me for a moment, Detective. I have to use the bathroom.'

Francis half ran towards the toilets down the hall. It was a good five minutes or more before he returned to the office. He apologised to Conor for keeping him waiting.

'Hey, I totally understand. I know this will have come as a big shock. For what it's worth, I have a pretty good idea what you are going through. I recently discovered that I have a sister I knew nothing about. She was adopted from Ireland in the same way just after the Second World War. Turns out she was stolen too. We only just found her. After all these years.'

'Really? You were able to find her?'

'Is it OK if I call you Francis?'

'Yes, of course. Sorry, I'm just in shock to be honest. Francis, of course.'

'Conor!' Conor smiled and leaned over the desk to shake his hand. 'I know how crazy all this must sound. My head was spinning when I first found out about my sister. I'd a million questions running around in here.' He pointed to his head. 'Francis, would you mind if I asked you another couple of questions?'

'Yeah. No, sorry, I mean, yes, go ahead.'

Conor could see he was a million miles away. 'How about your father, Michael Finnegan. Had he any clue about this? Did he ever speak to you about your adoption?'

Wherever Francis was, whatever he was thinking, the question literally snapped him to attention.

'My adopted father?' Conor noticed the definite use of the word 'adopted'. Not 'Father' or 'Dad' but 'adopted father'.

'No, we never spoke about it. I spoke to my mother about it once, but she just told me that all she knew was that my birth mother back in Ireland had willingly given me up for adoption.'

It was obvious from his reaction and his demeanour that Francis didn't want to talk about Michael Finnegan.

'When was the last time you saw your father?'

'What? My adopted father? Not for some time.'

'You two not close, then?'

'Look, Detective. I appreciate you coming out here to give me this information. It's a lot to take in. I need time to process it. If you don't mind, I think I'd like to go home and speak to my wife.'

'Of course, perhaps another time?'

Conor had seen him shut down at the first mention of Michael Finnegan's name. He wasn't about to tell Francis that they knew his adopted father was a paedophile. He didn't want to take any chances at this stage of the investigation that somehow Michael Finnegan would be alerted to their suspicions. Conor knew he would have to gain this guy's trust before he would open up.

'Listen, Francis, I understand. Here's my card. It has my personal mobile on it. Just give me a call if you can think of anything that might help. If there's anything you want to talk to me about, just give me a call, anytime, day or night.

'Maybe we can help you find your mother.'

He wanted to drop that pebble in the pool and let it ripple. Francis might just come back to him first.

That evening Conor drove to Maggie's. They had arranged a quiet intimate meal at home for them both and Karan. It was the first opportunity they had had to sit down and really talk about everything that had happened. They wanted Karan to see the house, to see some of their dad's things. For her to get to know him a little bit. And Conor had decided to tell her about their investigation into O'Rourke. Her support as District Attorney would be really helpful – if she was prepared to get involved.

*   *   *

Karan pulled up outside the house and sat in the car for a little while looking across the street before she went in. *So, this is where my father settled after the war?* she thought. *This could have been my mother's home, my home!*

For days, her emotions had been mercurial. One minute she felt like bursting into tears – and when she was alone, she frequently did – the next she was seething with rage and anger at the Catholic Church.

Karan had had a wonderful life in Boston, and wonderful parents who had loved her. She had wanted for nothing. But the horrible truth about Rose and James had shattered her peace of mind. Yes of course she had often wondered about her biological parents, about her mother. However, she had come to terms with what she thought was the truth, that she or they had simply not wanted her. Now she knew that her mother had loved her dearly and that these nuns, the Church, had stolen the life they should have had together.

For all her adult life she had endeavoured to stand with those who had been denied justice. She had always had this inner drive. She had witnessed injustice, institutional corruption, abuse and indifference, but only through the eyes of others. Now this was deeply personal. There was no way she was going to allow the Catholic Church to bury the truth, not this time.

Inside, the house was huge. Maggie explained to her that she and Conor had tried to persuade their dad to sell up and downsize, but he simply refused. He always said the house was still full, full of precious memories. It was like a book of short stories and every room had its very own chapter. As they waited on Maggie laying the table for dinner, Conor showed Karan into their father's study.

'There's a lot of Dad in this room. This was his favourite place in the whole house. After Mom died, he spent most of his time here, reading mainly. He has a great collection of books. His other passion was Irish whiskey. He became quite a collector of the stuff.

'I'll leave you alone. Take your time and have a look at anything you want.'

With a kind smile he added, 'You're family now, Faith.' And quietly shut the door behind her.

One side of the room was filled from floor to ceiling with books. The other side had dozens of full whiskey bottles displayed on rows of shelves. The shelves were lit from behind and threw the rich golds, bronzes, coppers and occasional dark browns of the various whiskies throughout the room, giving it a warm ambience, though it felt chilly. In between was a beautiful mahogany writing desk and worn leather armchair. Behind the chair was a wall covered in photographs. The room smelled of furniture polish, leather and, oddly, cinnamon.

She ran her fingers across the spines of the books closest to her. Lots on Irish history – *How the Irish Saved Civilisation*, *The Big Fellow*, *Goodbye Dearest Heart*, *Before the Dawn* – and what looked like hundreds more. But she was surprised to see a lot of poetry and prose too. *In the Skin of a Lion* by Michael Ondaatje, *And Still I Rise* by Maya Angelou, *Food for the Winter* by Geraldine Connolly, W.B. Yeats, Walt Whitman, Emily Dickinson and so many others. Lots of classics, old bound editions, but liberally sprinkled with contemporary writers. She smiled a melancholy smile. She had always loved poetry.

She stepped behind the chair to examine the photographs. There were a few very old black and white ones, the type that had a silhouette around the image and an aged wooden frame. Karan guessed these were taken some time in either the late nineteenth or early twentieth century. They were probably grandparents or great-grandparents. *My grandparents*, she thought.

She recognised her father straight away. There were some wonderful photos of him in his smart GI uniform. God, he was handsome. There was another of him and a group of his army buddies, all bunched together, amongst the ruins of an old building, with a French sign above the crumbling door frame. They all looked so young. There were lots of photos of Conor and Maggie, from babies to adults. Lots. But almost immediately she was drawn to what was clearly a new addition to the collection. A large photo of Rose and James together.

Rose was stunning, like a Hollywood movie star from the 1940s. She was dark and smouldering. Her smile sparkled and seemed to light up the photograph. Karan smiled at the thought. She was damn hot. She was leaning against James, who was dressed in his best US Army uniform. He was smiling at Rose as if no one else existed.

Karan sat in the chair, closed her eyes and imagined her father sitting here, reading a book, a glass of Jameson whiskey sitting on the desk in front of him. When she opened them, she leaned forward and lifted a clear glass jar that sat on the desk. It was filled with cinnamon sticks and ground nutmeg and smelled lovely.

There were old letters and bills piled on one side of the desk. There was a sheet of paper with ornate handwriting in the centre, a fountain pen resting at the top of the page. She assumed it was her father's. She lifted the paper and admired the script. The elegant curls, the sharp precise lines that ended in needlepoints or what looked like little fishhooks. When she looked closely enough, she could see the different shades of black ink within the pigment of each letter. In fact, each letter was a mixture of the deepest blacks and browns that faded into coppers. It was beautiful writing, rich and full of texture. She couldn't remember the last time she had seen such beautiful handwriting, thirty years, more possibly. The writing, the books, all of it said something about the man James was, but they were no more than glimpses, the faintest whispers. She wished she could have truly known him. She wished he could have known her.

There was a soft knock on the door and it was opened.

'Supper is served!' said Maggie. 'We're down the hall on the right.'

Karan closed the study door behind her and followed. The dining table was set family style with a large pot and dishes in the middle.

'The study smells lovely!'

'Yeah, Dad always kept freshly boiled cinnamon sticks and nutmeg about the house. I think he learned about it when he served in the Far East towards the end of the war. Apparently, it was good for keeping mosquitoes away. He refused to use air freshener. I've kept the tradition going,' replied Conor.

'OK, guys, I'm no gourmet cook, but I make a mean good old-fashioned Boston clam chow-dah. I hope you like fish, Karan?' Maggie laughed.

'I love it!' replied Karan with a huge smile.

They sat at one end of the large rectangular dining table, Conor on one side, Maggie on the other with Karan in between. They were silent for a few moments and just smiled at one another. A 'welcome home' smile. Karan reached out and took both their hands and Conor took Maggie's. No one said a word – they didn't need to.

'Right, Conor, you do the honours, please!' said Maggie, handing him a ladle. When it was all dished out, they tucked into the meal.

After dinner they sat around the table having a few beers, chatting, reminiscing about growing up in Boston. The close encounters. The absurdity of it all. It felt perfectly natural and relaxed. Of course, they spoke a lot about James and Rose. Maggie went and got the bunch of letters and photos that they had found in their father's old trunk in the attic. Karan picked her way through the letters, reading a paragraph or a line or two here and there.

'Why don't you take them home with you for a few days and read through them at your leisure?' offered Maggie.

'Yeah, that would be great. I'd really appreciate that, thank you both.'

'Listen, these are your letters and photos, as much as they are ours,' said Maggie.

'There's something else we wanted to talk to you about,' said Conor. He glanced at Maggie, who nodded, before proceeding.

Karan raised an eyebrow and replied, 'I'm all ears!'

Conor told Faith about Finnegan and O'Rourke, about the evidence they had uncovered and their strong suspicion that Finnegan, O'Rourke and probably others had sexually abused adopted children, certainly two that they knew of and possibly more.

Karan was appalled. But she agreed that it made perfect sense. Kids that could be adopted by a family simply on the recommendation of a Catholic priest, some of whom were themselves paedophiles. Vulnerable children, wrenched from their mothers in Ireland and effectively imported into the US, like precious livestock, for a price. No questions were ever asked about the suitability of adopting families. No police or social services checks were carried out. It made horrifying and terrible sense.

Conor continued, 'Think about it. Isolated children who could be "acquired" with no questions asked? Fuck, it's a paedophile's dream. I'm convinced Finnegan and O'Rourke co-operated in the violent sexual abuse of numerous children across Boston. Could there be other perpetrators involved? Absolutely, yes. Do we have conclusive, indictable evidence to convict them in a court of law? Not yet!

'Francis Finnegan is the key to this case. I'm sure of it. The likelihood is that Michael Finnegan and O'Rourke abused not just Peter Finnegan, or whatever the poor kid's real name was, but Francis as well. We must find a way to persuade Francis to open up and go on the record about these two scumbags.

'In the meantime, we are conducting a review of all the pre-existing cases involving incidents of sexual abuse by members of the Catholic Church going back decades. After the *Globe*'s exposé in 2002, the hierarchy effectively escaped prosecution for its role in covering abuse up. I intend to look at that again. We could do with your department's help?'

Karan paused for a few seconds just to absorb what Conor was telling her before she said, 'OK! I'm going to put one of my best prosecutors on the case with you – you'll already know her, Conor, or at least have heard of her, Martine Holden? She will have the full support of my department – and me personally.'

CHAPTER 15

BOSTON, PRESENT DAY

Conor told Detectives Washington and Goldberg to commandeer a room and make it their case room. He wanted to start holding weekly case reviews. They were making progress, but he wanted to step up the level of activity. He was bringing more detectives into the group. They were now, officially, a dedicated task force. He appointed Stacey Washington the lead detective in charge of the group.

'Stacey, I want the first case review tomorrow at 10am. The DA's office is on board and has appointed Assistant DA Martine Holden to work with us on the case. I think you've worked with her before?'

'Yeah, Chief, she's first class. Methodical, dedicated. She puts the time in.'

'Good. She'll be here in the morning for the review. Give her a call before if you want to let her know you're in charge.'

'Will do, Chief.'

Stacey Washington was thirty-four years of age and had been a Boston cop for fifteen of those years. Six as a patrol cop and nine as a detective. She had worked in both Homicide and Sexual Crimes. They were often two sides of the same coin and the same case. She was experienced, tough and intelligent.

Washington was quite tall and had an athletic figure. She was fast, wiry and strong. She jogged, lifted some weights and kickboxed. Like a lot of female cops, she felt the need to demonstrate that she was as tough as any of her male colleagues, and she was.

She had what many half-decent detectives didn't have, an attention to detail and instinct. A good detective's job was 90 percent thoroughness and attention to detail. Plenty of cases remained unsolved because someone missed something, someone didn't do something, the simple things, like canvassing potential witnesses, the full utilisation of good forensic science, searching the right places, a thorough examination of phone, computer and online activities, financial records, CCTV, etc. So much of a person's life now was recorded in some shape or form. You just had to know where to look for it. She did the A to Z by the book with no shortcuts.

But crucially she had what others lacked: instinct. Sometimes that extra 10 percent made all the difference. She questioned everything and everyone. She took no one and no situation at face value. She was suspicious of everything, a real doubting Thomas. In a partner or a lover, it could be a pain in the ass; in a detective, it was an asset. This was the type of thing that couldn't be taught – you either had it or you didn't. She was one of those cops, a 24/7 cop, totally dedicated.

Conor knew it was going to take attention to every little detail, and every ounce of instinct, to catch these devious bastards.

The next morning, they gathered in the taskforce room to review the case. He stood up and kicked the meeting off.

'OK, Detectives, let's get down to business. This is Assistant DA Martine Holden. She'll be working with us on this investigation.'

Martine nodded and said, 'Hi.'

'The rest of you know each other and have worked together before.

'I've appointed Detective Washington the lead detective responsible for this task force. She's in charge.

'Firstly, I want to make several things clear. This investigation is extremely sensitive and will require the maximum discretion. One of our suspects is a very high-profile figure. We cannot, absolutely cannot, afford to alert the suspect prematurely to this investigation. Outside of this room and outside of this team, I do not want O'Rourke's name mentioned. Get that? Is it loud and clear?

'The press must not get a sniff of this until we have the evidence we need and are ready to tell them.'

Conor looked around the room as everyone replied, 'Yes, Chief.'

'Secondly, I don't give a damn where this investigation takes us or who it takes us to. Bishops, priests, politicians, cops, even!

'No one is out of bounds. No one is above the law. I don't give a shit if we catch the Mayor or the Commissioner of Police with their pants down around their ankles. If they have molested or hurt children, or if they knowingly allowed children to be molested or hurt, I want us to find that evidence and put them behind bars.

'We have some circumstantial evidence on two suspects, but we also suspect that there were others involved. Let's do our jobs and find them, Detectives.'

Conor nodded to Stacey who stood up and took charge of the meeting.

'OK, everyone, let's review what we know and what else needs to be done.'

She opened a folder, lifted several photographs out and began to pin them on the large display board on the wall. First was a photo of Michael Finnegan, and second was a photo of the chess piece for the bishop.

'Given the need for secrecy, this will represent Bishop Timothy O'Rourke for now.'

She then pinned a number of head and shoulder silhouettes to the board alongside Finnegan and the bishop. Each of them had a question mark in the centre. Below them she pinned photos of two men, Peter and Francis Finnegan, and beside them she pinned a copy of Peter Finnegan's police statement.

'We have a statement that names Finnegan and O'Rourke as paedophiles, but we need corroborating evidence. The Chief is going to work on Francis Finnegan to see if we can persuade him to make a statement. So, consider that covered.' She then turned to Goldberg.

'Sam, I want you to double back, find out where both Finnegan and O'Rourke worked, what schools, what parishes. I want to know everything there is to know about these two men. Family, friends, colleagues, what they drive, where they live, phone records, everything. Did anyone else suspect they were molesting children? Was there talk, gossip? Let's see if we can find someone else who will go on the record.'

'Will do.'

'Gerry, I want you to check to see if we have any incidents of children being molested, going missing or even being murdered in any of the schools or parishes that Finnegan and O'Rourke worked in. These guys are predators, so my guess is that they have abused other children. Murder? Let's not rule any possibility out.

'Susan, for now I want you to work with Gerry, but we'll be impounding the Catholic Charities of America adoption records soon – Martine is going to prepare the warrant – I want to know how many kids were adopted from Ireland since the Second World War and what the Church was paid for these kids.'

'I'm on it, Chief.'

'Go through them and check to see if any known child abusers were allowed to adopt children. We need to know where that happened and who those kids were. They are victims, but we need to find out if they are potential witnesses.'

'Got it.'

'Joe, I want you to dig out all the stuff relating to the *Globe* exposé back in 2002. Go and talk to any of the guys who are still working there. Get your hands on any material they uncovered and review it. We need to know who the paedophile priests were. Are they still alive and can we bring them in and question them? Is there any connection to Finnegan or O'Rourke?'

'Will do, Chief.'

'And everyone, we need to know who knew what was going on and who covered it up, who turned the other way and let it happen. OK, guys, let's get busy!'

* * *

Detective Sam Goldberg had dug out all that he could find about both Michael Finnegan and Bishop Timothy O'Rourke. Finnegan had worked as a gardener for various schools in the area for over thirty years before retiring. His work had taken him all over the city including most Catholic schools and church grounds in the Diocese. He had been living in the Almont Park area of Mattapan for most of that time. He made a note in his diary to check out the ownership history of the property.

He made a list of schools to visit and brought the photograph of Michael

Finnegan. He had decided to speak to the school principals, any teachers that had been there long enough to maybe remember Finnegan and school maintenance.

He had been able to pull together a brief history of Father Timothy O'Rourke, from humble parish priest to bishop. The guy had gotten around. His first parish as a newly ordained priest was St Michael's in Charlestown. He had spent ten years there before being moved to Mattapan, then West Roxbury and Dorchester. It was from here that he was promoted to Monsignor. Cardinal Law had elevated O'Rourke to the position of bishop in 1999.

Sam visited the first four schools on his list. Nothing. Anyone who did remember Finnegan said he was a good worker. Friendly. The next day he visited a school in Dorchester. After talking to the principal, he spoke to a couple of the longest-serving teachers in the school. The last teacher he met was a woman, Mrs O'Reilly. She had taught there for more than thirty years. In fact, she was now just a few months away from retirement.

'Hi, I'm Detective Sam Goldberg, Boston PD.' He showed her his badge. She took it from him and looked closely at the photograph. She was a careful lady. And just right, thought Sam.

'The principal tells me you're due to retire very soon. How many years have you taught here?'

She handed him his ID back before replying. 'Thirty-seven years, Detective.'

'Wow. Congratulations. How'd you stay sane?' Both of them laughed. 'Well done. I really admire the job teachers do. My daughter's a teacher. I'm so proud of her. It's a tough job.'

Sam could see her relax a little and begin to open up to him.

'Thank you for your service.' And again, they both got the joke and laughed.

'Anyway. We are carrying out an investigation. Would you mind if I showed you a photograph of a person we are interested in?'

'Of course not, Detective.'

He handed her the photo of Michael Finnegan.

'Do you know this man? He used to work here off and on as a gardener some time ago?'

She looked at the photograph carefully before replying.

'Yeah, I remember him. Mr Finnegan? I think that was his name.'

'Do you remember anything unusual about him? Was there any sugges- tion that he might have been involved in criminal activities?'

'Criminal activities?' she asked.

'Was there any suggestion of inappropriate behaviour in relation to the children?'

'Oh, I see. No, not that I was aware of. Sorry, no.'

'Are you absolutely sure?'

'Yes, sorry, Detective.'

'OK, I appreciate you taking the time to talk to me.'

Shit, thought Sam, *nothing again*.

He was putting Finnegan's photo inside the breast pocket of his coat and rising to leave when Mrs O'Reilly spoke.

'He's not the one you should be investigating!'

Sam sat down again and asked, 'How do you mean?'

'It's Bishop Timothy O'Rourke you should be investigating.'

Sam opened his notebook and asked, 'Really? Why is that?'

'Detective, twenty-eight years ago I reported Father Timothy O'Rourke, before he was a bishop, to the old school principal. One of my boys came to me and told me that O'Rourke had been touching him inappropriately. I went straight to the principal and informed him.'

'What did he do? Was it reported to the police at the time, do you know?'

'I doubt it, Detective. Certainly, I was never interviewed by the police. I insisted that the boy's family were informed, and they were. Soon after, the boy left for another school. Within a month O'Rourke was promoted and I never saw him again, except on the television or in the newspapers.'

'Do you recall the child's name?'

'I certainly do. His name was Raymond McCarthy. He was a nice kid, quiet, polite. His family were local, lived just a few blocks away.'

'What age was he at the time?'

'Nine years of age, Detective.'

'Thank you very much. That's really helpful. I appreciate you confiding in me.'

'I'm retiring in a few weeks' time, Detective. I'll have my pension by then. They won't be able to touch it.'

'They?'

'The Church, the bishop, who else?'

* * *

Two weeks into the investigation, Conor and Karan, Detective Washington and Assistant DA Holden decided it was time to seize whatever material the Church and the bishop were holding. No arrests were to be made, yet!

Detective Susan Blake and Assistant DA Holden arrived at the headquarters of the Catholic Charities of America. They were accompanied by a dozen uniformed cops and a transit van. The charity did a lot of great work across

Boston, youth support, providing refugee services and affordable childcare, but this was where the bulk of the files relating to adoptions was kept.

Of course, the charity was one hundred years old and existed well before it had moved into the building on West Broadway. It was more than likely that those records were simply kept elsewhere, possibly at the bishop's residence.

The Assistant DA had asked to speak to the CEO, had shown him the warrant to search their adoption records and to confiscate any files relating to historic adoptions from Ireland. He was clearly shocked at the arrival of so many police officers to carry out the search but co-operated fully. However, it did not stop him from immediately ringing both the cardinal and Bishop O'Rourke and informing them that a police search was underway at the building and that the police were already removing filing cabinets containing material in relation to adoptions from Ireland.

'How dare they raid the building as if we were common criminals!' O'Rourke was furious at the other end of the line. 'Did they say who had authorised the search?'

'Yes, Bishop O'Rourke. The warrant was shown to me by an Assistant DA named Martine Holden.'

'The DA's office? How dare they! I will not stand for this!'

Before the CEO could reply, O'Rourke had slammed the phone down in a rage.

Later that morning the cardinal rang Karan to register his 'concern' at the search and the removal of church records. He was politely but firmly told, 'Cardinal, we have begun a very serious investigation into the illegal trafficking of children from Ireland to Boston by the Catholic Church. And I can tell you, this search is unlikely to be the last.'

Less than an hour after receiving the phone call from the charity's CEO, the bishop saw several police cars pull up outside his residence. He was still watching from his office when Detectives Conor McCann and Stacey Washington stepped out of their unmarked car. This time he would not have the luxury of denying he was at home.

CHAPTER 16

DUBLIN, PRESENT DAY

Maggie and Carole flew into Dublin airport and took a cab to their hotel, the Gresham, in the centre of the city. It was Carole's first visit, but Maggie and Conor had stayed there before with their parents. 'Donkey's years ago,' her dad might have said. They had visited Cork and met a few of their distant relatives, but nearly forty years had passed. The city had been transformed in the decades since.

As they stepped out of their cab, Maggie noticed something straight away, the diversity of nationalities passing up and down the street. In the time that it took them to pay the driver, and have their luggage carried into the hotel, she had heard three, four, maybe five different languages, Polish, Spanish, French, what sounded like Portuguese and an African language, but which one, she couldn't tell. Dublin had become a cosmopolitan city.

From New York she had cheered and cried tears of joy when the people of the Republic of Ireland had voted overwhelmingly in a referendum to legalise same-sex marriage. The first country in the world to do so by popular referendum. How deeply ironic but profoundly poetical given the history of religious conservatism in the country and among its diasporas. She had been reminded of Yeats's haunting poem, 'Easter 1916', which had described the violence of the rebellion, 'All changed, changed utterly. A terrible beauty is born.' But it had aptly described events and mindsets he could not have imagined, the incredible sea change in social and religious attitudes that had taken place in Ireland since then. Wonderful change, but change that had unearthed some of Ireland's darkest secrets in the process.

It was late afternoon. They were exhausted and jetlagged. They had a quick bite to eat in the hotel bar before retiring for an early night. They had a meeting first thing the next morning with the US Ambassador.

Not surprisingly the Ambassador was another Bostonian. President Joe Biden had appointed Kevin O'Sullivan soon after his inauguration. While vice president, Biden had visited Ireland himself and had a real *grá* for the place. O'Sullivan had served in President Obama's cabinet as Labour Secretary. When asked by President Biden to become ambassador, he had been keen to assist the ongoing efforts to consolidate the peace process in Ireland, particularly after the UK had left the European Union, taking the citizens of the North of Ireland with them, despite the fact that the majority of the state had voted to remain. He loved Ireland and he and his wife had relished the opportunity to move there for a few years at least.

Karan was an old family friend and when she had rung Kevin and asked for his help, he promised to do whatever he could. He had immediately contacted the Irish Minister for Children, Equality, Disability, Integration and Youth and asked for his department's co-operation with the DA's investigation into the historic adoptions. He was happy to oblige. He had directed one of his senior officials, who was responsible for supporting the ongoing Commission of Inquiry into the Tuam mother and baby home scandal, to liaise with Maggie and Carole.

The Minister had arranged a meeting between Maggie, Carole and the department official for that afternoon. He was going to give them a private briefing on the work of the Commission to date. Crucially he had also arranged for them to examine the historic adoption records the department had in its possession.

After Maggie and Carole had paid a courtesy visit to the US Embassy in the affluent Ballsbridge area of Dublin and met with the Ambassador, he had insisted that his official driver take them in his US government car to Government Buildings. When they had said that it was not necessary, he insisted and joked, 'It'll impress the hell out of the Irish officials, which won't do any harm.'

The Ambassador's car took them to the Department of Justice's headquarters. They were greeted in the private car park by the government official they were scheduled to meet, Sean Kelly. It seemed the Ambassador had been right – he looked suitably impressed as the large executive Mercedes-Benz drew up to the private entrance of the building.

Both Maggie and Carole had dressed for the occasion. Maggie wore a dark two-piece trouser suit, white blouse and flat shoes, while Carole wore a grey matching skirt and jacket with heels. Maggie carried an over the shoulder leather satchel. They wanted to make the right impression. They looked suitably important and professional.

They were escorted to a large meeting room with high bay windows that looked out across St Stephen's Green.

'Take a seat, ladies. Make yourselves comfortable and I'll serve the tea or coffee. What would you like?'

'Coffee, please,' both replied.

'Help yourselves to the milk and sugar on the table in front of you.'

Sean Kelly was accompanied by another official, a woman, whom he introduced.

'As I said downstairs, my name is Sean Kelly, and this is my colleague

Grainne Hargey. We were seconded from the Department to work with the Commission. If it's OK with you both, I'll give you an overview of the Commission's work to date and then Grainne will take you to have a look at the historical records in our possession. They are held in another building not far from here.'

'That's great. Would you mind if we took some notes?' Maggie asked.

'Not at all, feel free. OK, here we go. Bear with me.

'The Mother and Baby Homes Commission of Investigation was a judicial commission that was established in 2015. We had three Commissioners, Judge Yvonne Murphy, the Chairperson, Doctor William Duncan, an expert in child protection and adoption, and Professor Mary E. Daly, an eminent historian. The Commission had a budget of 21 million euros.

'They concluded their work in January 2021 and delivered the final report to the Minister. While the Commission has, of course, investigated the discovery of the human remains of around 800 children and women in Tuam, it was also given the remit to investigate the activities of another additional thirteen similar homes throughout the State.

'If you don't mind, I'm going to put up on the screen in front of you and read out what the Taoiseach, our Prime Minister of the day, said about what had occurred in these homes.

'I really don't want to simply rhyme off a lot of statistics because of course what occurred here was a horrendous human tragedy. These were innocent children, vulnerable young women. I don't know if either of you have heard or read his comments?'

'No, I don't believe we have.' Maggie looked to Carole, who shook her head.

'Well, this is what he said in the Dáil, our parliament.

'No nuns broke into our homes to kidnap our children. We gave them up to what we convinced ourselves was the nuns' care. We gave them up maybe to spare them the savagery of gossip, the wink and the elbow language of delight in which the holier than thous were particularly fluent.

'We gave them up because of our perverse, in fact, morbid relationship with what is called respectability. Indeed, for a while it seemed as if in Ireland our women had the amazing capacity to self-impregnate.

'For their trouble, we took their babies and gifted them, sold them, trafficked them, starved them, neglected them, or denied them to the point of their disappearance from our hearts, our sight, our country and, in the case of Tuam and possibly other places, from life itself.'

He paused for a few moments when he noticed that Maggie had become upset.

'Maggie, I'm very sorry if that upset you. Perhaps you'd like to take a few minutes' break?'

'No, I'm fine. I just hadn't heard that before. They are very moving words.'

'I don't mind admitting it myself that I cried the first time I heard those words. I think he spoke for a lot of us when he made that speech. If it's OK, I'll continue?'

'Yes, please, carry on,' Maggie replied.

'The Commission's terms of reference were quite broad, and I won't bore you with them all, but number seven deals with your area of specific interest, adoption practices. The Commission was asked to examine the extent to which the child's welfare was considered, if at all, in these adoption practices. The extent to which the mother's consent was sought, if at all, in these practices. Given that it appeared at the time that many children were adopted abroad, the Commission's remit covered domestic and international adoptions.

'Sorry for that rather long-winded introduction. But now let me get straight to the information that you are interested in. The Commission has found that thousands of children were taken from their mothers and placed for adoption with families in the US. Are we talking about five thousand, ten thousand? The Commission found that information – documentation, records – were in many cases incomplete or non-existent. Some homes kept few records; others kept a great deal. So as the information is incomplete, that figure has to be a conservative estimate. Remember also that the Commission's remit was restricted to a limited number of specific homes. There were other homes and institutions that were not included in its remit. If you want my opinion – but you cannot quote me on this – the real figure of adoptions to the US is more likely to be more than that.'

'That's incredible,' said Maggie.

'There is also considerable evidence, both witness evidence and documentary evidence, that in many of the homes, birth certificates were falsified. Children were in many cases given new names. This was done deliberately to disguise who the children were, who their mothers were. In very many cases the children were effectively stolen from their mothers, and mothers were given no choice or indeed were intimidated into signing consent forms. Without a shadow of doubt. However, the Commission was reluctant to state categorically that women were forced to give their consent to adoptions.

'The other thing that was apparent was that these institutions solicited money from the families of many young mothers, although the State was already funding the work that they did. We found some evidence that some of the institutions charged a fee whenever a child was placed for adoption.

Again, the Commission was unable to state this categorically because of the lack of definitive evidence.

'It would certainly be helpful to our investigation if you were able to corroborate this. There is anecdotal evidence that some families in the US were effectively charged a fee when adopting a child, in some cases thousands of dollars. But the bulk of that evidence will almost certainly have been kept in the US by the Catholic Charities of America or their subsidiary organisations in cities across the US.'

With a pause and a smile, he concluded. 'Anyway, I think I've gone on long enough, but we wanted to give you an overview of the Commission's findings. Copies of the full report are now available online. However, we'll let you examine the original documentation we hold. We have a huge amount of source material. We thought it would be better to let you look through that yourselves to see what might be of use. Grainne will take you over to see it now. We are happy to let you spend the afternoon going through the material, though you will not be able to remove any of it. If you need to return tomorrow, just let Grainne know and that can be arranged. We hope that helps!'

'You have been incredibly helpful. Thank you for taking the time to meet with us and sharing that information. We are really keen to look at the adoption materials. We can't thank you enough, Sean.'

They shook hands warmly and said their goodbyes before Grainne escorted them out of the building and across a few blocks to the offices where the materials were stored.

She led them into a large open-plan office. There was a long conference table with chairs in the centre. Along one side of the room were about a dozen large filing cabinets, each about five foot in height containing six deep drawers. Each of the cabinets was labelled and locked.

'This is only about one-third of what we have. Government documents, church records, paperwork directly from some of the homes, testimonies from mothers, adopted children and other witnesses. You could fill this entire room with the volume of the material we have gathered.'

She unlocked five of the cabinets and left them to it.

Maggie and Carole grinned at each other before Carole asked, 'Well, what exactly are we looking for?'

'Several things. First, obviously any material relating to adoptions from the Tuam home. Particularly between the years 1945 and 1964. We have a date when Faith was born and Rose died, and we can guess that Faith was adopted when she was very small or Karan would remember it. So, we have a precise time period to examine.

'We are also interested in finding any material relating to the adoptions of Peter and Francis Finnegan or whatever their real names were. Particularly Francis. If we can find information on his birth mother or his wider family here in Ireland, that could be the opportunity that Conor needs to persuade him to talk about Michael Finnegan and O'Rourke. We don't have their birth surnames, but we do at least know when they were born, when they were adopted and roughly what age they were when they were adopted. That should narrow our search down considerably.'

'Right. Got it. You start at one end, and I'll start at the other. Meet you in the middle.'

By the end of the afternoon, they had identified several potential candidates. There was an old grainy black and white photo of a young boy holding a little suitcase and a teddy bear. He looked as if he was four or five years of age. The name Peter Kavanagh was written on the back. There was another photo of a group of young children including the little boy. Written on the back was the word 'Boston'. There were dozens of old black and white photos of individual children and groups of children. Maggie took photographs of all of them with her mobile phone.

Carole had found several old ledgers that appeared to contain a register of births and deaths in the home. This was what they had been hoping for.

'Maggie, come see these!'

Carole lifted them from the cabinet to the table. They were large hard-backed books. And thick, very thick. Both of them started to thumb through the books searching for dates and years. They were recorded chronologically. The earliest entry appeared to be 1932 and they were able to fast forward to 1945. Maggie was running her finger down each page. She turned a page and ran her finger slowly through the names until she found them.

Rosaleen Rafferty, Belfast, aged 18, deceased 24.3.1945, cause of death: postpartum haemorrhage.
Faith Rafferty, daughter of Rosaleen Rafferty, Tuam, new-born, deceased 24.3.1945, cause of death: unknown.

Despite knowing exactly what they were looking for and what they might find, it was still shocking to read. That was all they were to these people. Two hastily scribbled lines in a book. That's what Rose Rafferty's beautiful life meant to these nuns. And there were thousands of entries in these four books. The simplicity of the lines reminded Maggie of Hannah Arendt's description of Eichmann, the Nazis and the nature of evil, during his trial: 'Evil comes from a failure to think. It defies thought for as soon as thought tries to engage itself with evil and examine the premises and principles from which it originates, it is frustrated because it finds nothing there. That is the banality of evil.'

'The banality of evil,' Maggie whispered aloud.

Below the two entries was another. This one a register of birth.

Mary Maguire, girl, born 24.3.1945. Mother, Mary Maguire, deceased 24.3.1945.

They took note of several entries that mentioned the name Francis, including one for a boy named Francis Keenan.

Francis David Keenan, boy, born 12.10.1959. Mother, Mary Keenan, Dublin, father unknown.

Below that entry was another line which read 'Moved to Castlepollard, County Westmeath'.

Before they left that afternoon, they took photos of all the entries and any photos of the children from all the years that might be relevant.

* * *

The next day they had arranged to meet a representative of the Mother and Baby Home Survivors' Group. They hoped they would get the opportunity to meet some of the survivors themselves, mothers and children. Maggie had explained that she was a journalist with the *New York Times* researching a piece about illegal adoptions to the US. The chairperson of the group, Paddy Cunningham, was to meet them in the lounge bar of their hotel.

Paddy was a middle-aged man who himself was a survivor of one of the homes. He had spent five years in a home in Dublin before being adopted by a family in rural Ireland. What followed was another tragic tale of neglect and abuse before he spiralled into alcohol abuse, petty crime and prison as a teenager and then a young adult. However, Paddy had pulled himself back from the brink of self-destruction, had turned his life around and was working as a counsellor for a homeless charity in the city. His biggest passion was now the search for truth and justice for the survivors of these homes.

Paddy spent an hour with Maggie and Carole, telling them about the group. He explained that in many cases where children had been adopted in the US, it was almost impossible for them to find information about the children. Paddy was adamant.

'Maggie, believe me, no one else gives a damn, not the Church, not the government. They all have a vested interest in covering it up or minimising their own role. They all pay lip service to the needs of victims. The Commission's report was another whitewash.

'Even here, after everything that has been said about the homes, the role of the orders, the State itself, the government is still trying to hide the full truth. When the Commission report first came out, all we heard was "we" were all to blame. We, my bollocks! The nuns were to blame, the Church and the government. They! They were to blame and we, the victims, want them to say it.

'No evidence? No evidence of forced adoptions, no evidence of fees being charged for adopting children? No evidence of systematic abuse? There was a mountain of evidence. Obviously, our testimonies, hundreds of first-hand accounts, weren't properly listened to by the Commission. That report didn't reflect what we'd told them. It felt like we were being screwed all over again.

'Just fucking say the words. It was our fault. We did it. We're sorry. That's what we want. And we want to know who we are. No more hiding behind the law. We have a right to our birth certificates. No right to privacy should deny me the right to my identity. To know who I am, to know where I come from.'

Paddy fumed and raged against the Commission report. 'Excuse my language, ladies.

'When you go home, think about forming a victims' and survivors' group. After all, what happened in the US is the other half of our story. How many kids were stolen from their mothers and shipped to the US? Thousands. We have mothers in our group who are desperately searching for children who were stolen from them seventy years ago. Seventy long years. But they still haven't given up hope of finding their children, children that they loved and wanted.

'Why don't you come and meet some of them? We've a meeting in town tonight at 7pm. We'd love to have you both.'

'Of course, we'd love to come,' replied Maggie.

'It's more of a get-together than a meeting, really. Some of the ladies are real characters,' said Paddy with a hoarse chuckle before saying his goodbyes.

They were able to walk to the meeting that night. It was being held just a few streets away in the headquarters of Ireland's largest trade union, SIPTU. They walked up O'Connell Street, linking arms and turned onto the quays. Maggie and Carole had become close friends since they had met. The past few months had been an odyssey, an emotional rollercoaster, but one that they were glad to have shared together.

It was a crisp autumn night. As they walked along the quays, they were struck by how beautiful the city looked. The moonlight and lamplight shimmered and rippled along a tranquil River Liffey. They crossed the road to walk along the boardwalk. Maggie noticed there were several rough sleepers, the homeless, wrapped in sleeping bags, tucked below public benches that lined the boardwalk. Dublin had well and truly become a European city.

Maggie felt joy, a sense of contentment, the first time she had felt that in a long time. *What was it about coming to Ireland that felt so much like coming home?* she wondered. Was there ever a race of people scattered across the globe who felt so connected to a place, a beginning? She doubted it. She felt rooted here. Paddy was right – what had begun here and continued in Boston, in New York, right across the States, was one half of the story. She felt a deep sense of purpose, of calling, as if she had been called by Rose to find Faith and bring her home to her.

After meeting Paddy, she knew that countless others were calling from that dark grave in Tuam and other haunted sites throughout this ancient island. That evening she resolved to do everything in her power to tell their stories and, if she could, bring some of those lost children home to their mothers.

The SIPTU building towered over the quays and the River Liffey. It was appropriately named Liberty Hall. Paddy and a handful of the group's members were also trade union activists and the union had agreed to allow the group the occasional use of one of the meeting rooms and kindly laid on tea, coffee and sandwiches for them.

As they entered the building there was a large image of one of the union's founders, James Connolly, on the front entrance. Connolly had been a familiar historical figure in the McCann household growing up. Maggie's dad had a portrait of Connolly on the wall in his study. She smiled when she remembered the stories he would tell of the great Dublin Lockout of 1913 and the 1916 Rising. They were raised on this stuff.

Before eventually being executed by a British Army firing squad for his part in the Easter Rising, Connolly had lived in the US. He was one of the founding fathers of the Wobblies, the Industrial Workers of the World trade union, America's first big militant general union. Connolly had been one of the Wobblies' first organisers in New York, learning Italian, German and Yiddish as he organised the poorest workers across the city. Not surprisingly, he had been a hero of her father's. Her dad would have loved to have visited this place.

Paddy met them at the front entrance and brought them upstairs to the meeting. There were about thirty or forty adults in the room. A dozen children of various ages chased each other about, laughing and occasionally screaming, before being chastised by a nearby parent. Trays of sandwiches sat on tables alongside paper cups of tea, coffee and soft drinks. There was a family atmosphere, as if it were a christening or a birthday party rather than a meeting.

Maggie and Carole were introduced to families, victims and survivors. Some of them were mature men and women, fathers, mothers, grandfathers and grandmothers themselves now, who had been adopted from the homes. All of them had been scarred by the experience of institutional abuse. Some of them had found their birth mothers but many of them hadn't, still. Some of those present were the siblings of children who had perished in the homes and were desperate to find out where they were buried. Desperate to lay them to rest and to have their remains close to them.

Paddy said to Maggie and Carole, 'There's someone in particular I want you to meet. She's nearly eighty now, but she's fit as a fiddle and bright as a button. Her name is Mary Fegan. She was sent to Tuam to have her baby when she was a teenager, and he was stolen from her. I'm not going to tell you her story – she'll tell you herself. She's an amazing woman. I told her your story about Rose and Faith, and she said she'd love to meet you.'

* * *

Mary sat in a booth chatting to her family. She noticed Paddy usher two women through the crowd to her table tucked into a corner of the room.

'Mary, this is Maggie and Carole, the ones I told you about earlier?'

Mary was a small woman, stick thin. She dressed plainly. Her hair was white, and she wore it in the style of her middle age, in tight curls. Her daughters took her to the hairdresser each month, where she had her hair washed and permed. Old styles, like old habits, die hard.

Mary wore her age well. She suffered from early-stage emphysema, which was beginning to affect her breathing and her health, but for now she was grand. She was what others called a 'character', which meant she had a strong will and a strong personality. She was quick to laugh but had a cutting wit. Some people who didn't really know her thought she was often rude. She wasn't deliberately so. She was simply blunt. Paddy had explained, 'If you didn't know her, you'd think she was a cheeky aul' bitch. She isn't. She's a heart of gold.'

Mary smiled at Maggie and Carole and one of the younger women asked them to sit down on two short stools they pulled up.

'Nice to meet you, girls.'

Maggie hadn't been called a girl by anyone in many years and smiled.

Paddy introduced the rest of the group to Maggie and Carole.

'These are Mary's daughters, Mairead and Lisa, and this is Máire Óg, Mary's granddaughter.'

There was a chorus of 'Hi's and 'Nice to meet ya's' around the table.

'Paddy told me about Rose and Faith. So sad. He tells me you'd like to hear my story?'

'We'd love to, we really would,' said Carole.

'These ones are sick hearing it,' she said with a chuckle.

'No, we are not, Nan!' said her granddaughter and you could tell she meant it.

Before she began, Mary closed her eyes momentarily and took a long breath. 'I grew up in different parts of Dublin, but I became pregnant when we were living in Mount Pleasant Buildings. It was a slum. You wouldn't believe just how bad it was – the place was filthy and overcrowded. Of course, when we were children, we hardly noticed it.

'What can I say? I was young. I fell in love and became pregnant. The father didn't know I was pregnant, wasn't told. He was a much older man, wealthy, and I was just a child. I was simply shipped off to Tuam to have my baby.

'The place was hell on earth. Some of the nuns were wonderful people, but most of them thought we were little sluts. Sinners. You wouldn't believe the foul names we were called by them. They thought we were there to be punished, not cared for. The Head Sister was the worst of all, a right bully.

'You know the whole time I was there, while I was pregnant, not once did I see a doctor. Not once did anyone in authority explain to me what was happening to my body, what childbirth would be like. I was terrified.

'Can you imagine? I was just a child myself. I genuinely believed I was going to die giving birth. Plenty of young mothers did, you know.

'I suppose I was lucky enough. When I went into labour, it happened very quickly. Francis was born after only a few hours with no complications. Thank God!

'As soon as I saw him, I fell in love with him. I can remember him as if it were yesterday. He was a beautiful little boy. So content, so well behaved.

'I remember wondering where my love for him had come from. It even took me by surprise. I wanted him by my side every minute of the day. Within twenty-four hours of the birth, I was sent back to work by the nuns, but every chance I got, I had him in my arms.

'Then they started talking to me about adoption. They started telling me how much better for him it would be. At first it was subtle, no, not subtle, sly. Yes, sly is a better word for it. Some of the nuns would ask me how I would support him, how I could afford to look after him? They reminded me I had no job, no money. That my parents didn't want him. That no man would want me.

'I just ignored them. As the days passed my bond with Francis grew stronger. I don't quite understand why or even how, but as the time went on, I became more determined to keep him. I was a quiet girl back then. Shy. Hard to believe, isn't it?' She laughed out loud and winked at her grand-daughter.

'I was called to the Head Sister's office and told I was going home. She announced – I was never asked, never once – that Francis was to be placed for adoption. She nearly had kittens when I told her, no, Francis was coming home with me. I remember I was trembling when I told her. I was wetting my knickers with fear. But I said it anyway.

'The next day my father and mother arrived and literally dragged me back to Dublin, without Francis. A few days later I stole money from my mother and got the bus straight back to Galway and to Tuam.

'I arrived there on the last bus that evening. I stood outside the home in the pouring rain most of the night and most of the next day. It was winter and bitterly cold. Finally, Sister Carmel came out and recognised it was me. The first thing I said was, "I want my baby!"

'She called the Guards, and they took me to the station. But I collapsed and had to be rushed to hospital. I'd caught a bad chill, which developed into pneumonia, and I was moved to a Galway hospital. I think I was there for eight or nine weeks. They told me afterwards that I had nearly died but that I kept asking for Francis.

'It was months before I was discharged and able to go home to Dublin. But as soon as I was well enough, I got the bus back to Tuam. This time I didn't stand outside. I banged the door until it was opened and ran straight to the nursery searching for Francis. But he wasn't there. He was gone.

'Of course, they wouldn't tell me where he was. Sister Carmel appeared and I called her all the worst names under the sky. I remember I screamed, "Where is my child? Where is Francis?" She simply refused to answer. "You are an evil bitch. Do you know that? Pure evil!" I screamed at her.

'Two Guards came and arrested me again. No one cared. No one wanted to help. I wrote to the cardinal. I wrote to the head of the Bon Secours order. I wrote to the newspapers. I wrote to my local politicians. No one cared. Most never even replied.

'When I turned seventeen, I caught the boat to Liverpool. I met my husband there. I told him about Francis, about being in the home, but God love him he didn't care. We never had any secrets between us. You know, despite it all, we always wanted to come home to Ireland and raise our children here. Isn't that ironic?

'I never forgot Francis. When we moved back to Ireland, I tried to find him, but the order refused point blank to tell me anything about his adoption. He was stolen from me and for more than sixty years they have kept him hidden from me. But I know he's out there somewhere.'

She pointed to the city skyline and the horizon beyond port.

'Thank you, Mary, for sharing your story,' said Maggie. 'I've given Paddy my email address. If any of you want to contact me and if we can be of any assistance, we'd love to help. My brother is a senior cop and my sister, Faith, is the District Attorney for Boston. We're going to fight to access the Church's records. If Paddy sends me the names and dates, we will do our best to find out whatever we can.'

Mary's daughters took her home, but before she left, she gave both Carole and Maggie a great big hug and said, 'Will you help me find my Francis, girls?'

CHAPTER 17

BOSTON, PRESENT DAY

Francis Finnegan was a quiet man. He was married to his college sweetheart, Millicent, or Milly, as he affectionately called her, for forty years and had three grown-up children, all of whom still lived in the greater Boston area. They were a very close family. Every Sunday after church they would have a traditional dinner all together in the family home in Cambridge. One or more of his children rang their parents every day and visited during the week.

Francis and Milly had three daughters, three sons-in-laws and, for now, four beautiful grandchildren and another on the way. The girls loved their parents and were particularly close to their father. He was an affectionate and tender man. They only ever remembered gentle words growing up, words of support, words of encouragement, love and lots of hugs. Not one of them could remember a single instance when their father had raised his voice to them, never mind his hand. It was their mother who was the first to say no or to chastise them for misbehaving. There was a vulnerability to their father that they never quite understood. He seemed fragile, as if a harsh word or a careless admonishment would hurt him deeply or even shatter him completely like a fallen glass.

The encounter with Detective McCann had sent him into a tailspin. With the passage of time and with practice, Francis had learned to push the horrible memories of abuse to the back of his mind. He had locked them away there and told himself that they could not hurt him anymore. But that was all – they had not been banished, they still lurked there, threatening, sneering, whispering horrible things to him. Over forty years after the last time he had been raped, Finnegan and the priests still visited him in the black of night, in his nightmares.

He had never told anyone about the abuse, not even his wife. She knew he had experienced a horrible trauma in his youth because she, too, lived with his nightmares, his periods of depression and self-medication, the long silences when he would retreat into himself. After years of trying to find out just what that trauma was and being told it was nothing, she had learned to stop asking.

Like every adoptee, Francis grew up wondering who he was. Wondering who his mother and father were and why she had given him up. Of course, he had come to what had seemed the most reasonable conclusion – she did not want him. Growing up in Boston had turned into a living hell for him between the ages of five and sixteen, when he had eventually left home, escaped through a scholarship. On countless lonely nights as a small child, he had cried himself to sleep whispering the word 'Mommy'.

Now he believed, he dared to hope, that his mother had loved him and had wanted him. Had he been stolen from her? That question grew louder and louder in his mind. Nothing could erase the horrors he had experienced at the hands of Finnegan, O'Rourke and those other priests. But what if his mother had truly loved him and had fought to keep him? Suddenly, unexpectedly, it was as if there had been a rare moment of calm in the terrifying storm. As the days passed, he felt this growing, almost overwhelming need to search for her, to find her. One week after he had first spoken to Detective

Conor McCann, he called him.

'Hi Detective, it's Francis Finnegan here. We met a week or so ago and you gave me your number?'

'Yes, of course, Francis, I remember. How can I help?'

'I was wondering if we could meet. I'd like to talk to you about my adoption?'

'Sure, Francis. Actually, my sister just flew back into Boston last night after spending a few days in Ireland gathering information on the adoptions from there to the US. It's Wednesday now – why don't we meet on Saturday for a coffee? I'll be able to speak to my sister and see what she might have learned.'

'That's great, Detective.'

'Conor!'

'That's great, Conor. Thank you.'

'Just text me where and I'll see you there about 11am, OK?'

'Perfect.'

*　*　*

That evening, Maggie had just printed off the information that Paddy Cunningham had sent as promised when Conor arrived to catch up with her and Carole.

'Fire's lit and the kettle is on in the hottest place in the house,' she said. They both laughed. It was one of their mother's frequent sayings. The wood-burning stove had been fired up and Maggie had the coffee ready. Conor sat down at the kitchen table.

'Grab yourself a coffee, bro.'

'Good trip, Carole? Maggie rang me this morning and told me it had been very productive. And good *craic*, I believe?'

'Absolutely! Very productive and great *craic*.' They both laughed.

'Great *craic*. Don't go repeating that too much now that you're both home,' chuckled Conor. 'It doesn't travel well!'

Maggie came back into the kitchen and handed them Paddy's email, which ran to about four pages. She said, 'There are a few hundred names here of mothers and children who spent time in one or other of the homes. Paddy explained that some mothers and some children spent time in more than one institution. Some were moved from one home to another – this must have added to their sense of abandonment and isolation, always the outsider, the loner. In a few cases, children spent the best part of their young lives being moved from pillar to post before eventually being adopted.'

'That must have been really hard for those kids – and it'll make it harder to find them,' Conor said, thinking of Francis.

'Well, we took copies of what we could so we can try to identify people in the files in Ireland,' said Carole. She handed Conor several sheets, each with a few grainy black and white photographs that they had taken on their phones in Dublin. There were dozens of images.

Maggie showed Conor the ledger entries, particularly the ones of Rose and Faith Rafferty, saying, 'It has to be more than a coincidence that there is an entry for a newborn the same date that Faith supposedly died. I think it's fair to assume that "Mary Maguire" is Faith.'

'Agreed. What about Francis Finnegan, any luck with him?' Conor asked.

'Well, we found an entry for a Francis Keenan that fits the timeline. It recorded that he was moved to another home, Castlepollard, a few months after he was born. But no photographs of him. At least not among the ones we found,' said Carole.

'What about the victims and survivors you met, any clues there?'

'We met a few dozen survivors, including several mothers. But Paddy Cunningham emailed this list of mothers and children. Let's go through it and see if there are any possible connections,' suggested Maggie.

They scanned the list of names. It was Carole who turned to Maggie.

'Maggie, look at the bottom of page two, Mary Fegan – neé Keenan. Mary Fegan? That was Mary's married name. Her maiden name was Keenan. Her son, Francis Keenan! And look at the date of birth? Same as the one in the ledger.'

'Holy shit!' Maggie exclaimed. 'I think we've found Francis Finnegan and his mother.'

* * *

Conor met Francis in the Cambridge Marriott Hotel just off Main Street. Francis had arrived early to pick a quiet corner of the hotel foyer and had ordered a coffee. He was nervous. Conor arrived just a few minutes later. They shook hands.

'How are you doin', Francis?'

'I must admit I'm a little bit nervous.'

'Yeah, I get that. It's perfectly understandable. Francis, I appreciate you reaching out to me.'

'I spent years, decades, trying to put this behind me and you walk in my door.' He lifted his hands as if to apologise. 'I hope you know what I mean. It was a shock.'

'No, I know, I get it. I've some important information for you. But before I give you it to you, Francis, I've got to ask – do you want to find your mother?'

Francis looked at him directly and replied in a quiet determined voice, 'Yes, yes, I do!'

Conor unzipped a black leather file he had placed on the table in front of him and removed several sheets of paper.

'We think we have found your mother.'

Maggie had emailed Paddy Cunningham back in Dublin and asked if he had any images with Mary Fegan in them. He had. Maggie had several glossy photos of Mary printed off a machine in the local store.

'Francis, this is your mother, Mary Keenan.'

Conor handed a photo to Francis, whose hand was shaking as he reached out to take it. Francis exhaled a deep shuddering breath as he stared at her photo. Tears welled up in his eyes.

'Mary Keenan gave birth to a baby boy, Francis, in the Tuam mother and baby home on 12 October 1959. We were able to check the adoption records held by the Catholic Charities of America and in 1964 a young boy named Francis Keenan was adopted from a mother and baby home in Castlepollard, County Westmeath. He had been moved there from Tuam just under four years earlier.'

Conor went to order a couple of fresh coffees from the bar. He wanted to give Francis a few minutes alone to digest the information. When he returned, he could see that the older man had been crying but had managed to compose himself somewhat. As Conor brushed by him, he gently placed his hand on his shoulder, to reassure him, before sitting down.

'Francis, your mother loved you dearly. She was just sixteen when she had you. Her parents had sent her to the home to have her baby because she wasn't married. It was tough on young girls back then in Ireland if they became pregnant out of marriage.

'After you were born, she fought hard to keep you, but her parents took her back to Dublin and left you in the home. She tried to get you back, but the nuns moved you to another home and they wouldn't tell her where. But she never gave up looking for you. For over sixty years she's been searching. She never once stopped loving you.'

Conor leaned forward and with a smile he repeated those words, 'She never once stopped loving you, Francis.

'Go home and tell your three daughters they have an Irish grandmother, two aunts and a half a dozen cousins.

'You can keep that photo. Call me during the week. In the meantime? Just enjoy it. Let it sink in.'

Conor decided that he would not raise the matter of Michael Finnegan, O'Rourke and the abuse with Francis that day. It was a day for him to enjoy, to share with his family. He didn't want to spoil the moment for him. It could wait another while.

* * *

A few days later Conor and Detective Washington held another case review. Conor told the team that he was sure Francis Finnegan had been abused by Michael Finnegan, Father Timothy O'Rourke and other priests and he planned to work on him to see if he'd admit it and testify in court.

'Sam, have you been able to trace this other boy, Raymond McCarthy, yet?'

'Yes, Chief. He's living in Dorchester. I have an address and I'm gonna go visit him this afternoon.'

'Good. We need another witness. Susan, what were you able to find out about the adoptions?'

Detective Susan Blake stepped forward.

'As far as we can tell from the records we have looked at, between the end of the war and today, something like over eight thousand kids were adopted from Ireland into Boston. I'll have a more exact figure for you in a few days when we have gone through all of the Church material.

'There is evidence in the form of letters, correspondence between the Church and adopting parents, that sums of money exchanged hands, and in some instances large sums. In some of the correspondence these are referred to as "fees", not donations. It's impossible at least at this stage to calculate just how much money exactly the Church was in receipt of, but given the figures I've seen and the number of adoptions, it has to be millions of dollars. This was big business, Chief.'

'OK, let's invite the FBI to join the financial part of the investigation. If it happened in Boston, it's happened elsewhere. They have the expertise we don't! What about the adopting parents and the priests who sponsored them, any known or convicted paedophiles?'

'I'm afraid the answer is yes. We cross-referenced our files with the names and details we have been able to lift from the adoption files. There were a lot of hits. O'Rourke himself sponsored lots of adoptions, over two dozen. Michael Finnegan had a conviction for indecent exposure to a minor dating back to the 1950s, but he was able to adopt through the Catholic Church, twice. On both occasions O'Rourke gave him glowing references.'

'First class. Go and talk to these people if they're alive. More importantly, go and talk to the adopted children and see if any of them were the victims of abuse. This is the priority now, guys, connecting the dots. Susan, you have the names, give everyone a list. Get out there and find out who else was a victim. Let's keep building the evidence. Joe?'

'Chief, some of the priests are now dead or were moved out of Boston a long time ago. But we managed to track down five of them who are now retired but still living in the Boston area. We are still talking to the victims named in reports to see if they are willing to give evidence against them. No mention of Bishop O'Rourke, yet!'

'Good work, Joe. OK, Sam, let me know how you get on with Raymond McCarthy. We need this guy's evidence. Peter Finnegan left us a damning statement, but he's dead and can't help us anymore. If McCarthy was abused and is prepared to go on record, we've got O'Rourke. He's going to go to prison for the rest of his life.'

* * *

That afternoon Francis rang Conor and invited him to his home in Cambridge. Francis lived in Somerville, a quiet middle-class suburb. Conor parked outside the house and walked up onto the large veranda. When he rang the doorbell, the door was opened by a young woman.

'Hi, Conor?' He was greeted with a warm smile. 'I'm one of Francis's daughters, Debra, but everyone just calls me Deb. Come in, please. Dad's waiting out back.'

It was a cold autumn evening. They stepped out onto a pretty patio that looked across a verdant garden, the trees dropping their leaves to the ground below. Two young girls chased each other around the lawn, laughing and screaming, kicking piles of dry leaves into the air. Francis was sitting on one of two chairs either side of a table with a mosaic top.

'Ah Conor, come on over. Please sit down. Thanks for coming out to visit. You met my lovely daughter Debra, I see?'

'Would you like something to drink, Conor?' Deb asked.

'Some hot coffee would be great, if you have it?'

'Yeah, of course. Would you like a coffee, Dad?'

'Yes, sweetheart.'

Debra brought a pot of hot coffee and two mugs, placed them on the table and left them alone.

'Conor, I really want to thank you for what you've done. I can't tell you how much it means to me. All my life I believed my mother had abandoned me. That she didn't want me. Does she know about me?'

'Not yet, Francis. That's up to you to decide. Do you want us to contact her and tell her about you?'

'Absolutely. I can't wait to meet her, to speak to her. Though I'm nervous as a kitten.'

'If you are happy for Maggie to reach out to your mother, she'll do it straight away. Might be nice to send her a photo of you and the family?'

'That's a great idea. I'd love that.'

'Francis, there is something else I wanted to discuss with you.'

'Yes?'

'When we checked the adoption records, we could see that Father Timothy O'Rourke sponsored your adoption and vouched for your adoptive parents. We have also uncovered disturbing evidence that Michael Finnegan and O'Rourke sexually abused your older brother Peter, and possibly other children.'

At the mention of O'Rourke's name, Francis froze and the mug in his hand dropped to floor and shattered.

Debra had heard the smash of the mug and appeared on the patio. Francis sat there immobile before finally speaking.

'I'm sorry, darling. The cup slipped from my hand. Would you mind clearing up for me? Myself and Conor will step down into the garden.'

'Of course, Dad. Girls, come inside and give your grandfather some peace and quiet.'

Conor followed Francis as he walked to the bottom of the garden and turned to him.

'I've got to ask, Francis. Did he abuse you too?'

Francis turned away from Conor, slipped both hands into his pockets and looked up at the blue sky. He was silent for a while. Conor couldn't see, but the tears streamed down both of Francis's cheeks. After a few moments of silence, he replied, 'Yes.'

He continued to stand there with his back to Conor, staring up at the sky.

'You know, Conor, I've never told a single person that, not even my wife. I've kept that secret for fifty years, more. Why you, why now? I haven't thought about Peter in all those years. Isn't that a terrible thing to say?' He paused as if thinking back.

'The abuse started almost as soon as I arrived. First Michael Finnegan and then the others. You do know there were others?'

He turned his head around slightly towards Conor before looking back to the sky above him.

'Yes, I do, Francis. You and Peter were not the only children.'

Francis lowered his head and began to sob.

'Francis, will you help us put these people behind bars where they can't hurt any other child? Will you testify in court?'

There was a long silence before Francis replied.

'I can't. No, I can't.'

* * *

That evening Karan met up with Conor and Maggie for dinner at Jamaica Plain. Martine had kept her informed of the investigation's progress, but Karan was keen to get a first-hand account from Conor. After they had settled back with coffees, she said, 'I've been thinking a great a deal about the case, everything you have uncovered to date, Conor, what we know about the abuse and the scale of these so-called adoptions. You aptly described them, Maggie, when you said they were organised on an "industrial" scale. Not just in Boston but across the US.

'Here's what I think we need to do, but it's not going to be easy, and I suspect there will be well-organised opposition.

'Firstly, I intend to establish a Grand Jury Investigation into both the abuse, and these so-called "adoptions" from Ireland. This time the hierarchy won't be allowed to escape the consequences of their actions.

'Secondly, that this happened on the scale that it did, across the whole of the country, I believe requires a federal investigation, a Congressional Inquiry!'

Maggie chuckled with glee and exclaimed, 'Now we're talking!'

'If Conor pursues the abusers through a criminal investigation, I can handle the Grand Jury and start to lobby my political contacts for a Congressional Investigation. If the Grand Jury does its job, it will help build momentum behind the demand for a Federal Congressional Investigation.

'But one last suggestion and this is for you, Maggie. We need publicity about all of this, national coverage. We need to shine a spotlight onto these adoptions. Adoptions? This was kidnapping, pure and simple! Human trafficking by one of the most powerful and respected institutions in the US. We need to get the public on our side. We need the victims to get angry and to get organised!'

*　*　*

Sam Goldberg waited until later that evening to call to Raymond McCarthy's home. Dorchester had a large Irish-Catholic population. Before the war it had had a thriving Jewish community, but that had declined rapidly from the late 1950s. The fifties and sixties saw an influx of black families. Many of the Irish had moved out to the more affluent districts such as Ashmont Hill, Neponset and Savin Hill.

Raymond McCarthy lived in Savin Hill. Sam parked opposite the three-story building, climbed the steps to the front door and pressed the intercom.

'Hello, can I help you?'

'Yes, I'm looking for Raymond McCarthy?'

Sam flashed his badge up to the camera in the corner above him.

'Detective Sam Goldberg, Boston PD. I'd like to speak to you, sir.'

'Come on up. I'm on the second floor.'

The intercom buzzed and the door unlocked. When Sam got to the second floor Raymond McCarthy was standing at the open door of his condo with a quizzical look on his face. Sam showed him his badge again.

'Don't worry, Mr McCarthy, you're not in any trouble at all. But you might be able to help us with an investigation we are carrying out. Would you mind if I came in and asked you a few questions?'

Raymond smiled with visible relief and replied, 'Thank God you said that, Detective. My heart was in my throat when you mentioned police. Sorry, but I'm sure you get that all the time. The bringer of bad news and all that. Of course, come in.'

He led Sam into a large open-plan living room and kitchen. There was another guy there.

'This is my partner, Matt. Please, take a seat. How can I help?'

Matt said, 'Hi.'

Sam nodded to him and turned back to Raymond. 'It's a relatively sensitive matter. It might be better if we spoke in private?'

'No, it's OK. I'd like Matt to be here.'

'It's in relation to Father Timothy O'Rourke, or Bishop O'Rourke, as he is now. I spoke to your old teacher from elementary school recently, Mrs O'Reilly, and she has told us that when you were in fourth grade you reported that Father O'Rourke sexually assaulted you.'

'It's OK, Matt knows about it. I told him years ago. Yes, I did report him, and he did molest me. Several times.

'I told Mrs O'Reilly and she took me to the school principal, and I told him. I told my parents. I even told the police. Apart from Mrs O'Reilly, no one seemed to give a damn and I include my parents and the police in that. Do you know they even accused me of making it up?

'You see, Detective, they were devout Catholics. As far as they were concerned "Father Timothy"' – he gestured quotes with his fingers – 'couldn't possibly have been responsible for molesting a child. Therefore, I was lying, or I was confused and misinterpreted something innocent.

'He pulled my trousers and pants down and fondled my penis. How is it possible to misinterpret that? I was nine years of age.'

Matt crossed the living room, sat beside Raymond and put his arm around his shoulders.

'The next ten years of my life were a mess. O'Rourke and my parents made sure of that. Do you know that right after it happened, they still made me go to mass every Sunday? They even made me go to confession every month. Every time I closed the confessional door behind me and sat in that darkened space, I was terrified. All I could see, all I could hear from behind that screen was O'Rourke's face and O'Rourke's voice. The first time I sat there, I wet myself with fear. Not metaphorically, Detective, but literally. I actually wet myself with fear.

'Twenty years of counselling, thousands of dollars of therapy later, I've finally learned to accept that it wasn't my fault, that I didn't make it up.

'I haven't spoken to my parents in nearly twenty years, Detective. If I passed them on the street and said, "Hello Mom, Hello Dad" – and believe me I've tried – they would walk around me like I was dog shit on the sidewalk.

'You see the "lifestyle" that apparently I have "chosen" is an abomination, as far as the Church is concerned. I'm the abomination, not O'Rourke. How fucked up is that?'

'Raymond, we now know O'Rourke abused kids. Not just you but many others. If you help us, we'll put him behind bars once and for all. I give you my word on that. Will you help us? Will you give evidence against him?'

'Damn right I'll give evidence against him. I only wish my mom and dad could be made to sit in the front row.'

'Make no mistake about it, Raymond, when he's convicted and sent to prison, they'll know all about it. It'll be over every front page in every newspaper in Boston.'

* * *

After Maggie had arrived back from Ireland, she had rung her editor at the *New York Times* and run him through the story of Rose, her father James and Faith. She withheld Faith's identity. She explained that she was certain that the Catholic Charities of America had trafficked thousands of stolen Irish children from mother and baby homes to the US and that huge sums of money had been paid to the organisation by the adopting parents.

'That is powerful stuff, Maggie. Write it, let me see your sources and if it stacks up, I'll put it on the front page.'

'Thanks, Boss. I'll send it through to you tomorrow.'

Maggie rang Karan and Conor and told them.

'We've got to get this out to the public. We want television, radio shows, talking about these adoptions. We want victims, adoptees writing to newspapers, ringing up talk shows. We want them calling their Congressmen and women calling for a federal investigation.

'Maggie, if you have any contacts in CNN or Fox, get on to them. I've a couple of favours in Congress I can call in. I'll make sure a few of them issue statements calling for an investigation,' said Karan.

Two days later Maggie's piece appeared on the front page of the *New York Times*. The editorial addressed the matter with the headline 'The Stolen Children of Ireland'. The issue exploded onto the media and spread throughout the country, as they had hoped. The epicentre of the explosion was Boston, but its shockwaves rumbled across the US and the Atlantic to Ireland, Britain, most of Western Europe and to the Vatican.

* * *

Later that evening, Conor's cell phone rang on his bedside locker. The vibration woke him from his sleep. He lifted it and squinted at the time, 2.45am. The number was withheld. He turned on his side to shield the sound from Brenda sleeping soundly beside him.

'Hello?'

There was no reply.

'Hello?'

After a long silence, a voice spoke.

'Conor, it's Francis, Francis Finnegan.'

Conor sat up in bed.

'Yes, Francis. Is something wrong? Are you OK?'

'I'm OK. I've had a few drinks, but I'm OK.'

There was another long silence.

'Francis?'

'I've decided I'm going to testify!'

'Are you sure, Francis?'

'Yes! I'm not going to run away. Not anymore. They don't get to walk away this time!'

CHAPTER 18

BOSTON, PRESENT DAY

Karan, Conor, Detective Stacey Washington and Assistant DA Martine Holden sat around the large meeting table in Karan's office. They were about to review the evidence they had gathered in the case. Karan began the meeting.

'OK, everyone, where are we with the case?'

Conor replied first.

'Well, we have solid witness evidence against O'Rourke and Michael Finnegan that they collaborated in the abuse of several children. We have Peter Finnegan's police statement, given the day he took his own life, and we have Francis Finnegan and Raymond McCarthy, who are prepared to give evidence in court that Finnegan and O'Rourke molested them.'

'What sort of witnesses are they, Martine?'

'Solid! Respectable. Articulate. No criminal records.'

'Good.'

Conor said, 'We haven't searched Finnegan's place yet. We are hoping we will find something connecting him to O'Rourke and these other priests when we do.'

Stacey Washington interjected, 'Peter Finnegan mentions other priests in his statement and Francis Finnegan is adamant that there were at least two other priests who molested him, but he doesn't know who they were or their names.

'We've arranged for Francis to come in and go through photos that we have compiled of older priests who served in the greater Boston area in the past. We are hoping he will be able to identify them. If he can and they are still alive, we'll lift them for questioning. If he's certain, we'll put them in a line-up.'

Conor continued, 'When we ran a check on Michael Finnegan, we learned that the home where he has lived for thirty-odd years belongs to the Catholic Diocese of Massachusetts. It used to be a retirement home for elderly priests before O'Rourke decided to give it to Finnegan. Rent-free, it seems. We can find no record of Finnegan paying rent over that entire period.'

'What do you think, Martine? Sounds like a solid case. Do we have enough to arrest and convict these two?' asked Karan.

'We have a solid case. We have statements and we have credible witnesses. I say we go.'

Karan considered carefully before turning back to look at Conor and Stacey. 'OK, you two. Let's bring them both in for questioning. Let's charge them. Let's go back and search O'Rourke's residence, this time for other incriminating evidence.'

* * *

The following morning Conor assembled two groups of detectives. One to arrest Michael Finnegan and the other to search the bishop's residence. Everyone in the team was experienced and had been briefed to conduct a meticulous search of the building, especially O'Rourke's private rooms and office. Any mobile phones were to be confiscated so that data or images they held could be checked. They were looking for anything unusual, photographs, diaries, written correspondence, anything that would connect him to Finnegan. And trophies – paedophiles sometimes felt compelled to record their activities, to keep mementos of the experience so that they could relive the pleasure they had felt. Conor and Stacey would arrest O'Rourke. Goldberg would deal with Finnegan.

The small convoy of unmarked police cars pulled up outside O'Rourke's residence. It was a large, detached building with extensive gardens. The bishop had a sizeable staff working for him. A receptionist, his personal assistant, a housekeeper, a cook and two cleaners. On any given day, O'Rourke would hold a series of meetings in his office, and he would receive visitors. Today was no different. The place was busy.

Conor led the team in. As he passed reception, he showed his badge and asked where the bishop was. There was a look of confusion on the receptionist's face, as if her brain couldn't compute what appeared to be happening.

'He's in a meeting in his office, Detective.'

Conor and Stacey mounted the stairs as the rest of the team gathered in the reception area. Of course, Conor knew where O'Rourke's office was – he had been there many times in the past. He passed Dolores, the bishop's personal assistant, who appeared equally confused. She had only just begun asking them a question when Conor and Stacey entered the bishop's office.

O'Rourke was seated behind his large desk and two other priests sat facing him. When the bishop recognised Conor he slowly and calmly stood up and said, 'Ah, Superintendent, how can I help you?'

There was a quizzical and annoyed expression on his face. The penny had not dropped that he was about to be arrested. Conor stepped behind his desk and drew close to his face.

'Bishop Timothy O'Rourke, you are under arrest.'

'Excuse me?' was all the bishop could say before Conor told him firmly, 'Turn around and place your hands behind your back.'

The two priests stood up, in shock.

'You have the right to remain silent. Anything you say can be used against you in court.'

The bishop muttered angrily, 'This is outrageous!'

'You have the right to talk to a lawyer for advice before we ask you any questions. You have the right to have a lawyer with you during questioning. If you cannot afford a lawyer, one will be appointed for you before any questioning, if you wish.'

Conor placed the handcuffs on each wrist one by one, snapping them in place.

'If you decide to answer questions now without a lawyer present, you have the right to stop answering at any time.'

Conor turned him towards the door and said, 'Let's go.'

As they led O'Rourke from his office, past Dolores, down the stairs towards the exit and the waiting police car, some of the staff, having heard the commotion, gathered in the reception area and watched in bewilderment.

*   *   *

O'Rourke and Finnegan were placed in cells at either end of the custody suite. Conor had given strict instructions to everyone responsible for both suspects to make sure neither was aware that the other had been arrested and was being held just a few cells away. Under no circumstances were they to be moved to and from the cells at the same time. No one was to mention the name of one in the presence of the other.

O'Rourke was escorted to the interview room and left there alone. Conor and Stacey waited and watched from the CCTV room. He sat in his seat with his back straight and his two arms resting on the table, hands clasped. He didn't appear agitated or discomforted. At one point he lifted his face and stared unblinking at the camera positioned in the corner of the ceiling above him.

'He seems to be quite calm. No sign of nerves,' she said.

'Stacey, he's arrogant. He's too arrogant to be afraid or nervous. He'll be a hard nut to crack. I'll do the talking. You watch his reactions closely. He's too calm.'

The image on the screen was jarring, an oxymoron. O'Rourke was dressed in his dark priestly garb, including his white collar and bishop's cross and chain, and sat quietly. This was someone whom Conor had been taught to respect, to revere even. This was a person whom, prior to this investigation, he would have been content to leave his two children alone with.

What he had learned about the bishop and the Church in recent months, the horrible reality he had come to understand at first hand, had shaken his faith. Not in God, but in the institution of the Church.

He felt like walking into that interview room and physically ripping the priest's collar and the crucifix from O'Rourke's body. But he knew he couldn't, and he wouldn't. There wasn't the slightest chance that O'Rourke would break down and confess. He realised now that O'Rourke was a sociopath. He was incapable of feeling guilt or remorse.

Conor's objective was to try to provoke him into letting something slip. Short of that, to do the interview by the book so that the bishop could not escape punishment later, claiming his legal rights were impugned in some way. A few minutes later Conor and Stacey entered the interview room and sat down at the table.

'Interview with Bishop Timothy O'Rourke by Superintendent Conor McCann. Also present: Detective Stacey Washington. Interview commenced at 11.15am.'

'Superintendent, this is quite ridiculous!'

'Bishop O'Rourke, you have already been informed of your rights. Before we begin, you have the right to have an attorney present. Do you wish to exercise that right?'

'Detective, I have absolutely nothing to hide. As you well know, I have always supported the police. I am happy to assist your investigation in whatever way I can. I have no need of a lawyer.'

The bishop appeared totally composed, unconcerned.

'For the record, Bishop Timothy O'Rourke has declined to have an attorney present during questioning. This interview began at 2.17pm.'

'Bishop O'Rourke, could you tell us when you became a priest and what parish you served in when you were first ordained?'

'I was first ordained in 1956, Detectives, and my first parish was St Michael's in Charlestown.'

'How long were you there, Bishop O'Rourke?'

'Around ten years.'

'And after that?'

'I served in St Mary's parish in Mattapan.'

'For how long?'

'For six years, if my memory serves me correctly.'

'Can you tell us how many different parishes you served in before being confirmed as a bishop?'

'Well, after that I served in West Roxbury and then Dorchester before becoming a monsignor and then a bishop.'

'It seems quite a lot. Was there a particular reason why you moved parish so frequently over the years?'

'No particular reason, Detective.'

'Bishop O'Rourke, do you recall when you were a priest in Dorchester, an allegation being made against you that you had sexually molested a nine-year-old boy?'

'Certainly not!'

'We have a statement here from a Mr Raymond McCarthy, who was a nine-year-old pupil at St Joseph's elementary school, alleging that on three separate occasions you sexually assaulted him.'

'That's preposterous!'

'We have a statement from Mrs O'Reilly, a teacher in the school, confirming that Raymond McCarthy told her that you had sexually assaulted him and that she reported the matter to the school principal. Are you aware that these allegations were reported to the principal?'

'No, I was not. Because they are not true!' He yawned and sat back in his chair.

'You left that parish soon after these complaints were made. Were you moved by the bishop because of these complaints, that you had sexually abused a nine-year-old boy?'

'No!'

He continued to deny everything. Conor decided to change tack.

'Bishop O'Rourke, have you helped arrange the adoption of children from Ireland over the years?'

'Yes, I have of course.'

'How many, would you say?'

'I do not recall. Several.'

'We have checked the adoption records, and would it surprise you to know that you were directly involved in the adoption of twenty-five children, from Ireland to Boston?'

'I have no recollection of that number, but if you say so, perhaps I did. There have been very many adoptions from Ireland over the years. It's work that I am very proud of. We found good Catholic homes for those children.'

'Did you sexually assault and rape any of those children, Bishop O'Rourke?'

'Absolutely not. I find these allegations deeply offensive.'

'Did you collaborate with others to sexually assault and rape children who had been adopted from Ireland?'

'Certainly not.'

'Do you know a man named Michael Finnegan?'

'Michael Finnegan? Yes, I believe he was employed as a gardener by some schools in the area for some years.'

'Did you and Michael Finnegan assault and rape his adopted son, Peter Finnegan?'

'Of course not!'

'Are you aware that Peter Finnegan took his own life while in police custody? Have you no remorse for the part you played in driving this young man to take his life?'

O'Rourke merely shrugged his shoulders. Conor persisted, undaunted.

'Did you and Michael Finnegan assault and rape his second adopted son, Francis Finnegan?'

'Of course not, Detective.'

'Did you, Michael Finnegan and other individuals collaborate to assault and rape these boys?'

'This is ridiculous, Detective, of course not.'

'Are you prepared to name those other men who, along with Michael Finnegan and yourself, sexually assaulted and raped these boys?'

This time O'Rourke sat back in his chair and paused for a few moments before replying.

'These unfounded and untrue allegations are becoming tiresome, Detective, they really are.'

'What is the nature of your relationship with Michael Finnegan?'

'None. I hardly know the man.'

'If that is the case, can you explain why Mr Finnegan appears to have been living in a Church-owned property rent-free for the past thirty years?'

'I have no idea, Detective.'

'Did Michael Finnegan, yourself and other priests take children to his home, a Church-owned property, to sexually abuse them?'

'No, we did not.'

Conor watched the bishop. He was calm. Any innocent person would be outraged, would be offended by the accusations. The bishop seemed unconcerned. In fact, he appeared smug. Conor felt like reaching across the table and slapping the look off his face.

There was a knock on the door and Conor was called out. A few minutes later he returned with a slim cardboard box under his arm. It had the word 'Evidence' stamped across it in red lettering. He placed it on the table between himself and the bishop. Conor then leaned forward and lifted the lid. There was a slim Mac notebook inside.

Conor and Stacey watched the bishop carefully for his reaction. O'Rourke's eyes snapped on the laptop straight away. They widened just for a moment. Despite his outward composure, Conor knew he had recognised it and was worried. Let's see just how worried you are, Bishop, Conor said to himself.

'Do you recognise this laptop, Bishop O'Rourke?'

'Not particularly, no.'

'This laptop was removed from your residence. Do you recognise it now?'

'Detective, I have several laptops and PCs in my rooms and offices. I have no idea if this is one of them.'

'This laptop was removed from your private rooms. Are you aware that it contains hundreds of illegal and obscene images, of a graphic sexual nature, of children?'

Conor could see a very thin layer of sweat bead on the bishop's forehead.

'Detective, I have no knowledge of any such images. In fact, many people have access to my rooms and to my computers, my PA, housekeeper, cleaners. I have absolutely no idea how or why those images would be on that computer. But I can assure you categorically that I had nothing to do with them.'

The bishop began to fidget in his chair. Conor thought, *Gotcha, you fucking asshole, and you know it now, don't you?* He allowed himself a momentary smile. He could see a trickle of sweat run down the side of O'Rourke's neck and below his priestly black and white. *Gotcha!*

'Bishop O'Rourke, we want to go back to your role in organising adoptions. Would it be fair to say that in one form or another you have been directly involved in organising adoptions from Ireland for over fifty years now?'

'I suppose you could say that, yes.'

'And for the last twenty of those years your role has been to oversee, to supervise, the work in Boston of the Catholic Charities of America, which has had responsibility for those adoptions?'

'That is correct.'

'Are you aware that many of those adoptions were effectively illegal because few of those children had passports and many of them were taken from their mothers without their consent?'

'Oh please, that is nonsense. A fiction spun by atheists, homosexuals and communists. Spare me the bleeding-heart liberal platitudes, Detective.' He almost spat the words. It was the first time that he had visibly lost his temper.

'During your time as a Catholic priest and a senior clergyman in Boston, how many children would you say were adopted from Ireland? Hundreds?'

'I have no idea, Detective.'

'Would you be surprised if I told you thousands? Closer to ten thousand children? Stolen from their mothers and shipped from Ireland.'

O'Rourke scoffed and replied, 'Now you are being ridiculous, Detective. Stolen? These children were given up by their mothers of their own free will. We saved them from a life of shame and poverty and placed them with decent Catholic families here in the US. These mothers were sinners, fallen women. We gave them an opportunity to start a new life. To put their sins behind them and start again. Why should we apologise for that?'

O'Rourke's voiced quickened as he spoke. He leaned forward on the table to stare directly at Conor.

'For God's sake, you of all people should know better, Detective. Haven't you seen at first hand the moral chaos out there? Where this liberal ideology is leading us? The prostitution, single drug-addicted mothers, children roaming the streets at night like feral cats, robbing and assaulting at will?

'And what do you think the remedy is? More welfare cheques? Parenting classes? Homosexual adoptions? Bleeding hearts? No, we need to restore respect for the institutions of authority. The Church, the police, the officer on the beat. Men like you, Detective. And yes, men like me.'

He stopped abruptly, realising that he had lost control for a few moments. He smiled and withdrew slowly back into his chair. Conor paused and looked at Stacey. At last, they had caught a glimpse of the real Timothy O'Rourke. Conor remarked to himself, perhaps this was his weakness, his pride? He tucked the idea away in his mind and told himself to speak to Karan about it. He continued his questioning.

'Did the Catholic Charities of America charge adopting families a fee for the service? Did these families pay the Catholic Church for children? Did you sell these children for cash, Bishop O'Rourke?'

'Of course not. Some families may have made a voluntary donation to the Church, but there was never any question of fees.'

'Did Michael Finnegan and other adopting parents pay you large sums of money to adopt these children?'

'No, not at all!'

'Was it not the case, Bishop O'Rourke, that the Catholic Church did expect families to donate large sums of money for these children? Was it not in fact the case that this was a lucrative business for the Church in Boston, a multimillion-dollar business?'

'Absolutely not!'

Both detectives gathered their papers together. Conor looked at his watch and then at the clock on the wall and said, 'We are terminating the interview at 2.53pm. Please stand up, Bishop O'Rourke.'

O'Rourke stood. From the look on his face, it appeared that he thought he was about to be released or returned to his holding cell before being released. Instead, Conor stepped around from behind the desk that separated them until he was standing just inches from his face.

'Timothy Sean O'Rourke, you are being charged with the following felony counts.

'That you had in your possession indecent images of children.

'That you did repeatedly rape a child, namely Peter Finnegan, between the years 1956–1966.

'That you did repeatedly rape a child, namely Francis Finnegan, between the years 1964–1975.

'That you did carry out an indecent assault and battery of a child, namely Raymond McCarthy, between the months of February and October 1994.'

Bishop O'Rourke's face registered with shock that he was being charged, but within seconds he had composed himself and replied, 'I categorically deny these charges.'

* * *

The following day, O'Rourke and Finnegan appeared in Suffolk County Court in downtown Boston for their arraignment. The superior courtroom was jampacked with press, legal teams and spectators. Among the crowd were Francis Finnegan and Raymond McCarthy. Conor, Maggie and Carole sat in the front row together. Who knew if other victims, as of yet unidentified, had decided to attend? Conor and his team hoped the publicity would encourage other victims to come forward, though he knew it was notoriously difficult to get men to admit what had happened to them as children in cases like this.

Conor watched the bishop and Finnegan as they took their seats. It galled Conor that the bishop still wore his priestly garb. *What an insult to everything it stood for*, he thought to himself.

O'Rourke and Finnegan sat together, but neither acknowledged the other and sat looking straight ahead. O'Rourke was represented by Barbara Clarke and her formidable team of attorneys. Finnegan was represented by a different firm and lawyer, though no less formidable. Both were expensive.

Across the room sat Martine Holden and another Assistant DA. When the judge entered the room, the court clerk announced, 'All rise for the Right Honourable Judge R.J. Feeney! This court is now in session.'

The judge looked at both tables and asked, 'Shall we proceed, ladies and gentlemen? OK. Could I ask the clerk to read out the charges against both defendants?'

'In the case of Timothy Sean O'Rourke, he is charged with four felony counts.

'That he had in his possession indecent images of children.

'That he did repeatedly rape a child, namely Peter Finnegan, between 1956–1966.

'That he did repeatedly rape a child, namely Francis Finnegan, between 1964–1975.

'That he did carry out an indecent assault and battery of a child, namely Raymond McCarthy, between February–October 1994.'

There were loud exclamations of surprise, followed by whispers and comments from the press and public present. The judge intervened.

'I'm instructing everyone in the courtroom, particularly those in the public gallery, to remain quiet. I will not tolerate interruptions from the gallery. Please remain quiet or I will be forced to clear the press and the public.'

The judge turned his attention to the defendants.

'Mr O'Rourke, please stand!'

'It's Bishop O'Rourke, Bishop Timothy O'Rourke.'

The judge looked at the bishop and paused before replying.

'How do you plead to the charges, Mr O'Rourke?'

'Not guilty.'

Conor wasn't the least bit surprised that O'Rourke was going to fight the case against him. There was no way he would simply plead guilty. Why would he? His conviction was far from a certainty. He'd told them all, but particularly Francis and Raymond, not to expect O'Rourke to make it easy for them. Despite this, he could see that Francis in particular was in shock. There was no question now, no doubt or hope to the contrary, that he would have to take the stand and give his evidence in open court.

The judge said, 'Take a seat, Mr O'Rourke.' Then he turned back to the clerk.

'In the case of Mr Michael Finnegan, he is charged with three felony counts.

'That he had in his possession indecent images of children.

'That he did repeatedly rape a child, namely Peter Finnegan, between 1956–1966.

'That he did repeatedly rape a child, namely Francis Finnegan, between 1964–1975.'

The judge looked at Finnegan.

'Mr Finnegan, please stand. How do you plead to the charges?'

'Not guilty.'

'Take a seat, Mr Finnegan. In the case of both defendants, are they making an application for bail?'

'Yes, yes, we are,' replied their two attorneys.

'What is the District Attorney's attitude to bail?'

Martine Holden stood up.

'We are vigorously opposed to bail for both defendants, Your Honour. These are very serious charges involving the violent assault and rape of a number of young children. We believe that both individuals would be a danger to other children and there would be a real possibility that either would abscond.'

'Would the defendants' attorneys care to respond?'

'Yes, Your Honour,' said Barbara Clarke standing up. 'We represent Bishop O'Rourke only. The bishop has no criminal convictions of any sort. Indeed, he has an exemplary record of community service going back over sixty years. As a Catholic bishop we would assert, without fear of contradiction, that there is no question of Bishop O'Rourke absconding. In fact, he is eager to have his case heard at trial as soon as possible so that these charges can be challenged by him. We would ask that you grant our client bail.'

'Mr Lawrence?' The judge gestured to Finnegan's attorney, who rose from his seat.

'Yes, Your Honour, we are asking that our client be released on bail. Mr Finnegan has only one minor conviction going back over sixty years. An action that he deeply regrets. For over sixty years Mr Finnegan has been a good father and husband. He has been a stalwart of the Church and given a great deal of his spare time to serving the local community. We would like to present a number of character references from individuals of good standing, including his local parish priest, who are prepared to vouch for Mr Finnegan and to post bail for him.'

'Thank you, both. These are very serious charges in both cases. Mr Finnegan, I see, has a previous conviction for exposing himself to a minor, though as you say that was a very long time ago. However, given the seriousness of the charges and the real possibility that Mr Finnegan could abscond. I am refusing him bail.

'As for Bishop O'Rourke, I am prepared to release him on bail and bail will be set at fifty thousand dollars. He has no previous convictions and, given his prominent position within the Catholic Church, I doubt there is much risk of him absconding.

'And Assistant District Attorney Holden, I want the evidence in this case to be presented as quickly as possible. It is my intention to set a date for early trial of the accused at the next arraignment. Is that clear?'

'Yes, of course, Your Honour.'

One hour later, bail was posted for Bishop O'Rourke, and he was released from custody. The cardinal had asked Barbara Clarke to make it clear to the bishop that upon release he was to make no statement to the press. He was to leave the building as quietly and discreetly as possible. An officer of the court had offered the bishop the opportunity to exit via a private car park, but he had declined. Instead, he had left through the front entrance. A large press group had gathered there hoping to film and question him. As Barbara tried to usher him quickly through the crowd of journalists and reporters, to her surprise and annoyance O'Rourke stopped at the top of the steps outside the court and proceeded to make a statement.

'Ladies and gentlemen, let me say categorically that I am innocent of these charges. I have never harmed a child, never! I do not know any of the men who have made these horrible accusations against me. I cannot see into their hearts and discern their motivation. Perhaps they are acting maliciously; perhaps they are simply mistaken. I do not know.

'Perhaps in this public climate of liberal ideology and fake news, some people might think that now is the time to manufacture damaging accusations against the Catholic Church. I really do not know but what I do know is I am innocent of these charges and intend to prove my innocence as soon as I have an opportunity to do so in court.'

He said thank you and smiled confidently as he pushed his way through the waiting press pack. Barbara thought to herself, *What an arrogant prick.*

* * *

That afternoon Conor and Detective Washington joined the team searching Michael Finnegan's home. So far, they hadn't found anything of significance, but it was early days. Conor had asked that cadaver dogs be brought in to search the house and the extensive back garden. Anything or anyone could be buried out there. The guy had been living here forever.

The place was damn creepy, thought Conor. Even in broad daylight, the rooms seemed dark and menacing. They felt more like cells than bedrooms. Each one had a single bed, a bedside locker and a small desk and chair. Above the headboard of each bed hung a large crucifix. He wondered if children had been brought here by O'Rourke and Finnegan to be raped. He was certain they had. Just standing in one of the rooms sent a chill down his spine.

The uniformed sergeant came in to tell him that the dog team had arrived. Conor went down to give them instructions.

'Take one out to the back garden, Jack. And then do the house.'

* * *

The team had been working most of the day. Detective Sam Goldberg was overseeing the search. Detective Stacey Washington stood in the middle of Finnegan's bedroom. She pulled a set of surgical gloves on before handling anything. She picked up various things that were sitting on his bedside locker and examined them. She opened several of his drawers and lifted out some of his personal items. She opened the large wardrobe and ran her finger across the clothes hanging there. There were several boxes sitting under them. She called out to Sam in the next room.

'Sam, have we searched these boxes in the wardrobe?'

Sam walked in from next door.

'Yeah, Boss. There's a few pairs of old shoes and an ancient camera in one of them. Don't worry – we checked it. It's one of those old Instamatics, the ones that feed a developed photograph out the front. It's empty.'

Stacey lifted the top box onto the bed. Standing behind it in the corner of the wardrobe was a camera tripod. She pulled it out and stood it nearby. When she opened the box, she found a large plastic camera. On the side it read 'Polaroid 600'. This model was red and black with a folding flash that sat on top. She picked it up. It was big and bulky but in very good condition. Probably made sometime in the early 1980s, she thought. She noticed that there were no photographs in the box. Not a single one.

'Where are the photographs?' she asked.

'The photographs? There were none.'

'No instant photographs? None at all?'

'There were some old photos in another box, family photos, but no Instamatic ones.'

Stacey handed Sam the camera.

'It's in remarkable condition. Don't you find that … unusual?'

He shook his head and replied, 'No, why?'

'Well, where are the photographs? He's used it. He went out of his way to take care of it. So where are the photos?

'Sam, get a team in here now. And when they are finished in this room, I want them to search every other room again. But this time, I want them to check for wall cavities. I want them to check under the floorboards. Rip the place apart if you have to.'

'OK, everyone, you heard the detective. Take it apart.'

* * *

Conor was standing on the back patio watching the dog do its work when one of the search team in Finnegan's bedroom shouted, 'Got something!'

As he walked back into the room, a young detective was pointing down to the side of the bed. The bedside locker had been moved and the detective had pried the baseboard from the wall where it met the floor. There was an open cavity behind it. Stacey Washington removed a small torch from her pocket, got down on her knees and shone a light inside.

'There's something there.'

Conor knelt beside her and took the torch.

'Go ahead!'

She pulled out a cardboard container about the size of a donut box. She sat it on the bed and opened it. Inside were dozens of Instamatic photographs. She lifted one and passed it to Conor. It showed a naked man raping a child.

CHAPTER 19

BOSTON, PRESENT DAY

The trial date was set, and a jury selected. Karan was to present the case for the state, with Martine acting as her assistant. They had spent half a day choosing the jury and had gone through all the usual questions. Did anyone know the accused? Had anyone been the victim of sexual abuse? And so on. The numbers had gradually been whittled down to the remaining twelve.

Privately Karan had one objective: to try to weed out as many Catholics and middle-aged or older demographics as they could. They needed as few middle-aged conservative Catholics on the jury as possible. The younger, the better and the more diverse religiously and racially, the better. And mothers. They wanted empathetic mothers who would look at Raymond McCarthy and Francis Finnegan and see in them their own children.

Their case against O'Rourke and Finnegan was solid but not airtight. It relied on the physical evidence – the laptop and photographs – and the two witnesses, Raymond and Francis.

They knew the Defence would argue that others had access to O'Rourke's laptop, that he hadn't downloaded the images of child sexual abuse onto it. They would try to sow seeds of reasonable doubt in the minds of the jurors.

Goldberg's team had found photographs in Finnegan's house that were damning for him. They were hidden in his room. His fingerprints were all over them, and he was clearly identifiable in several of them.

In O'Rourke's case there were no fingerprints on the photographs and the few shots of him were taken from behind. They had body and facial recognition experts who would testify that it was him. But they knew the Defence team would have their own experts who would testify that it was not. In his case everything hinged on the quality of the witness evidence and who the jury believed.

On paper Raymond and Francis appeared strong. Neither had a criminal conviction and both were middle-class professionals. But who knew what could go wrong? Karan had seen witnesses crumble or be discredited before now. The men had practised taking the stand and giving their evidence. Karan and Martine had aggressively questioned them about their witness testimonies. Both had performed remarkably well. They had prepared them as best they could. However, Raymond had lost his temper several times. He was angry and who could blame him? But it was a danger and could be exploited by the Defence.

'You must not lose your temper, Raymond. The defence attorney will try to provoke you. You can be sure of that. We do not want any of the jurors thinking, *This guy is so angry he would say anything!* or *This guy simply hates the Catholic Church.* We know how you feel, but do not be drawn into a discussion about the Catholic Church. Got it?'

'OK. I get it.'

'Just try to stay calm and stick to what he did to you. That's all the jury needs to hear.'

Francis, on the other hand, was quiet and soft-spoken. He appeared vulnerable, damaged by what had been done to him. This was something the jury might empathise with. After Finnegan and O'Rourke had been arrested and charged, Francis had grown in confidence and determination. He had told Conor that he was ready to face them both and to help put them behind bars.

'You know, Conor, my brother Peter tried to look out for me. He tried to protect me. For over fifty years I tried to bury the memories, the nightmares, of what they did to me. But in the process, I buried the memories of my brother. Even the good ones. And I pretended that it didn't matter. Shame on me. But not anymore.

'I got to live my life. To have a family. He was denied both. They took his childhood – and more than that. They drove him to destroy his own life and two other innocent lives. God knows I thought about taking my own life more times than I care to remember. But I'm still here. I survived.

'I want to tell the court; I want to tell the jury who Peter Finnegan was. That he was a sweet kid, who tried to protect me. I want to tell them he was my big brother and he loved me.'

Karan knew a trial was like a drama, a grand stage and they were the actors. Yes, physical evidence often played a crucial role, but in many instances, it simply came down to which side could be the most convincing. Who were the best actors? She had had bigger cases than this, cases that had changed the law of the land. But for her, this time, this case, this was the most important one she had ever fought. This was what separated the stars from the supporting cast. She knew everything depended upon her performance and she had no intention of losing.

*   *   *

The morning of the trial was dark and stormy, but it didn't keep the crowds away. The general public queued outside the courtroom to try to get a seat. All sorts of crazy people attended trials, especially the high-profile ones. Centuries ago, thousands of people would gather to watch public executions. They would bring their packed picnic baskets and their children. Now they watched them on Netflix or sat in the public galleries of high-profile trials.

Conor had made sure Maggie and Carole had a front seat beside him. Karan and Martine stood directly ahead of them discussing the case. To the right Barbara Clarke and the Defence team milled about chatting and leafing through legal papers.

Conor reached across and squeezed Maggie's hand. They turned and looked at each other. Maggie smiled and slipped her fingers between Conor's and held his hand the way she used to when she was just a child. They both looked at their clasped hands and silently, simultaneously, thought of their father.

Karan turned and glanced at them both. They had found her. They had found Faith. They exchanged a single but somehow meaningful glance before Karan nodded to them and then turned back to face the judge and the jury. Now, together, they were about to hold the Church to account for its own sins.

When the last few seats were filled, the jury filed into the courtroom through a side door. A few minutes later, O'Rourke and Finnegan were escorted to their seats by several armed guards. At one minute to ten the court clerk rose and called 'All rise for the Right Honourable Judge R.J. Feeney.'

Judge Robert James Feeney was Irish American and Catholic. He was a patron of several Catholic charities, some of which worked with disadvantaged children across the city. He attended his local Catholic church in Cambridge with his family every Sunday morning without fail. He was conservative and Republican. He had a reputation for tough sentencing, but in Karan's experience he was fair.

She had no idea what his attitude might be to O'Rourke and the fact that he was a Catholic bishop. Would that influence him in any way? It might but Karan wasn't sure in what way. He was, at least as far as appearances went, a devout Catholic. But what did that mean in this day and age? Would he be unduly sympathetic to the bishop's testimony, or would he be outraged at O'Rourke's betrayal of his priestly vocation and the Catholic Church? All she could hope for was that it was the latter of the two.

'Pleased be seated. Members of the jury, this morning you will hear opening statements from the District Attorney and from the Defence. This is not evidence. This is merely a summary of their respective arguments.

'I hope both attorneys will excuse me when I say to you all, do not pay much attention to what they say at this opening stage.

'Your job is to listen to the evidence in this case, which will take the form of witness testimonies, physical evidence and so called "expert evidence". Listen to that evidence, assess that evidence very carefully and when you have heard all the evidence, you must decide – beyond a reasonable doubt – that both or either defendants are guilty or innocent of each of the charges.

'Because you might conclude that one, either or both, are guilty of one charge does not mean that they are automatically guilty of the other charges. Consider each of the charges separately and decide on each of those charges whether the defendant is guilty.

'If there is anything that is not absolutely clear to you or you would like further clarification on, please write those questions down on a note and during recess have them forwarded to me via the foreperson of the jury. If I deem it appropriate, I will then ask your questions on your behalf. You are not permitted to ask a question directly yourself during the course of the open proceedings.

'Madam District Attorney, would you like to make your opening statement?'

The courtroom was completely silent for a few moments, and only the low vibration of the fluorescent lights could be heard.

'Thank you, Your Honour.'

Karan rose from her seat and walked towards the jury. She was dressed in a dark trouser suit and a white blouse buttoned to the neck. She had chosen the dark suit to complement her plain white hair, which she wore layered with a simple side parting. She looked serious and professional.

She walked slowly along the full length of the jury's enclosure looking each of the jurors directly in the eye. She didn't smile. She wanted them to know that this was a serious business and that she understood they had a difficult job to do. She stopped at the other end of the enclosure with O'Rourke and Finnegan sitting to the left of her. She exuded a quiet confidence. Her movements were considered. Fluid.

'Thank you, each of you, for participating in this jury. The judge is right. My opening remarks don't matter very much. What matters most will be the evidence, the extensive and irrefutable evidence, which we will present to you during this trial.

'We will present to you conclusive evidence that these two men, Timothy O'Rourke and Michael Finnegan, sexually assaulted and violently raped at least two young children. We will present overwhelming evidence that both these men continued to rape these two young children, repeatedly, from the age of five years through to their teenage years.

'I want each of you to think about that for one moment. I want you to look at both defendants.' Karan stepped back and pointed to the men.

'Both men are six feet or more in height. Both men easily weigh more than two hundred pounds. Now I want you to imagine, and I'm sorry to have to ask you to do this, but I want you to imagine these two men, these large men, standing over a five-year-old child and taking turns raping him.'

Karan saw some of the female jurors physically recoil from her words. *Good*, she thought, *I have their attention*. Some of them looked directly at the bishop.

There was a flurry of gasps and comments from the public gallery before the judge intervened and ordered the public to remain quiet so Karan could continue.

'We will present corroborating evidence, not just one piece of evidence but first-hand witness accounts from the victims themselves, photographic evidence and expert evidence that supports our contention that Timothy O'Rourke and Michael Finnegan collaborated together to adopt vulnerable children from Ireland, collaborated and acted in a joint endeavour to sexually abuse these children and in fact raped these children on multiple occasions over many years.

'When you hear this evidence, when you see this evidence, you will be shocked, you will be sickened by the horrible detail of what these men did to these innocent children. Find them guilty as charged. And most importantly of all, we ask you to send them to prison, where they will not be able to rape or hurt another child.'

Karan looked at each of the jurors again before turning to stare at O'Rourke and Finnegan. She then walked slowly back to her table and took her seat.

'Thank you, Your Honour.'

'Miss Clarke, please make your opening statement.'

Barbara Clarke stood up. 'Ladies and gentlemen of the jury, you have been asked to carefully consider each of the charges, to carefully consider the actual evidence presented during this trial. The District Attorney will try to persuade you that there is conclusive evidence to convict Bishop Timothy O'Rourke of the charges.

'There is no such evidence. No such evidence. You will be told that Bishop O'Rourke had hundreds of images of child sexual abuse on his computer. But we will demonstrate that numerous people in the bishop's residence had access to that computer and could have downloaded those images without the bishop's knowledge. Remember what the judge told you. Beyond reasonable doubt. If there is even the slightest possibility that someone else downloaded those images, you must reject the suggestion made by the District Attorney.

'We are told that there are two witnesses who are prepared to give evidence against Bishop O'Rourke. But who are these witnesses and why has it taken them almost thirty and almost sixty years to come forward? How seriously can we take their evidence? We will present such evidence that will call into question the motivation and indeed the honesty of those witnesses.

'Remember what the judge said. By all means, remember what the District Attorney said. You must examine the evidence, you must consider each of the charges separately, and at the end of this trial, if you have a reasonable doubt, a reasonable doubt, if you are not one hundred percent sure of his guilt, you must acquit him of these charges.

'Thank you, members of the jury.'

'Mr Lawrence, would you like to make your opening statement on behalf of Mr Finnegan?'

Finnegan and his attorney were huddled together in conversation.

'Mr Lawrence?'

Finnegan's attorney stood up; it was clear that he was agitated.

'Your Honour, my client has just instructed me to change his plea. He wishes to plead guilty!'

There was consternation in the court. Conor immediately turned to Milly, Francis's wife, who sat directly behind him with her three daughters. She grasped his hand and began to cry.

He whispered to her, 'It's OK. We'll get word to Francis before he comes out to give evidence. Don't worry.'

Conor stood up and quickly left the courtroom to speak to Francis. He was shocked. So was Maggie. So was Karan, though she hid it well. The only person who didn't appear to be surprised was Bishop O'Rourke.

'OK, Mr Lawrence. Is your client absolutely sure he wishes to change his plea at this late stage?'

The attorney turned and looked at Finnegan, who nodded.

The judge continued, 'Mr Michael Finnegan has lodged a plea of guilty. Mr Finnegan, you will be returned to prison pending the conclusion of these proceedings. At which point you will be returned for sentencing. Officer, return Mr Finnegan to the custody suite, please.'

Finnegan was handcuffed before being led away. O'Rourke was left sitting alone with his Defence team. Karan looked across to him and inwardly cursed to herself. She didn't know how he had persuaded Finnegan to plead guilty and remove himself from the trial, but she knew he had. He was a clever and devious bastard for sure. With Finnegan gone, there was no question O'Rourke's odds had improved.

'Madam District Attorney, are you ready to proceed?'

'Yes, we are, Your Honour. We would like to present the statement of Mr Peter Finnegan, deceased, as evidence.'

Barbara Clarke immediately stood up.

'Objection, Your Honour. If I may?'

'Carry on, Miss Clarke.'

'Your Honour, this statement is over fifty years old. Peter Finnegan is not here to be cross-examined. These dying declarations are notoriously unreliable. We have no idea as to the mental state of the individual at the time and we have no idea of his motivation. He may have been acting out of malice or madness. We would ask that the statement be deemed inadmissible.'

'Madam District Attorney?'

'Your Honour, this statement is entirely relevant to the case. The passage of time is neither here nor there. The statement was made to police officers less than twenty-four hours before he took his own life. It is a dying declaration and therefore carries considerable weight.

'What is more, Your Honour, Peter Finnegan was the older adopted brother of Mr Francis Finnegan, who will testify that both he and his brother were assaulted and raped by Mr Finnegan and Bishop O'Rourke.

'Therefore, not only is the statement itself compelling evidence, but we have the testimony of Francis Finnegan, which will corroborate that statement. We would ask Your Honour to admit the statement as evidence.'

'Thank you both for your opinions.'

The judge scribbled some notes on the paper in front of him as he considered the matter.

'In light of the fact that Francis Finnegan will be giving evidence supporting the claims made in the statement, I'm going to allow it. You may proceed, Madam District Attorney.'

'Thank you, Your Honour. I have copies of Peter Finnegan's statement. If it pleases you, I'll hand copies for yourself and for the members of the jury to the clerk?'

'Yes, that's fine.'

'I'd like to read from the statement if that's OK, Your Honour?'

The judge nodded his assent.

'Ladies and gentlemen of the jury, you have in front of you the sworn statement of Peter Finnegan. He was just eighteen years of age when he made the statement and less than twenty-four hours later, he took his own life while in police custody. He hung himself in his cell.

'Peter was adopted from Ireland in 1956 by Mr Michael Finnegan. He was able to adopt Peter, a five-year old child at the time, because Father Timothy O'Rourke, the defendant, recommended him as a suitable parent for adoption. Mr Finnegan has today pleaded guilty to repeatedly raping both Peter and his brother Francis – another child who was adopted from Ireland on the recommendation of Father Timothy O'Rourke.

'You will read a graphic description by Peter Finnegan of how Michael Finnegan and Father Timothy O'Rourke brutally raped him. Violently and repeatedly. It was this treatment that drove him to take his own life.

'I do not intend to read the whole statement to you, but I would like to read just one paragraph from it. If I could draw your attention to the third paragraph.

'And I quote "But he wasn't the worst. The worst was the parish priest, Father Timothy O'Rourke, from St Michael's parish where I lived. When

I became a little older, O'Rourke asked me if I wanted to become an altar boy and I said yes. Straight after saying my first mass, O'Rourke raped me in the sacristy.

"'O'Rourke was an animal, a real nasty piece of work. He would bite me while he raped me. He would leave bite marks on me, deliberately. For years I wouldn't undress unless I was alone because that animal would bite me when he raped me. He left me with scars. He enjoyed hurting me. I remember he was always laughing, enjoying it. When I cried, he seemed to enjoy it more. He was *pure evil*.'"

The two words seemed to echo around a stunned courtroom.

Karan pointed at O'Rourke. 'He was pure evil.'

She paused and looked at the jury. 'Father Timothy O'Rourke, Bishop Timothy O'Rourke, was in his words, "pure evil".

'Thank you, Your Honour.'

'Miss Clarke?'

'Your Honour, members of the jury, what the District Attorney has failed to mention is that at the time that Mr Peter Finnegan made this statement he had just been charged with the murder of a male transvestite. He had already served a year in juvenile detention for grievous bodily harm, and he had several convictions for theft and burglary.

'The witness statement was given by a convicted criminal, a proven liar and a thief. Members of the jury, when considering this statement, we would ask that you set it aside and attach no weight to it. Had he not taken his own life at the time, he would most certainly have been convicted of first-degree murder.' She sat down.

The judge looked across to the jurors. 'OK, ladies and gentlemen of the jury, you have heard the views of both the District Attorney and the

Defence. It is entirely up to your own judgement the weight you attach to the statement of Peter Finnegan, but consider it you must.

'I want to move to direct witness evidence now. Madam District Attorney, would you like to call your first witness?'

'Yes, Your Honour, thank you. The Prosecution calls Francis Finnegan.'

* * *

Not long after being told about his mother in Ireland and the Boston PD's plan to arrest and charge Michael Finnegan and Bishop O'Rourke, Francis had gathered his family together and told them about how he was sexually abused as a child by both men. Of course, they were horrified and devastated but instantly rallied round him. He told them he wanted to give evidence against both men, but he would only do so if they agreed. He knew the case would attract huge media attention that would impact not just him but the whole family. One of his children asked him, 'Dad, why do you want to do this, to put yourself through this?'

He looked at his three beautiful daughters and said, 'For nearly sixty years I hid the truth. I convinced myself that it was the best thing to do. God knows how many other children these men abused in the intervening years. I'm deeply ashamed of that, deeply ashamed. It's time for me to do the right thing, to help put these monsters behind bars. I owe it to Peter.'

They gathered round him and locked their arms. They cried and told him how much they loved him and how proud they were of him as their father and their children's grandfather. If he wanted to sit in that courtroom and confront O'Rourke, they would be incredibly proud of him and would be there with him.

Francis was sitting waiting in a small room off the courtroom. He was still partly in shock at Conor's news that his adopted father had changed his plea to guilty. His hands were clasped as if in prayer and his head was bowed. He could feel his nerves increase. His left leg began to tremble against his will. The door opened and a police officer in uniform called his name.

'You are wanted in court now, Mr Finnegan.'

Francis took a deep breath, stood up and followed him into the court.

*   *   *

When Francis took his seat, Karan rose and walked to stand in front of him.

'Thank you, Francis, for taking the stand today. I know this is extremely difficult for you. Can you tell us your full name and occupation please?'

'My name is Francis David Finnegan. I work in Harvard University as a bio-tech researcher.'

'Can you tell us a little bit about how you came to be adopted by the Finnegans?'

'I was born in Ireland and adopted by the Finnegans when I was five. I don't remember very much about Ireland or the adoption itself.'

'And your adopted father, Michael Finnegan, raped you. Is that correct?'

'I remember that soon after arriving in Boston, he raped me in my bedroom.'

'When did you first meet the defendant, Father Timothy O'Rourke?'

'It was only a few weeks after I arrived in Boston. He called to the family home, took me to my bedroom and he raped me.'

'Francis, I know this is very difficult, but I must ask you. What exactly did Timothy O'Rourke do to you?'

Francis drew a deep breath and the tears welled in his eyes. He looked at his three daughters before turning his attention back to Karan.

'He made me perform oral sex on him, then he forced me over the bed and penetrated me from behind.'

Karan paused to let the image sink into the jurors' minds before she asked her next question.

'Can you tell us about your brother, Peter? What type of boy was he?'

'Peter was a few years older than me. I remember he was kind to me. I remember he tried to protect me. We would try to make excuses not to be at home. We played outside as much as we could. We joined sports teams, after-school clubs. Anything to get us out of the house and to keep us out. Peter took me everywhere with him.'

'Did you ever see Father Timothy O'Rourke with Peter?'

'Yes, he would visit our house on a regular basis. He and my adopted father, Michael Finnegan, were good friends. They managed the local base-ball team together.'

'Did Peter tell you that O'Rourke had raped him? Did you ever see any-thing happen to Peter?'

'Yes. I came home from school early one day and went straight to my room to leave my schoolbag there. When I opened the bedroom door, I saw my adopted father and O'Rourke standing there naked and Peter lying on the bed. I just froze when I saw them.'

'What did they do, Francis, when they saw you?'

'O'Rourke walked towards me and just smiled. And then he slowly closed the door. As if he hadn't a care in the world.'

Karan looked at the jury and asked, 'He smiled at you?'

'Yes, he simply smiled at me.'

'Are you absolutely certain it was Father Timothy O'Rourke?'

'Absolutely!'

'Can you point him out to the jury?'

He pointed at O'Rourke and said, 'That is the man who raped Peter and that is the man who raped me. Bishop Timothy O'Rourke.'

'One last question, Francis. How often were you raped?'

'It continued from when I was five, right through until I was about fifteen. Hundreds of times.'

'Thank you, Francis.'

Karan smiled sympathetically. She looked him directly in the eye for a few moments. She wanted to reach out and embrace him. Instead, she turned and walked slowly back to her seat.

'Your witness, Miss Clarke.'

'Thank you, Your Honour.' Barbara Clarke walked over to Francis.

'Good morning, Mr Finnegan. Did you ever tell anyone about these allegations?'

'No.'

'Did you confide in a single person about these allegations?'

'No.'

'Surely, you confided in your wife?'

'No, I did not.'

'Did you confide in a close friend?'

'No.'

'Did you tell a teacher?'

'No.'

'Did you report these allegations to a social worker? To the police?'

'No.'

'Is it not the case, Mr Finnegan, that the real reason you did not report these allegations to another single person, in nearly sixty years, is because they never happened? That for some perverse reason, an imagined slight, a personal dislike, you have concocted these allegations against Bishop O'Rourke?'

'No!'

'No more questions, Your Honour.'

Francis turned to the judge and in a quiet voice he asked, 'Can I answer the question, Your Honour? I would like to.'

'Of course, Mr Finnegan.'

Barbara Clarke immediately objected.

'Your Honour, we have–'

The judge interrupted her.

'Take a seat, Miss Clarke. You asked the question. I'd like Mr Finnegan to answer it.'

There was silence in the court as Francis spoke in a quiet voice.

'Your Honour, who would I have told? My adopted father, who raped me? The parish priest, who raped me? My adopted mother, who knew but did nothing? Peter tried his best to protect me, but when he was old enough, he ran away from home. I was alone. Completely alone.

'I was afraid. I was ashamed. For years I wondered, had I encouraged it in some way? Had I deserved it? When I escaped, when I was older, I should have told someone. I know that now. I have had to live with the knowledge, with the guilt, that Father O'Rourke and my adopted father probably molested other children while I remained silent.'

Barbara Clarke sprung to her feet and immediately objected.

'Objection, Your Honour, that is prejudicial speculation.'

'Objection sustained. Members of the jury, you will ignore that last remark. Thank you, Mr Finnegan. You can take a seat in the public gallery now if you wish.'

'Thank you, Your Honour,' he said in a soft whisper.

The judge looked at his watch and checked the court clock.

'It is almost one o'clock. We shall recess for lunch and proceedings will resume at 2pm this afternoon. Court is adjourned.'

* * *

During the lunch recess Barbara Clarke had a meeting with Bishop O'Rourke to discuss their strategy. She was reasonably content that she had sowed sufficient doubt in the minds of the jury in relation to Francis Finnegan's testimony, but he had been a strong, credible witness.

They had agreed before the trial that the bishop would not take the stand and give evidence on his own behalf. She had been relieved. There was something about him, his manner, that rubbed people up the wrong way. He came across as haughty and arrogant. Ironically, his own arrogance prevented him from seeing this weakness in his own personality. He had no self-awareness. Towards the end of their consultation, O'Rourke dropped his bombshell. He had changed his mind. He now intended to take the stand and testify in his own defence. Barbara was horrified.

'Bishop O'Rourke, I want to advise you, in the strongest possible terms, not to take the stand. Karan O'Loughlin is incredibly skilled when it comes to cross-examination. It's one of her strongest courtroom attributes. I've seen her perform many times and she is razor sharp, brutal and incisive. We do not need to take that risk!'

Her remarks only seemed to aggravate the bishop. He appeared offended at the suggestion that 'that woman' could in any way get the better of him.

He made it clear to her that his mind was made up. Of course, he could deal with Karan O'Loughlin. Barbara got the distinct feeling that what the bishop really wanted to say was that no woman would get the better of him. Not for the first time she thought to herself, *What an arrogant and sexist prick.*

'OK, Bishop O'Rourke, but I want to make it clear that it is against my direct and explicit advice. And for the record, I intend to inform the cardinal that I advised you otherwise.'

'Yes, yes, Miss Clarke. Inform whoever you wish. I am more than capable of dealing with Miss O'Loughlin.'

* * *

The trial resumed at 2pm and the judge asked Karan to call her next witness.

'The Prosecution calls Mr Raymond McCarthy.'

After swearing in, Raymond took his seat in the witness stand. Karan stood up and approached him.

'Could you state your full name and occupation, please?'

'Raymond John McCarthy, and I'm a senior nurse at Boston General Hospital.'

'What elementary school did you attend, Raymond?'

'I attended St Joseph's in Dorchester.'

'Do you recognise the defendant, Raymond?'

'I do.'

'Can you tell us how you know the defendant?'

'He was the parish priest in our school. When I was nine years of age, Father Timothy O'Rourke sexually assaulted me in his office.'

Raymond took a shuddering deep breath. He knew the next question that Karan was going to ask him. He looked to his partner Matt, who sat in the public gallery. Matt nodded in reassurance. For a moment, Raymond closed his eyes. He could feel his fists clench uncontrollably.

'I realise that this will be difficult for you, but can you tell us how Father O'Rourke assaulted you?'

'On three separate occasions he pulled my trousers and pants down and fondled my penis.'

'Raymond, did you tell anyone at the time? Did you report it?'

'Yes, I did. I told my teacher, Mrs O'Reilly. She took me to the principal, and I told him. I also told my parents.'

'Your Honour, we have a sworn statement from Mrs O'Reilly confirming that she took the nine-year-old Raymond McCarthy to see the principal and he repeated the same allegations, that Father Timothy O'Rourke had sexually assaulted him on three separate occasions. You have it there in the case file.

'Should the Defence wish to challenge the statement, Mrs O'Reilly is willing to attend and be cross-examined.'

'Miss Clarke?'

'No, that is not necessary, Your Honour. We do not dispute that Mr McCarthy told both his teacher and the principal that he had been molested. We do, however, dispute the truthfulness of the witnesses account, but we will reserve any further comment until we have the opportunity to cross-examine the witness.'

'Carry on, Madam District Attorney.'

'Raymond, just one last question. What impact did these assaults have on you growing up?'

'They destroyed the next twenty years of my life. I lost all interest in my schoolwork. I lost a great deal of weight in my teens and suffered a form of anorexia. Worst of all, for many years I lost my faith in God. I blamed myself for letting it happen and I blamed God for allowing one of his priests to do that to me.'

'Thank you, Raymond.'

'Your witness, Miss Clarke,' said the judge.

Barbara Clarke approached the witness stand.

'Mr McCarthy, what is your relationship with your parents?'

'My parents? We do not speak.'

'Why is that?'

'They do not approve of the fact that I am gay and that I live with my partner.'

'Is that the only reason?'

'I'm not sure what you mean?'

'How did your parents feel about these allegations when you told them?'

Raymond looked at Karan before he spoke. He looked at Francis, at Maggie and at Connor. Tears welled in his eyes. He felt trapped. He didn't want to say the words. He knew exactly how they would sound.

'They didn't believe me.'

Barbara Clarke turned and looked at the jury.

'They didn't believe you,' she repeated. 'No more questions, Your Honour.'

The rest of the afternoon was taken up with expert evidence in relation to the photographs found in Finnegan's home. Karan knew the evidence was inconclusive. Their expert said it was O'Rourke in the photographs. The Defence expert said it was not.

Barbara Clarke had informed the judge that Bishop O'Rourke had decided to testify in his own defence and the judge had scheduled the trial to resume the following morning at 10am. There was excited anticipation at the announcement, especially among the journalists present and the reporting media. This was exactly the type of drama they had been waiting and hoping for.

Karan was surprised, very surprised. The bishop was not the most sympathetic personality. If Barbara Clarke had advised him to testify, it was a huge mistake. She relished the prospect of confronting him in open court.

'Hubris!' In ancient Greek, the term had had sexual connotations. It sometimes described the act of shaming or humiliating a victim for one's own sexual gratification, a form of rape. She recalled Aristotle's quote: 'To cause shame to the victim, not in order that anything may happen to you, nor because anything has happened to you, but merely for your own gratification. Hubris is not the requital of past injuries; this is revenge. As for pleasure in hubris, its cause is this: naïve men think that by ill-treating others they make their own superiority the greater.'

This time the bishop's hubris might just be the cause of his own downfall.

* * *

The next morning court resumed, and Barbara Clarke called her witness. Bishop Timothy O'Rourke swore the oath and took the seat on the stand. Anticipation filled the courtroom.

'Bishop O'Rourke, could you state your full name and occupation?'

'Timothy Sean O'Rourke, and I am the Catholic Bishop of Massachusetts.'

'How long have you been a priest?'

'I have been a priest for more than sixty years.'

'And why did you become a priest?'

'I became a priest because I felt a profound love for Jesus Christ and from a young age, I knew I wanted to serve God and his community.'

'So, it was love and a sense of responsibility that moved you to become a priest?'

'Yes, it was.'

'And during those years, Bishop O'Rourke, what sort of pastoral work have you been responsible for?'

'For the past twenty years I have overseen the work of the Catholic Charities of America here in Boston.'

'What sort of work does the charity do?'

'We give support for the homeless of our great city. We run a number of shelters, we provide food and warm clothing. We also work with young people across Boston, organising breakfast clubs in the most deprived communities. We provide safe spaces where young teenagers can congregate and play. We also do a great deal of work with our new immigrant communities, helping them integrate, find work, etc. And of course, we also work with the Children and Welfare Services to find foster families and place children for adoption.'

'Why do you do that work, Bishop O'Rourke?'

'Why?' O'Rourke turned and looked directly at the jury. This was his stock in trade. He felt confident. He smiled. He'd smiled this smile a million times. Not too much teeth. Not a happy smile. A modest smile. A soft and sincere tone of voice. 'Because our Lord Jesus Christ preached a gospel of love and of charity. I've always believed that the Church has a responsibility to love and care for our most vulnerable in society.'

'And during those sixty plus years of ministry, of helping the poor, the homeless, has anyone ever made a complaint against you?'

'No! Not that I am aware of. No, absolutely not.'

'For the record, Your Honour, we wish to state that there is no record of a single complaint being made against Bishop O'Rourke to the Church authorities or indeed the police.'

Karan rose and objected.

'Your Honour, the Prosecution has already placed on record Peter Finnegan's statement to the police and Raymond McCarthy's complaint to his school principal.'

'Miss Clarke, would you care to qualify your assertion?'

'Yes, Your Honour, setting aside the dubious statement of Peter Finnegan and Mr McCarthy's allegation, which we dispute.'

'Thank you, Miss Clarke. Carry on.'

'I have to ask you this, Bishop O'Rourke. Have you ever touched, molested or raped a child?'

Again O'Rourke turned directly to the jury. His face appeared to register a look of shock and horror. He paused dramatically for a few moments. Some of the jurors thought they detected a tremor of emotion in his voice when he replied, 'Absolutely not. Never!'

Bravo, thought Karan. Only the crocodile tears were missing from the performance.

'Thank you, Bishop O'Rourke.'

'Your witness, Madam District Attorney.'

'Thank you, Your Honour.'

Karan rose from her seat and walked closer to the bishop. She stopped about a metre away, looked at him directly and paused. They stared at one another for a few moments.

'Do you prefer to be called Bishop or Father O'Rourke?'

O'Rourke stared at Karan for a few moments. A look of disdain flashed across his face, as he turned to the jury.

'"Bishop" is my proper title.'

Karan thought to herself with some satisfaction, *That's it, Bishop O'Rourke. Let the jury see this pride of yours.*

'Bishop, then. Bishop O'Rourke, what is your relationship with Michael Finnegan? How would you describe it?'

'I know Michael Finnegan, not particularly well. He was employed by schools in the Diocese for a number of years.'

'Would you describe him as a close friend?'

'No, I would not!'

'Would it be accurate to say that you have been acquainted with him for more than sixty years?'

'I suppose so.'

'In 1956 you sponsored Michael Finnegan's adoption of Peter Finnegan. Isn't that correct?'

'It is but–'

'Just a yes or no will suffice, Bishop O'Rourke.'

He glared at Karan as he replied, 'Yes.'

'You must have known Michael Finnegan quite well if you were willing to recommend that he was suitable to adopt a child?'

'I knew him reasonably well as a parishioner. I knew him and his wife.'

'Did you know that Michael Finnegan already had a conviction for exposing himself to a child?'

'I did not.'

'Do you like sports, Bishop O'Rourke?'

'I do.'

'What's your favourite sport – football, basketball, baseball?'

'Baseball. The Red Sox, of course.' He smiled at the jury.

'Did you and Michael Finnegan manage the school baseball team?'

'Well, I wouldn't say I managed it. I was a supporter of the team.'

'Would it be fair to say you were a strong supporter of the team and regularly travelled to games across the city?'

'I wouldn't say regularly. Occasionally, yes.'

'You and Michael Finnegan?'

'Yes.'

'And was Peter Finnegan a member of the baseball team?'

'I cannot remember.'

'Your Honour, I'd like to draw your attention to item 52 in the evidence list. It's a school Yearbook for the year 1962. Bishop O'Rourke, on page twelve there is a photograph. Can we have that item shown on the large screen, Your Honour?'

The judge nodded to the clerk.

'Can you tell us, Bishop O'Rourke, is that you in the centre of the photograph?'

'Yes, it is.'

'And who is the boy standing next to you holding the other side of the trophy?'

O'Rourke hesitated before answering the question. 'I couldn't be sure.'

'Can you read the small print below the photograph, Bishop O'Rourke?'

The bishop removed glasses from his inside pocket and placed them on his nose.

'It reads …' – again O'Rourke hesitated, this time staring malevolently at

Karan – 'Father Timothy O'Rourke presents the tournament trophy to the captain of the baseball team, Master Peter Finnegan.'

'And do you recognise the individual standing to the left of the photograph, Bishop O'Rourke?'

O'Rourke snapped, 'No, I do not.'

Karan looked at the jury.

'The caption clearly refers to the Team Coach, Mr Michael Finnegan. Bishop O'Rourke, do you still insist Michael Finnegan was only an acquaintance?'

'Yes.'

'Bishop O'Rourke, did you later sponsor Michael Finnegan to adopt another child from Ireland. In 1964, to be precise?'

'If you say so. There were quite a lot of adoptions from Ireland during that period.'

'Let the record show that Father Timothy O'Rourke sponsored a second adoption, this time of Francis Finnegan. A copy of the adoption application is item 53 in the evidence book, Your Honour, members of the jury. Would it not be fair to assume that you knew Michael Finnegan very well, given that you had sufficient confidence in him to recommend him for adoption twice?'

'Ah, well, of course I knew both parents, but not particularly well.'

'But yet you thought Michael Finnegan was a suitable person to adopt a child, not once, but twice? May I remind you, Bishop O'Rourke, that Michael Finnegan has already pleaded guilty to the rape of both children, Peter Finnegan and Francis Finnegan.'

O'Rourke's face reddened for the first time since taking the stand. Karan knew he wasn't a man who was used to admitting mistakes.

'I may have made an error of judgement.'

'An error of judgement?'

Karan stepped closer to the dock and placed her two hands on the rail. In a quiet voice she asked, 'Bishop O'Rourke, isn't it true that both you and Michael Finnegan conspired together to adopt these vulnerable children from Ireland?'

'No!'

Karan raised her voice and said to O'Rourke, 'Bishop O'Rourke, isn't it true that you and Michael Finnegan violently and brutally raped both these boys?'

'Absolutely not!' he spat back in an angry tone.

Barbara Clarke sprung to her feet.

'Objection, Your Honour. The District Attorney is baiting the witness!'

'Madam District Attorney, please take the tone down a notch and do not try to provoke the witness.'

'Of course, Your Honour.'

'Carry on.'

'Bishop O'Rourke, which school did you minister to when you were a parish priest in Dorchester?'

'St Joseph's elementary.'

'Did you have a private office there?'

'I did.'

'For what purpose?'

'For pastoral support.'

'So, you would have had pupils in your office, alone, unsupervised?'

'What do you mean "unsupervised"?'

'Without another adult or teacher present.'

'Sometimes. But–'

'Just a yes or no answer will suffice!'

'Yes!' O'Rourke almost barked the words back at Karan.

'Did you invite nine-year-old Raymond McCarthy into your office, unsupervised?'

'I have no idea. It was a long time ago.'

'Did you invite nine-year-old Raymond McCarthy into your office on three separate occasions, unsupervised, and sexually assault him?'

'Absolutely not.'

'Bishop O'Rourke, have you any idea why this boy would make these allegations against you?'

'None whatsoever.'

'Really? A nine-year-old boy simply decides to make up this story and tells his schoolteacher, then the principal? It would be remarkable, would it not, for a nine-year-old child to make up such a story and repeat it in person to both his teacher and then again to the school principal?'

'Madam District Attorney, it did not happen and there is no school record of any such complaint being made.'

'Bishop O'Rourke, we have a sworn statement from Mrs O'Reilly, Raymond's teacher, that he made these complaints and that she informed the principal. Are you saying that she is lying too?'

'I'm saying she is mistaken. I have no idea of the reason why she has said this. But she is mistaken. Perhaps the child lied to her also. I have stated from the start that Raymond McCarthy is lying about these allegations.'

'What possible motivation or reason would Raymond McCarthy have for making up his statement? What had he to gain then? And what has he to gain now?'

'Again, I have no idea why he is lying.'

'Bishop O'Rourke, Peter Finnegan did not lie when he made his last statement. Francis Finnegan did not lie when he gave evidence. Mrs O'Reilly did not lie when she made her statement and Raymond McCarthy did not lie when he gave evidence. You lied, Bishop O'Rourke, didn't you?'

'I did not.'

'Wouldn't it be fair to say, Bishop O'Rourke, that your whole life has been one big lie? That you masqueraded as a man of God but, in reality, you perpetrated evil on these children? Isn't that the truth?'

'No.'

'Isn't it true that these children were stolen from their mothers in Ireland and shipped to Boston, only to be abused by you and Michael Finnegan?'

'No!' he snapped.

Karan leaned closer to O'Rourke. 'You raped these children, didn't you?' she almost whispered. 'DIDN'T YOU?' she shouted.

Before Barbara Clarke could rise and open her mouth to object, O'Rourke had already jumped to his feet in a rage and raised his hand as if to strike Karan.

'You …!' O'Rourke froze as he realised that the jury and the judge were staring at him in horror. He looked as if he had been seconds away from lashing out at the District Attorney. He slumped back down into his seat.

After a few moments, Karan asked O'Rourke, 'Bishop O'Rourke, do you recall your Proverbs? Proverb 16:18, to be precise?'

O'Rourke was speechless.

'Pride goes before destruction, a haughty spirit before a fall. No more questions, Your Honour.'

The court erupted into a cacophony of noise before the judge slammed his hammer and shouted for quiet. When the public and press had settled down, he said, 'Bishop O'Rourke, you are excused. Resume your seat, please. This court will recess and resume tomorrow morning when we will hear concluding statements from the District Attorney and the Defence.'

* * *

The next morning the Defence and Prosecution were asked to make their final concluding remarks. The judge addressed the jury one last time before he sent them to consider their verdict in the case.

'Ladies and gentlemen of the jury, thank you for your patience and your valuable time. The case is now concluded and having heard the arguments by the Prosecution and the Defence, you must retire to consider the evidence and reach a decision. Do you find the defendant guilty or not guilty of the charges?

'The defendant is charged on four separate counts. Consider each of them in turn and come to a verdict on each of them. You must consider the evidence, not the opinion of either the District Attorney or the Defence Attorney, but the actual evidence presented to you and then decide "beyond a reasonable doubt" whether the defendant is guilty.

'I wish you well in your deliberations. Court is adjourned.'

The judge looked at his watch and recorded the time. It was 11.27am.

At 3.30pm that afternoon he was informed the jury had arrived at unanimous verdicts. He scheduled the court to resume at 4.30pm.

Once again, the courtroom was packed. Karan had explained to Conor, Maggie, Carole, Francis and Raymond that it was impossible to make any assumptions about the verdict. It was an uncomplicated case and therefore there was no reason for the jury to deliberate for days. She did not want them to read anything into the relatively quick decision.

The jury filed into court, followed by the defendants. Conor, Maggie, Carole, Ray and Matt, and Francis and his family all looked at each other in apprehension as they took their seats.

'All rise for the Right Honourable Judge R.J. Feeney.'

'Please be seated.'

This was it, the moment of truth. Karen sat poised and straight, outwardly calm, but waiting to hear if she'd won the most important case of her life.

The foreperson of the jury stood up and the judge asked him, 'Has the jury reached a unanimous verdict in each of the counts?'

Instinctively Conor reached out and took Maggie's hand, and Maggie Carole's, and so on until they all held hands.

'We have, Your Honour.'

'On count one, the possession of indecent images of children, how do you find the defendant?'

'We find the defendant Not guilty.'

There was a wave of cries and expletives around the court. The judge had to intervene to restore order. Maggie and Conor looked at each other in surprise.

'On count two, that the defendant did repeatedly rape a child, namely Peter Finnegan, how do you find the defendant?'

Everyone held their breath for those interminable few seconds.

'We find the defendant Guilty.'

'On count three, that the defendant did repeatedly rape a child, namely, Francis Finnegan, how do you find the defendant?'

'We find the defendant Guilty.'

Francis closed his eyes and squeezed his wife's hand.

'On count four, that the defendant did carry out an indecent assault and battery of a child, namely Raymond McCarthy, how do you find the defendant?'

'We find the defendant Guilty.'

Raymond McCarthy let out a 'yes' before bursting into tears of joy and relief. The courtroom exploded into spontaneous applause and cheers behind him.

'Order! Order! Orrrrrrder!!' the judge shouted.

It took some time to restore calm. Eventually, the judge instructed the guards to bring up Michael Finnegan from the cells for sentencing alongside Bishop Timothy O'Rourke. O'Rourke's face was ghostly white against his black suit. Finnegan was remarkably calm.

The judge began, 'Both of you have been found guilty of one of the most reprehensible crimes, the rape of an innocent child. Your evil behaviour drove one young person to take his own life, Peter Finnegan. Had he not fallen into your depraved hands, he might still be alive today living a normal life with his own children and grandchildren. I pray that with this verdict his soul may at last rest in peace.

'I want to thank the witnesses, Francis Finnegan and Raymond McCarthy, for showing courage, remarkable courage, for giving evidence against the defendants. Are the two individuals present, Madam District Attorney?'

'Yes, Your Honour, they are seated behind me.'

Judge Feeney looked directly at both men in turn and said, 'Thank you, Mr Finnegan. Thank you, Mr McCarthy. I hope that you will both take some solace from this verdict. You will both be in my prayers at church this Sunday.'

The judge turned his attention back to Finnegan and O'Rourke.

'The harm that you have both caused is immeasurable, simply immeasurable. That you both conspired to adopt vulnerable and isolated children from Ireland, only to sexually exploit those children, is simply evil. There is no other word to describe your depravity. And that you, Mr O'Rourke, stand there in your sheep's clothing only serves to highlight that depravity.

'Guards, have both defendants stand, please.

'Mr Michael Finnegan, I sentence you to life in prison, to serve a minimum of twenty years before you may be considered eligible for parole.

'Mr Timothy O'Rourke, I sentence you to life in prison, to serve a minimum of twenty years before you may be considered eligible for parole.

'Take the prisoners away.'

*　*　*

When Karan left the court, there was a huge media presence waiting in the public reception. She had hugged Conor, Maggie, Carole, Francis and Raymond immediately after the proceedings had ended. She was elated. She had never been this personally invested in a case. Though she knew O'Rourke could not be blamed for Rose's death or her own adoption, he represented everything that was rotten about much of the Church's hierarchy.

The room was in chaos as journalists and camera crews fought each other for the front row. She shouted that she intended to make an announcement. She gathered Conor, Maggie, Carole, Francis and Raymond behind her and her two Assistant DAs beside her before making her statement.

'Thank you, everyone. If you would please be quiet, I'd like to make a statement?

'Today, justice was done. I want to thank the jury for the verdicts and Judge Feeney for the sentences. They were no more than were deserved. I especially want to thank Francis Finnegan and Raymond McCarthy for having the courage to give evidence against both men. It took incredible courage.

'I also want to announce today that I will be establishing a Grand Jury to investigate the role of the Catholic Church here in Boston in the illegal human trafficking of thousands of vulnerable children from Ireland. Who were stolen from their mothers in Ireland and sent to the US.

'We know from previous cases and this case today that the sexual abuse of children was prevalent within the Catholic Church here in Boston. We also know that many within the hierarchy of the Church covered up that abuse. However, to date no one has been held accountable for that cover-up.

'Well, no more. The Grand Jury will be asked not just to examine and investigate instances and patterns of abuse but to investigate who was responsible for covering up that abuse. The conviction and sentencing of Bishop Timothy O'Rourke today is an illustration of our determination to uncover those who sexually molested children and also those men who enabled those horrible crimes by their silence.'

* * *

A week later Maggie organised a press conference attended by Carole, Karan, Francis and Conor. The meeting room in the Four Seasons Hotel in downtown Boston was crowded with journalists from the newspapers, radio and television. Maggie passed copies of a press statement to the people at the front and asked them to pass them back.

'Thank you, folks, for attending today. I've handed out a press statement you can take with you, and we are available for interviews after I make a brief statement.

'Following the trial and conviction of Bishop Timothy O'Rourke and Michael Finnegan, and the uncovering of evidence of large-scale human trafficking by the Catholic Church, a number of victims and survivors have decided to establish a campaign group, which we have named S-T-O-L-E-N.

'Following the Second World War, the Catholic Church in Ireland and here in the US sent tens of thousands of children from Ireland to cities like Boston. These children were shipped to the US like prize cattle for sale.

'The mothers of these children were confined in so-called mother and baby homes run by the Catholic Church, where they were treated horribly, where thousands of women and children died of malnutrition, disease and medical neglect.

'In many of these cases children were taken from their mothers against their wishes, stolen, and sent to the US for adoption. Mothers and children were torn apart and then kept apart for decades.'

Maggie turned and looked at Karan and Conor. She smiled at them both. Tears brimmed in her eyes as she announced, 'The Catholic Church stole my sister Faith – you know her as Karan O'Loughlin, the District Attorney for Boston.'

There was rumble of shocked exclamations and comments among the assembled media. A dozen photographers rushed forward to photograph Karan. Both Maggie and Karan were bombarded with a frenzy of questions.

'Today in the US and here in Boston there are thousands of adoptees who are totally unaware of who they are, or the circumstances under which they were adopted, just as my sister was until very recently. In Ireland there are thousands of mothers and siblings who have been searching for these beloved children, brothers and sisters. To date the Catholic Church have point-blank refused to open up their records and assist both mothers and children find their loved ones. In some cases, mothers have been searching for their children for seventy years.

'We are calling on the Catholic Church to open up its historic adoption records and to make that information available to those children who were adopted and those mothers or siblings who are searching for them here in the US.

'My family only recently discovered our sister Faith here in Boston. We have decided to donate one million dollars from the sale of our late father's home to the group STOLEN. We have appointed the organisation's first Chief Executive, Carole McKenna, to manage and develop the campaign group. Carole is an expert on adoption practices here.

'STOLEN will seek to assist victims and survivors to find their adoptive parents and siblings. The organisation will work closely with victims and survivors in Ireland to reunite families who were torn apart by the Catholic Church. We intend to organise support groups across the US, not just in Boston. We would appeal to victims to contact Carole and help us in this work.

'We also wish to announce that we intend to launch a class action against the Catholic Church. We are appealing to the victims of sexual abuse and the victims of this policy of human trafficking to contact us and join us in this legal case. Karan, acting in a private capacity, will be leading this class action.

'We are also calling on our political representatives in Congress to establish a federal investigation into the activities of the Catholic Church, particularly in respect of its historic adoption practices. This is a national scandal that requires a national response from our government.

'Thank you. Now any questions?'

POSTSCRIPT

When they landed in Dublin airport it was a cold, crisp December day. On board the flight were Maggie, Karan, Conor, Carole and Danny. Seated a few rows behind them were Francis, Milly and their three daughters.

The Ambassador had arranged for a luxury coach to bring them to their hotels. By the time they made their way through Dublin city centre it was late afternoon and the Christmas lights were flickering into life. As night eventually fell, the group exchanged glances and smiles. There was something magical about the atmosphere. They all felt it.

Carole had been in contact with Paddy Cunningham from the victims' and survivor's group and he had booked a large meeting room in Wynn's Hotel for that evening and an evening meal for a party of twenty for 7.30pm. But before the meal he had arranged for Mary to be there with her daughters to meet Francis and his family.

Francis was incredibly nervous but equally excited. He felt as if he were being born again. Mary was overwhelmed with emotion at the prospect of finally being reunited with the boy she had always loved and wanted.

* * *

Earlier that evening Mary sat on a little stool in front of her bedroom dressing table preparing for the meeting. She looked at herself in the mirror, at the fine wrinkles and white hair. Where had all those years gone? They had flown by in an instant, it seemed now. She thought, *Sure isn't that the wisdom of old age. We only look back with our regrets when there is so little time ahead.*

At one period in her life she had thought she had been cursed, but then she realised she had been blessed in so many ways, by her late husband, her daughters and her grandchildren. And now she had finally found Francis, her only boy.

She pushed herself up off the stool and crossed the room to the side of her bed.

With some difficulty she knelt down and began a prayer of thanks.

'Hail Mary full of grace, the Lord is with thee ...'

*   *   *

That evening Francis and his family waited in the room for Mary to arrive. As the time of the meeting approached, their excitement grew. Milly could feel Francis shaking.

Finally, the door opened, and Mary entered, followed by her daughters and granddaughter. Across the room Mary and Francis locked eyes upon one another and began to cry. They walked slowly into each other's arms and embraced. They held each other, quietly. Both of them had waited a lifetime for this moment. Mary spoke aloud.

'My beautiful boy.'

She placed her two aged and fragile hands on his face and looked him in the eye.

'My darlin' Francis. The nuns took you from me, my love. I have searched for you for more than sixty years. Welcome home. *Fáilte abhaile, mo chroí.*'

The next day Danny picked up a hire car and drove the five of them to Tuam in the West of Ireland. The Gaelic word 'Tuam' meant, somewhat prophetically, 'mound' or 'burial ground'.

It had been nearly thirty years since Danny had visited the shrine that had sat on the former grounds of the mother and baby home, but he had no difficulty in finding the place again. In the years since the home had been demolished, houses had been built on most of the former grounds. In addition, the local authority had built a children's play park beside the little shrine to Our Lady that had been constructed by some local residents.

Some of the older residents told of occasionally hearing the ghostly sounds of happy children laughing and playing late at night and had built the shrine close to the septic tank where the poor 'illegitimate' babies had been secretly buried.

Danny turned into the old Dublin Road estate and parked beside a narrow lane that ran between two houses that led into the children's park.

Everyone got out of the car and followed Danny along the lane, across the park, to a section of ground that was now sealed off by a high wooden fence. Karan had spoken to the US Ambassador, who in turn was able to arrange access to the site.

They were met at the entrance by a security guard and a civil servant who had travelled from Dublin to escort them onto the site. He explained that they would have to be careful because the site was effectively an archaeological dig. However, the shrine had been left intact.

Danny and Carole stepped back and told Maggie, Conor and Karan to go in alone. The civil servant led them around the edge of what must have been a large rectangular hole. The location of the underground septic tank. It was now covered to prevent the excavated space from flooding or being damaged. He took them to the small shrine that sat in the corner of the space directly behind some of the homes on the estate.

It was beautiful. She was beautiful. The statue of Our Lady was perhaps about two-thirds of a metre in height standing on a raised mound surrounded by rough stone that had been built in the shape of a covered grotto. The inside of the grotto had been painted a pristine white, silhouetting the figure, giving her a luminous glow. The figurine was immaculate, despite the excavation work that had taken place around her. White wildflowers and purple heather grew either side of the grotto.

Karan, Maggie and Conor stood in front of the shrine and reached for each other's hands. Each of them was lost in their own private thoughts. Karan thought about her mother. Why had she named her Faith? She realised that the name had significance for her. It was more than just a name; it was a testament, a prayer from the grave. A statement of her love for James and for her that had whispered faintly across the decades and halfway around the world but had still somehow, beyond reason and understanding, found Maggie and Conor and then her. The three of them wept softly for Rose and for their father. But it was Faith who knelt and placed a bouquet of yellow roses and a little black and white photo of Rose and James at the foot of the shrine and whispered softly to her mother, 'I love you.'

AUTHOR'S NOTE

Between 1922 and 1998, approximately 56,000 women spent time in eighteen mother and baby homes across the twenty-six counties of Ireland. Thousands more passed through similar homes in the North of Ireland. Many thousands more passed through other institutions, such as the Magdalene laundries. It would be reasonable to suggest that close to 100,000 women were dispatched to one of these institutions.

These were harsh places where unmarried women were sent to have their babies or after they had their babies. They often arrived alone and destitute, having been denied support by either their child's father or their own family simply for falling pregnant outside of marriage.

Many of the women who were sent to these homes suffered terribly. In countless cases their children were taken from them against their wishes and sent illegally to the United States for adoption.

Today, this is considered child trafficking.

* * *

In the following pages two courageous campaigners, as well as victims and survivors themselves, describe how the brutal experience of these mother and baby homes impacted upon them and their families.

ANNA'S STORY

My name is Anna Corrigan, and both my parents were survivors of Ireland's regime of institutional abuse. I also have other family members who were touched by and lost to this system, two brothers born to my mother Bridget Dolan in the Tuam mother and baby home. One of my brothers lies in a septic tank together with the other 795 angels, and my other brother has been a missing person since the age of seven months, probably illegally adopted. My father's sister Aunt Mollie died aged thirteen in an industrial school in Loughrea, County Galway, and the nuns will not tell me where she is dumped.

My father, William Corrigan, together with his siblings were incarcerated for ten years each in industrial homes after their mother died of TB, when they were taken from their father aged seven, six and five, and sentenced through the courts and handed to the Religious to 'rear' them. Somebody, in their wisdom, thought that they would do a better job than leaving them in the bosom of their family.

My mother had two journeys through Ireland's mother and baby home system. She gave birth to my brother John in 1946 and spent one year there working and slaving to pay for her keep and her 'sin'. She left in 1947 and went to care for a nun's mother and remained there till the woman died in late in that year. She then moved on again to work in service, where she fell pregnant once again in 1950 and returned to the Tuam mother and baby home and gave birth to my brother William. William is marked as 'dead' in the ledgers of the home but does not have a death certificate, a reason for death or a medical certification of death and is not listed as having been one of the 796 who died in the Tuam home.

I sound very knowing of all these facts, but I only learned this in 2012 when I decided to do some family research. My father had died in 1975 and my mother in 2001, and I knew nothing of the lives they had led before they married and had me, which led me on a journey at the age of fifty-six to discover a family history that was both shocking and sad.

Ireland, the so-called Land of Saints and Scholars, had a very, very dark underbelly and if you fell foul of the system, you could suffer a fate worse than death.

I know now that what they went through led them to keep this part of their lives secret. This was a part of their lives that could not be spoken about in polite company. The stigma that was attached to those who went through this system was a burden that was to be carried as a penance. 'Fear' and 'shame', 'suffering' and 'silence', all words synonymous with the stigma of having been part of the network of these so-called 'homes'.

In 2013 I brought the matter of my brother to the police and in May 2014 I brought my story to the attention of journalist Alison O'Reilly. Together with the research of Catherine Corless, she ran an article in the *Mail on Sunday* on 25 May 2014 with the headline 'A Mass Grave of 800 Babies'. The world responded with shock and horror.

On foot of this a Commission of Inquiry was set up to look into a select number of mother and baby and county homes. It commenced its work in 2015 and trundled on till 2020 with delay after delay. It had great difficulty getting access to records – one has to wonder why – and eventually produced a report that wasn't fit for purpose.

We are still here and none the wiser. I have had to work diligently in the background digging and searching for any scraps that would lead me closer to answers about my family because I never believed that the Commission would provide them.

What occurred in these so-called homes has left a legacy of intergenerational damage and hurt. Here I am now, sixty-five years of age, a mother to two and a grandmother of four and the clock is ticking. My family has been robbed of the right to know their own, for my children to have uncles and cousins and my grandchildren to know their history. I believe that my brother was illegally trafficked to the US for adoption, based on what I was told by a family member, perhaps to Boston, but who knows? The Catholic Church knows – the records of these adoptions are hidden somewhere.

The Government in Ireland has failed to give us answers. It was so deeply enmeshed with the Church that it is in fear of getting to the truth. We lived in a country where Church and State worked hand in hand to deprive women of their basic human rights and to deprive their children of those same rights and, in a lot of cases, even their precious lives. The State has prevaricated; it has obstructed and denied us what was our due, justice for the egregious breaches of our family's human rights.

Reading *Stolen Faith*, I see my mother in all her youthful innocence, a young woman full of hopes and dreams. Was she deeply and blindingly in love like Rose? Was she let down and forced to travel this dark road on her own, to give birth to her children alone and afraid? Did she reach out again blindly in the hope of finding some comfort only to find herself right back where she started? Did her family and the Church interfere and end those dreams just like what happened to Rose? Or were her pregnancies a result of rape or abuse? I choose to believe that it was love's young dream, but we simply do not know.

Rose paid the ultimate price for love, her dreams crushed by those same ingrained misogynistic and patriarchal beliefs that rule the lives of women. Read this book and cry and never forget her. *Stolen Faith* is a very powerful and moving story that speaks a dark and troubling truth.

Anna Corrigan
2021

JOAN'S STORY

My name is Joan McDermott. I am a survivor of the Bessborough mother and baby home in Cork.

My story begins in 1967, when at the age of seventeen and a half I became pregnant. My boyfriend had no means to support me; I had just left school and was unemployed. I was three months pregnant when I informed my mother. The next day she asked me to pack a bag, as I could not stay at home. I would only bring disgrace to my family.

I sat in the car, not knowing where I was being taken. The journey was unfamiliar to me. The car turned in through large gates, down a very long driveway, to a bleak-looking Georgian house with broad steps leading to a red door. The house was surrounded by beautifully manicured lawns.

My mother walked me to the door. Her silence was deafening. A stern-faced nun opened the door and my mother turned on her heel and left me there without saying another word.

Once inside, I was terrified. The nun said, 'Now that you are here, there are three things you must obey. One, I will give you a false name which you must use at all times. You are not to divulge your real identity to anyone. Two, you will have no contact with the outside world. Three, if you attempt to escape, the Guards will catch you and return you.'

I slept in a four-bed dormitory, which was cold and sparsely decorated. The routine was monotonous and mundane. Mass every morning. All meals eaten in silence. Only one hour of free time in the evening before bedtime strictly at 9pm.

All the young women were allocated chores. As I had arrived in the home mid-summer, along with the other pregnant women, I was assigned the job of cutting the lawns on my knees with a small pair of scissors. During the winter, my job was washing and then polishing the wooden floors in the long corridors.

One day ran into the next. My pregnancy progressed, but I was clueless as to what was to come. One day in December while I was washing a floor, I felt a sharp pain. When I told the nun, she told me my suffering was paying for the awful sin I had committed. She was so unkind and showed me absolutely no compassion.

That evening my pains became much worse. I told another nun. She put me in a small room with a single bed, locked the door behind her and left me there until 8am the next morning. By then I was almost ready to give birth. I begged for pain relief but was denied it. I was told I had done the Devil's work and now I could repent for my sins.

I gave birth to my son, but I was only allowed access to him when the bell rang for feeding. All babies were locked in a nursery and the mothers were not allowed in except at feeding time.

I breastfed my son. One day whilst breastfeeding, a nun bent over me and tore my son from my arms. She ran down a long corridor and disappeared through a large set of double doors with him. He was seven weeks old, and I was never allowed to see him again.

Two days later my mother arrived at the home and collected me. Soon after I was sent to stay with an aunt who lived in the UK. I was forbidden to ever speak of the child. My body and soul were screaming out for my son. I was silently grieving, but my grief was never acknowledged.

My life in the UK spanned over forty years. I learned to live with what others told me was to be kept a 'secret', with my 'shame'. I coped, but I always had this pain in my heart. I always had this belief, this vision, that I would return to Ireland and search for answers about what had happened to my son. My son was stolen from me without my consent, without my permission.

I returned to Ireland in 2000. A year later I began to search for my son. From the outset I was met with strong opposition. I was told I was wasting my time because all the records had been destroyed in a fire. I continued to navigate my way through a dysfunctional bureaucratic system, but I persevered for fifteen years, and my persistence finally paid off.

I received a phone call from a social worker informing me my son had been found. The sad irony was that for nine of those fifteen years that I was searching for him, he was also searching for me.

Five years ago, I finally met my son after forty-seven years. I cannot articulate the mixture of emotions I felt, but now he is an integral part of my family and is very much loved.

I opted to give my testimony to the Commission of Inquiry. It retraumatised me by revisiting the depths of my emotions, but I was determined to tell the truth in order to get justice.

Its report was finally published on 12 January 2021, but it failed to address the violation of my human rights and that of my son. From the very first page it was clear the report wasn't going to address the fundamental injustices I had experienced. The opening few sentences had already contributed to the narrative that has denied survivors of the justice they deserved, including the many hundreds of babies who did not survive.

The mealy-mouthed apologies from some religious orders as well as the Catholic hierarchy feed further into the same narrative. Misogyny was the reason and the only reason why shame and stigma were attached to any woman who became pregnant out of marriage. The valley of squinting windows, created by a misogynistic Church and State, forced them to treat women and their children as outcasts.

The injustice and cruelty with which women and babies were treated was manifest. It may not have been enshrined in statute – it was unwritten – but it was sacrosanct. A land where politicians did the misogynistic Church's bidding.

They say all fiction reflects life in some way and *Stolen Faith* is a book with an unapologetic and thoroughly realistic portrayal of how an oppressive and brutally misogynistic culture led to the stigmatisation of unmarried mothers and their children. The novel depicts the real complicity of the religious orders in arranging the trafficking of thousands of children to America for adoption. With tragic consequences for many.

It is a poignant, emotive read of a dark and shameful period in our history that must never be forgotten.

Joan McDermott

2021

CHRONOLOGY

1925

A former poorhouse in Tuam is taken over by the Catholic Bon Secours order and turned into a mother and baby home for unwed mothers and their children. A harsh and cruel regime is established by the order. The order is paid a fee by the county council for each mother and child they take in.

1939

Department of Health Inspector Alice Litster reports to government:

> The chance of survival of an illegitimate infant born in the slums and placed with a foster-mother in the slums a few days after birth is greater than that of an infant born in one of our special homes for unmarried mothers.

She is ignored.

1943

By 1943 death rates of children born in the Tuam home reach a staggering 34 percent, many times the national average.

1947

The Tuam home records its highest number of infant deaths in a single year, 52.

1950

Adoption legislation is introduced by the government. In the following years there is a significant drop in the number of recorded deaths of children in the homes, indicating that the nuns may have been registering some previous adoptees as deceased and falsifying death certificates before sending the children to the US, including the city of Boston, for adoption.

1961

Tuam mother and baby home closes.

1972

The Tuam home is demolished.

1975

Children playing on the grounds of the former home in Tuam discover an underground chamber 'filled to the brim' with human bones. The Gardaí and parish priest attend the site but indicate that the remains are most likely a Famine grave, despite the fact there is no record of such a grave existing. Some residents erect a shrine to Our Lady on the site of the find. Rumours persist that the bodies of poor 'illegitimate' babies were secretly buried there.

2002

The Boston *Globe* Spotlight team publishes an exposé that proves that the Catholic hierarchy and Cardinal Bernard Law were aware that some priests had abused children but simply moved them to other parishes within Boston, where they went on to abuse more children, including altar boys. One priest, John J. Geoghan, who was a prolific and persistent child abuser, was moved to several different parishes across Boston over a thirty-year period. During that time, he abuses over 100 children.

The *Globe* uncovers sealed legal files that indicate that Cardinal Law and five other senior clerics, who were subsequently promoted to bishops in other parts of the US, were aware of Geoghan's activities but did nothing to stop him.

2010

The remains of 222 children are discovered in an unmarked grave on the grounds of the Bethany mother and baby home in Dublin.

2012

Local historian Catherine Corless publishes a piece in the *Journal of the Old Tuam Society* claiming that as many as 796 children may have been secretly buried in an old septic tank in the grounds of the former Tuam mother and baby home.

2013

The popular film *Philomena* is released and tells the story of one courageous Irish mother's fifty-year-old quest to find the child who was taken from her and adopted against her wishes.

2014/2015

Following public outrage at the allegations, such as cruelty to women, forced adoptions and child trafficking across borders, the government appoints a Commission of Investigation to examine the claims.

The Commission is asked to examine eighteen mother and baby homes in total across the State, including the one in Tuam. However, it is not asked to investigate either the Magdalene laundries or industrial schools, where thousands of mothers and children were also held.

2015

The *Irish Examiner* publishes a report that, following the discovery of old adoption records, the HSE now believes that up to 1,000 children may have been illegally 'trafficked from the Home' for adoption, many of them to the US. The HSE internal report on the adoptions states:

> This may prove to be a scandal that dwarfs other more recent issues with Church and State.

2017

An Expert Technical Group is appointed to begin examining the site in Tuam. During an examination of the sceptic tank pathologist Professor

Marie Cassidy records seeing in one chamber identifiable skulls and long bones. 'The bones were in a haphazard arrangement, with no indication of having been encoffined or laid out.'

The *New York Times* publishes an in-depth piece on the Tuam mother and baby Home entitled 'The Lost Children of Tuam' by Dan Barry. The piece documents the horrific treatment of the mothers and children by the nuns and the extraordinarily high level of infant mortalities. Children regularly died of measles, influenza, gastroenteritis, meningitis, whooping cough, tuberculosis and, frequently, severe undernourishment or 'marasmus', as it was euphemistically called. The piece records one local resident who remembers the children within the home being described by one teacher in a nearby school as 'The children of the devil'.

The Northern Ireland Executive commissions an investigation of the mother and baby homes and Magdalene laundries from 1922 to 1990 within its jurisdiction. This includes both Catholic- and Protestant-run institutions. Between those dates over 10,500 women entered these institutions; 58 percent of those women were aged between twenty and twenty-nine. Another 38 percent were under nineteen. According to the report:

> In the majority of testimony gathered on these four homes, women provided vivid accounts of being made to feel ashamed about their pregnancy and suggested that the atmosphere was authoritarian and judgemental.

The harsh treatment experienced by many young women led to a legacy of mental health issues for many of those who gave birth there.

There were records of dozens of children being moved across the border to the Republic of Ireland and subsequently being adopted by couples there. Given the number of recorded examples, it would be reasonable to assume that the actual figure may have numbered in the hundreds over the decades in question. There were a small number of recorded adoptions to the US.

2018

The book *My Name is Bridget* is published and tells the tragic story of Bridget Dolan and her two sons, both of whom were born in the Tuam home, one of whom perished and is believed to be buried there.

Pope Francis visits Ireland but declines to visit Tuam or to meet with the victims and survivors of the mother and baby homes.

2021

Following the initial North of Ireland report in 2017, the Executive agrees to establish a full independent investigation into the mother and baby homes and Magdalene laundries in the Northern jurisdiction. The Executive appears to have learned some valuable lessons from the experience and the criticisms from victims of the report delivered by the Commission in the Republic. A team of experts is asked to work with victims and survivors of the homes to help co-design an agreed terms of reference for the investigation.

The Commission of Investigation into the mother and baby homes in the Republic of Ireland finally delivers its report to the government and it is published.

It finds that approximately 56,000 women and 57,000 children passed through the homes. More than 25,000 other women and many more children again passed through other institutions not investigated by the Commission. This Commission concludes that this was probably the highest number of unmarried women that passed through similar institutions anywhere in the world. Of those women, 80 percent were aged between eighteen and twenty-nine; 11.4 percent of the documented cases were under eighteen years of age.

A total of approximately 9,000 children died in the 18 mother and baby homes under investigation. According to the report:

In the years before 1960 mother and baby homes did not save the lives of 'illegitimate' children; in fact, they appear to have significantly reduced the prospects of survival.

The highest rate of infant mortality was recorded in the Bessborough home in Cork in 1943, when 75 percent of all children born that year died before their first birthday.

By 1967 the proportion of 'illegitimate' children being adopted was 97 percent, the highest in the world.

The Commission identifies 200 women who died in the mother and baby homes.

It states that institutional records show that just 1,427 children were officially placed for adoption in the US. The Commission records that there were many 'allegations' of large fees being paid by adopting parents to church institutions but despite the volumes of testimony evidence, states that:

Such allegations are impossible to prove and impossible to disprove.

Following the publication of the Commission report, victims and survivors condemn its findings as incomplete, a copout and worse. The Commission had received 550 witness testimonies and statements from victims and survivors but had decided to categorise them as allegations and not as witness evidence. The extensive witness evidence of cruelty and abuse, of forced adoptions and the illegal trafficking of adopted children was largely ignored.

Catherine Corless, who did so much to uncover the scandal of the Tuam burials, said that the response from the survivors whom she knew was one of deep disappointment. That disappointment soon turned to anger. She also criticised the Commission for skimming over the issue of illegal adoptions. She wanted to know if the Commission would identify who was responsible for discarding the bodies of babies and toddlers in a sceptic tank in the Tuam home.

It did not!

DEATH RECORDS

MOTHER AND BABY HOME, TUAM, GALWAY

These deaths are listed from the first, Patrick Derrane, aged five months, who died on 22 August, 1925, to the last, Mary Carty, aged 4½ months, who died on 15 January, 1960.

Patrick Derrane, 5 months
Mary Blake, 3½ months
Matthew Griffin, 3 months
Mary Kelly, 6 months
Peter Lally, 11 months
Julia Hynes, 1 year
James Murray, 4 weeks
Joseph McWilliam, 6 months
John Mullen, 2½ months
Mary Wade, 3 years 3 months
Maud McTigue, 6½ years
Bernard Lynch, 3 years
Martin Shaughnessy, 1½ years
Bridget Glynn, 1 year
Margaret Glynn, 1 year
Patrick Gorham, 1 year 9 months
Patrick O'Connell, 1 year
John Carty, 1 year 9 months
Madeline Bernard, 2½ years
Maureen Kenny, 8 years
Kathleen Donohue, 1 year
Thomas Donelan, 2¼ years
Mary Quilan, 2½ years
Mary King, 9 months
Mary Warde, 1¾ years
George Coyne, 2½ years
Julia Cummins, 1½ years
Barbara Folan or Wallace, 9 months
Pauline Carter, 11 months
Mary Walsh, 1 year
Annie Stankard, 10 months
John Connelly, 9 months
Anthony Cooke, 1 month
Michael Casey, 2 years 9 months
Annie McCarron, 2 years 3 months
Patricia Dunne, 2 months

John Carty, 3 months
Peter McNamara, 7 weeks
Mary Shaughnessy, 4½ months
Joseph Coen, 5 months
Mary Murphy, 2 months
Patrick Kelly, 2½ months
Martin Rabbitte, 6 weeks
Kathleen Quinn, 7 months
Patrick Halpin, 2 months
Martin McGuinness, 6 months
Mary Kate Connell, 3½ months
Patrick Raftery, 7 months
Patrick Paterson, 5 months
James Murray, 1½ months
Colman O'Loughlin, 5½ months
Agnes Canavan, 1½ years
Christina Lynch, 1¼ years
Mary O'Loughlin, 6 months
Annie O'Connor, 1 year 3 months
John Greally, 11 months
Joseph Fenigan, 3 years 9 months
Mary Connolly, 2 months
James Muldoon, 4 months
Joseph Madden, 3 months
Mary Devaney, 1½ years
Michael Gannon, 6½ months
Bridget Cunningham, 2 months
Margaret Conneely, 1½ years
Patrick Warren, 8¼ months
James Mulryan, 1 month
Mary Kate Fahey, 3 years
Mary Mahon, 1¼ months
Martin Flanagan, 1 month
Mary Forde, 4 months
Patrick Hannon, 1 year 8 months
Michael Donellan, 6 months

Joseph Ward, 7 months

Walter Jordan, 3 years

Mary Mullins, 35 days

Peter Christian, 7 months

Mary Cunningham, 5 months

James Ryan, 9 months

Patrick O'Donnell, 9 months

Mary Monaghan, 4 years

Patrick O'Malley, 1 year

Philomena Healy, 11 months

Michael Ryan, 1 year

Patrick J Curran, 6 months

Patrick Fahy, 2½ months

Laurence Molloy, 5 months

Patrick Lynskey, 6 months

Vincent Nally, 1¾ years

Mary Grady, 1½ years

Martin Gould, 1¾ years

Patrick Kelly, 2½ months

Bridget Quinn, 1 year

William Reilly, 9 months

George Lestrange, 7 months

Christy Walsh, 1¼ years

Margaret Mary Gagen, 1 year

Patrick Moran, 3½ months

Celia Healy, 4¾ months

James Quinn, 3½ years

Bridget Walsh, 1¼ years

Patrick Shiels, 4 months

Mary Teresa Drury, 1 year

Peter O'Brien, 1½ years

Peter Malone, 1½ years

Mary Burke, 10 months

Carmel Moylan, 8 months

Mary Josephine Garvey, 4½ months

Mary Warde, 10 months

Catherine Howley, 8½ months

Michael Patrick McKenna, 3 months

Richard Raftery, 2½ months

Margaret Doorhy, 8 months

Mary McDonagh, 1 year

Patrick Leonard, 9 months

Mary Coyne, 1 year

Mary Kate Walsh, 2 years

Christina Burke, 1 year

Mary Margaret Jordan, 1½ years

John Joseph McCann, 8 months

Teresa McMullan, 1 year

George Gavin, 1 year

Joseph O'Boyle, 2 months

Peter Nash, 1 year

Bridget Galvin, 3 months

Margaret Niland, 2½ years

Christina Quinn, 3 months

Kathleen Cloran, 9½ years

Annie Sullivan, 8 months

Patricia Judge, 1 year

Mary Birmingham, 9 months

Laurence Hill, 11 months

Brendan Patrick Pender, 1 month

Kate Fitzmaurice, 4 months

[None] Mulkerrins, 5 days

Angela Madden, 3 months

Mary Christina Shaughnessy, 36 days

Mary Moloney, 11 months

Patrick Joseph Brennan, 5 weeks

Anthony O'Toole, 2 months

Mary Cloherty, 9 days

Joseph Fahy, 10 months

Mary Finola Cunniffe, 6 months

Martin Cassidy, 5 months

Francis Walsh, 2½ months

Mary Garvey, 4 months

Kathleen Gilchrist, 8 months

Mary Kate Walsh, 6 weeks

Eileen Fallon, 1½ years

Harry Leonard, 3/12 years

Mary Kate Guilfoyle, 3 months

John Callinan, 3 months

John Kilmartin, 2 months

Julia Shaughnessy, 3 months

Patrick Prendergast, 6 months

Bridgid Holland, 2 months

Bridgid Moran, 1 4/12 years

Margaret Mary Fahy, 1½ years

Bridgid Ryan, 9 months

Mary Brennan, 4 months

Mary Conole, 1 month

John Flattery, 2 2/12 years

Margaret Donohue, 10/12 year

Joseph Dunn, 3 years

Owen Lenane, 2½ months

Josephine Steed, 4/12 years

Mary Meeneghan, 4/12 years

James McIntyre, 3/12 years

Sheila Tuohy, 9 years

Margaret Mary O'Gara, 2 months

John Joseph Murphy, 4 months

Eileen Butler, 2 months

Thomas Molloy, 2 months

James Joseph Bodkin, 6 months

John Kelly, about 2½ months

Mary Walsh, 6 months

Mary Josephine Colohan, 4 months

Florence Conneely, 7 months

Norah McCann, 6 weeks

Mary Kelly, 9 months

Rose O'Dowd, 6 months

Mary Egan, 4 months

Michael Concannon, 4 months

Paul Joyce, 10 months

Mary Christina Kennedy, 4 months

Bridget Finnegan, 2½ months

Mary Flaherty, 3 months

Thomas McDonagh, 4 months

Joseph Hoey, 13 months

Teresa Cunniffe, 3 months

Joseph Clohessy, 2 months

Mary Kiely, 4 months

Thomas Cloran, 6 months

Mary Burke, 3 months

Mary Margaret Flaherty, 4 months

John Keane, 17 days

Luke Ward, 1¼ years

Mary O'Reilly, 5 months

Ellen Mountgomery, 1½ years

Mary Elizabeth Lydon, 4 months

Brigid Madden, 1 month

Mary Margaret Murphy, 4 months

Mary Nealon, 7 months

Stephen Linnane, 3½ months

Josephine Walsh, 1 year

Kate Cunningham, 2 months

Mary Bernadette Hibbett, 1 month

Thomas Linnane, 3½ months

Patrick Lane, 3 months

Mary Anne Conway, 2 months

James Kane, 8 months

Christopher Leech, 3 months

Elizabeth Ann McCann, 5 months

Margaret Mary Coen, 2 months

John O'Toole, 7 months

John Creshal, 3½ months

Mary Teresa Egan, 3 months

Michael Boyle, 3 months

Anthony Mannion, 6 weeks

Donald Dowd, 5 months

Peter Ridge, 4 months

Eileen Collins, 2 months

Mary Brennan, 2 months

Michael Linnane, 1 year 3 months

Bridget Glenane, 5 weeks

James Fahy, 5 months

Bridget Geraghty, 11 days

Patrick Joseph Hynes, 4 months

Martin Hannon, 6 months

Martin Coyne, 7 months

Mary Nuala Leech, 1 year

Michael Monaghan, 3½ months

Patrick Aiden O'Donnell, 2 months

Martin Baker, 3 months

Mary Browne, 4 months

Angela Daly, 1 year

Mary Teresa Joyce, 5 months

Francis Coy, 6 months

Margret Rose McLoughlin, 4 months

Mary Philomena Walsh, 7 months

Joan Gleeson, 14 months

Michael Joseph Fahy, 1 year 5 months

Michael John Walsh, 7 months

Annie Corcoran, 11 months

Michael Mee, 13 months

Kathleen Hynes, 10 months

John Coyne, 1 year 4 months

Michael O'Toole, 1 year 5 months

Michael Edward Feeney, 13 months

Alfred Conroy, 1 year 8 months

Margaret Ryan, 1 year 10 months

Mary Kate O'Reilly, 1 year

Patrick Joyce, 13 months

Edward Munnelly, 7 months

Bernadette Leech, 1½ years

Thomas Flaherty, 3 years

Teresa Cummins, 3 weeks

Edward Desmond Kilbane, 2½ years

Margaret Scanlon, 3½ years

Mary Bridget Larkin, 8 months

Brian O'Malley, 4 months

Michael Madden, 6 months

Mary Kate Cahill, 2 weeks

Mary Margaret Lydon, 3 months

Festus Sullivan, 1 month

Annie Curley, 3 weeks

Nuala Lydon, 5 months

Bridget Collins, 5 weeks

Patrick Joseph Coleman, 1 month

Joseph Hannon, 6 weeks

Henry Monaghan, 3 weeks

Michael Joseph Shiels, 7 weeks

Martin Sheridan, 5 weeks

John Patrick Loftus, 10 months

Patrick Joseph Murphy, 3 months

Catherine McHugh, 4 months

Mary Patricia Togher, 3½ months

Mary Kate Sheridan, 4 months

Mary Flaherty, 1 year 7 months

Eileen Conroy, 1 year

Mary Anne Walsh, 1 year 2 months

Eileen Quinn, 2 years 6 months

Patrick Burke, 9 months

Margaret Holland, 2 days

Joseph Langan, 6 months

Sabina Pauline O'Grady, 6 months

Patrick Qualter, 3¾ years

Mary King, 5 months

Mary Nee, 4 months

Martin Andrew Larkin, 14 months

Mary Keane, 3 weeks

Kathleen Veronica Cuffe, 5½ months

Margaret Linnane, 3½ months

Teresa Heneghan, 3 months

John Neary, 7 months

Patrick Madden, 4 months

Mary Cafferty, 2 months

Mary Kate Keane, 3 months

Patrick Hynes, 3 weeks

Annie Solan, 2 months

Charles Lydon, 9 months

Margaret Mullins, 6½ months

Mary Mulligan, 2 months

Anthony Lally, 5 months

Joseph Spelman, 6 weeks

Annie Begley, 3 months

Vincent Egan, 9 days

Nora Murphy, 5 months

Patrick Garvey, 6 months

Patricia Burke, 4 months

Winifred Barret, 2½ years

Agnes Marron, 3 months

Christopher Kennedy, 4½ months

Patrick Harrington, 7 days

Kathleen Devine, 2 years

Vincent Garaghan, 22 days

Ellen Gibbons, 6 months

Michael McGrath, 4 months

Edward Fraser, 3 months

Patrick McLoughlin, 4½ months

Bridget Lally, 1 year

Martin Healy, 4 months

Nora Duffy, 3 months

Margaret Higgins, 5 days

Patrick Egan, 6 months

Vincent Farragher, 11 months

Patrick Joseph Jordan, 3 months

Michael Hanley, 21 days

Catherine Gilmore, 3 months

Unknown (boy) Carney, 7½ hours

Annie Coyne, 3 months

Helena Cosgrave, 5 months

Thomas Walsh, 2 months

Unknown (boy) Walsh, 10 minutes

Kathleen Hession, 3½ months

Brigid Hurley, 10½ months

Ellen Beegan, 2 months

Mary Keogh, 1 year

Bridget Burke, 2½ months

Martin Reilly, 9 months

Martin Hughes, 11 months

Mary Connolly, 1 month

Mary Kate Ruane, 41 days

Joseph Mulchrone, 3½ months

Michael Williams, 14 months

Martin Moran, 7 weeks

James Henry, 5 weeks

Josephine Mahoney, 2 months

Bridget Staunton, 5 months

John Creaven, 13 days

Peter Lydon, 6 weeks

Patrick Joseph Ruane, 3½ months

Michael Quinn, 7½ months

Julia Coen, 6 days

Annie McAndrew, 5 months

John Walsh, 3 months

Patrick Flaherty, 6 months

Bernadette Purcell, 2½ years

Joseph Macklin, 33 hours

Thomas Duffy, 2 days

Elizabeth Fahy, 3½ months

James Kelly, 2 months

Nora Gallagher, 3½ months

Kathleen Cannon, 4 months

Winifred Tighe, 8 months

Christopher Williams, 1 year

Joseph Lynch, 1 year

Andrew McHugh, 1¼ years

William Glennan, 1½ years

Michael J Kelly, 5 months

Patrick Gallagher, 3 months

Michael Gerard Keane, 2 months

Ellen Lawless, 5½ months

Mary Finn, 2½ months

Martin Timlin, 3 months

Mary McLoughlin, 20 days

Mary Brennan, 5 months

Patrick Dominick Egan, 1 month

Nora Thornton, 1 5/12 year

Anne Joyce, 1 year

Catherine Kelly, 10 months

Michael Monaghan, 8 months

Simon John Hargraves, 6 months

Unknown (girl) Forde, 7 hours

Joseph Byrne, 2 months

Patrick Hegarty, 4 months

Patrick Corcoran, 1 month

James Leonard, 16 days

Jane Gormley, 22 days

Anne Ruane, 11 days

Patrick Munnelly, 3 months

John Lavelle, 6 weeks

Patrick Ruane, 24 days

Patrick Joseph Quinn, 3 months

Joseph Kennelly, 15 days

Kathleen Monaghan, 3 months

Unknown (girl) Quinn, 2 days

Anthony Roche, 3½ months

Annie Roughneen, 3 weeks

Anne Kate O'Hara, 3¾ months

Patrick Joseph Nevin, 3 months

John Joseph Hopkins, 3 months

Thomas Gibbons, 1 month

Winifred McTigue, 6½ months

Thomas Joseph Begley, 1½ months

Kathleen Heneghan, 25 days

Elizabeth Murphy, 4 months

Nora Farnan, 1 month

Teresa Tarpey, 1 month

Margaret Carey, 11 months

John Garvey, 6 weeks

Bridget Goldrick, 3½ months

Bridget White, 2½ months

Noel Slattery, 1 month

Mary Teresa Connaughton, 3½ months

Nora McCormack, 6 weeks

Joseph Hefferon, 5 months

Mary Higgins, 9 days

Mary Farrell, 21 days

Mary McDonnell, 1 month

Geraldine Cunniffe, 11 weeks

Michael Mannion, 3 months

Bridget McHugh, 7 months

Mary McEvady, 1½ years

Helena Walsh, 2½ months

William McDoell, 2 days

Michael Finn, 14 months

Mary Murphy, 10 months

Gertrude Glynn, 6 months

Joseph Flaherty, 7 weeks

Mary O'Malley, 4½ years

John Patrick Callanan, 13 days

Unknown (girl) McDonnell, ½ hour

Unknown (girl) McDonnell, ½ hour

Christopher Burke, 9 months

Stephen Connolly, 7½ months

Mary Atkinson, 6 months

Mary Anne Finegan, 7 weeks

Francis Richardson, 15 months

Michael John Rice, 6 months

Nora Carr, 3½ months

William Walsh, 16 months

Vincent Cunnane, 14 months

Eileen Coady, 10 months

Unknown (girl) Roache, 23 hours

Unknown (boy) Roache, 23 hours

Patrick Flannery, 2 months

John Dermody, 3 months

Margaret Spelman, 3½ months

Austin Nally, 3 months

Margaret Dolan, 2½ months

Vincent Finn, 8½ months

Bridget Grogan, 6 months

Thomas Patrick Cloran, 9 weeks

Catherine Devere, 1 month

Mary Josephine Glynn, 24 hours

Annie Connolly, 9 months

Martin Cosgrove, 7 weeks

Catherine Cunningham, 2½ years

Bridget Hardiman, 1½ months

Mary Grier, 4½ months

Mary Patricia McCormick, 2 months

Brendan Muldoon, 5 weeks

Nora Moran, 7 months

Joseph Maher, 20 days

Teresa Dooley, 3 months

Daniel Tully, 6½ months

Brendan Durkan, 28 days

Sheila O'Connor, 3 months

Annie Coen, 5½ months

Patrick Joseph Kennedy, 6 days

Thomas Walsh, 2 months

Patrick Rice, 11½ months

Edward McGowan, 10¾ months

Brendan Egan, 10½ months

Margaret McDonagh, 35 days

Annie Josephine Donellan, 10 months

Thomas Walsh, 14 days

Bridget Quinn, 5¾ months

Mary Mulkerins, 5 weeks

Kathleen Parkinson, 10 months

Sheila Madeline Flynn, 3½ months

Patrick Joseph Maloney, 2 months

Bridget Carney, 7 months

Mary Margaret O'Connor, 6 months

Joseph Geraghty, 3 months

Annie Coen, 10 months

Martin Joseph Feeney, 3½ months

Anthony Finnegan, 3 months

Patrick Coady, 3 months

Unknown (male) Cunningham, 1½ hours

Annie Fahy, 3 months

Unknown (girl) Byrne, 18½ hours

Patrick Mullaney, 1 1/12 year

Thomas Connelly, 2½ months

Mary Larkin, 2 months

Margaret Kelly, 3½ months

Barbara McDonagh, 4 months

Mary O'Brien, 3¼ months

Keiran Hennelly, 1 1/6 years

Annie Folan, 3½ months

Unknown (girl) McNamara, 12 hours

Julia Murphy, 2½ months

John Rockford, 4 months

Vincent Geraghty, 1 year

Anthony Deane, 2 days

Unknown (boy) O'Brien, 2¼ days

Mary Teresa O'Brien, 15 days

John Connelly, 2¼ months

Bridget Murphy, 2¼ months

Patricia Dunne, 2 months

Francis Kinahan, 23 days

Joseph Sweeney, 20 days

Josephine O'Hagan, 6 months

Patrick Lavin, 1 month

Annie Maria Glynn, 13 months

Kate Agnes Moore, 1¾ months

Kevin Kearns, 1¼ years

Thomas Doocey, 1¼ years

William Conneely, 8 months

Margaret Spelman, 15½ months

Mary Kate Cullen, 1 5/6 years

Kathleen Brown, 3 years

Julia Kelly, 1 7/12 years

Mary Connolly, 7 years

Catherine Harrison, 2¼ years

Eileen Forde, 1¾ years

Michael Monaghan, 2 years

Mary Frances Lenihan, 3 days

Anthony Byrne, 6 months

Jarlath Thornton, 7 weeks

John Kelly, 6 days

Joseph O'Brien, 1½ years

Anthony Hyland, 2½ months

Unknown (boy) Murray, 8 hours

Unknown (girl) Murray, 10 hours

Joseph Francis McDonnell, 11 days

Mary Walsh, 1¼ years

Unknown (boy) Glynn, 16 hours

James Gaughan, 14½ months

Margaret Walsh, 3½ months

Mary Philomena Moran, 9 days

John Francis Malone, 7 days

Michael Francis Dempsey, 7 weeks

Christina Martha Greally, 3½ months

Teresa Donnellan, 42 days

Rose Anne King, 5 weeks

Christopher John Joyce, 1½ months

James Mannion, 7½ months

Mary Teresa Sullivan, 3 weeks

Patrick Holohan, 11 months

Michael Joseph Keane, 24 days

Bridget Keaney, 2 months

Joseph Flaherty, 8 days

Unknown (boy) Mahady, 3 days

James Rogers, 10 days

Kathleen Frances Taylor, 9 months

Gerard Christopher Hogan, 6½ months

Kathleen Corrigan, 2 months

Mary Connolly, 3 months

Patrick Joseph Farrell, 5 months

Patrick Laffey, 3¼ years

Fabian Hynes, 8 months

John Joseph Grehan, 2 years

Edward O'Malley, 2½ months

Mary Fleming, 5¾ months

Bridget Frances McHugh, 2½ months

Michael Folan, 1½ years

Oliver Holland, 6 months

Ellen Nevin, 7 months

Margaret Horan, 6 months

Peter Mullarky, 4 months

Mary Philomena O'Brien, 3¾ months

Teresa Frances O'Brien, 3½ months

Mary Kennedy, 18 months

Sara Ann Carroll, 3½ months

Unknown (girl) Maye, 5 days

Mary Devaney, 21 days

Anthony McDonnell, 6 months

Vincent Molloy, 7 days

John Patrick Lyons, 5 months

Gerald Aidan Timlin, 3 days

Patrick Costelloe, 17 days

Martin Dermott Henry, 43 days

John Francis O'Grady, 1 month

Bridget Mary Flaherty, 12 days

Josephine Finnegan, 1 year 8 months

Martin McGrath, 3 days

[None] Haugh, 10 minutes

James Frayne, 1 month

Mary Frances Crealy, 14 days

Mary Davey, 2 months

Patrick Joseph Hoban, 11 days

Angela Dolan, 3 months

Mary Lyden, 5 months

Bridget Coneely, 4 months

Austin O'Toole, 4 months

Bernard Laffey, 5 months

Mary Ellen Waldron, 8 months

Terence O'Boyle, 3 months

Mary Frances O'Hara, 1 month

Mary Devaney, 3 months

Bridget Foley, 6 months

Martin Kilkelly, 40 days

Thecla Monica Hehir, 6 weeks

Patrick Anthony Mitchell, 3 months

John Kearney, 4 months 3 weeks

John Joseph Kelly, 3 months

John Conneely, 4 months

Stephen Laurence O'Toole, 2 months

Thomas Alphonsus Buckley, 5 weeks

Michael John Gilmore, 2½ months

Patrick Joseph Monaghan, 2½ months

Mary Teresa Murray, 2 months

Patrick McKeighe, 1½ months

John Raymond Feeney, 2½ months

Finbar Noone, 2 months

John O'Brien, 21 days

Beatrice Keane, 5 years

Mary Philomena Veale, 5 weeks

Winifred Gillespie, 1 year

Anthony Coen, 10 weeks

Michael Francis Sheridan, 3 months

Anne Holden, 3 months

Martin Joseph O'Brien, 7 weeks

Winifred Larkin, 1 month

Patrick Thomas Coen, 1 month

Mary Bridget Joyce, 8 months

Geraldine Collins, 13 months

Mary Flaherty, 5 days

Vincent Keogh, 5 months

John Francis Healy, 10 days

Martin Jarlath Kennelly, 24 days

Patrick Keaveney, 1½ months

Philomena Flynn, 2 months

William Reilly, 8½ months

Margaret Nuala Concannon, 12 months

Patrick Joseph Fitzpatrick, 14 days

Joseph Cunningham, 2 months

Mary Josephine Flaherty, 13 months

Kathleen Murray, 3 years

John O'Connell, 2¼ years

Alphonsus Hanley, 1¾ years

Bridget Pauline Muldoon, 11 months

Patricia Christina Higgins, 5 months

Catherine Bridget Kennedy, 1½ months

John Desmond Dolan, 1¼ years

Stephen Joynt, 2 years

Catherine Teresa Kearns, 2 years

Margaret Hurney, 2 years

John Patton, 2 years

Patrick Joseph Williams, 1¼ years

Nora Hynes, 8 months

Anthony Donohue, 2½ years

Brendan McGreal, 13 months

Anthony Cafferky, 23 days

Nora Cullinane, 1½ years

Kathleen Daly, 2 years

Nora Conneely, 1¼ years

Mary Teresa Joyce, 13 months

Kenneth Anthony Ellesmere, 1 day

Mary Patricia Carroll, 4 months

Thomas Collins, 1 year 5 months

Margaret Mary Moloney, 3 months

Josephine Tierney, 8 months

Margaret Mary Deasy, 3 months

Martin Francis Bane, 3 months

Bridget Agatha Kenny, 2 months

Unknown (boy) Kelly, 14 hours

Mary Teresa Judge, 1¼ years

Paul Dominick Bennett, 2½ months

Mary Bridget Giblin, 1 1/12 years

Sarah Carroll, 8 months

Francis Brehany, 1 year

Patrick Kelly, 2½ years

James McDonnell, 4 months

Anne Conneely, 6 weeks

Josephine Staunton, 5 days

Kathleen Madden, 2 months

Mary Philomena Byrne, 8 weeks

Joseph Byrce, 3¾ months

Joseph Byrne, 10½ months

Kathleen Glynn, 3½ months

Augustine Jordan, 9 months

Michael Francis Dwyer, 1½ years

Noel Christopher Murphy, 1 1/6 years

Margaret Mary McNamee, 5½ months

Patrick Grealish, 6 weeks

Bernadette O'Reilly, 6½ months

John Joseph Carr, 3 weeks

Paul Gardiner, 10 months

Simon Thomas Folan, 9 weeks

Joseph Ferguson, 3 months

Peter Joseph Heffernan, 4 months

Patrick Joseph Killeen, 14 weeks

Stephen Halloran, 7 months

Teresa Grealish, 5 months

Mary Joyce, none given

John Keane, 3½ months

Mary Burke, 8½ months

Brigid McTigue, 11 weeks

Margaret Rose Broderick, 8 months

Martin Mannion, 2¼ months

Mary Margaret Riddell, 8 months

Thomas Joseph Noonan, 7 weeks

Peter Casey, 10 months

Michael Scully, 3 months

Unknown (boy) Lyons, 5 days

Hubert McLoughlin, 4 months

Mary Margaret Finnegan, 3 months

Nicholas Patrick Morley, 3 months

Teresa Bane, 6 months

Patrick Joseph Kennedy, 5 weeks

Michael Francis Ryan, 3 days

John Forde, 2 years

Mary Patricia Cunnane, 2½ months

Margaret Patricia Sheridan, 3½ months

Patrick Joseph Nevin, 3 months

Joseph Nally, 4½ months

Christopher Burke, 3 months

Anne Madden, 7 weeks

Bridget Teresa Madden, 1¾ months

Thomas Murphy, 3 months

Francis Carroll, 1½ months

Bridget Josephine Linnan, 9 months

Josephine Staunton, 8 days

Mary Ellen McKeigue, 7 weeks

Mary Josephine Mulchrone, 2¼ months

Catherine Higgins, 4¼ years

Catherine Anne Egan, 2½ months

Thomas McQuaid, 3 months 23 days

Dermott Muldoon, 3¾ months

Martin Hanley, 9 weeks

John Joseph Lally, 3 months

Brendan Larkin, 4½ months

Unknown (boy) Bell, 3 hours

Mary Josephine Larkin, 6½ months

Annie Fleming, 8¾ months

Colm Alphonsus McNulty, 1 month

Walter Flaherty, 3 months

Sarah Burke, 15 days

Mary Ann Boyle, 5 months

John Anthony Murphy, 4½ months

Joseph Augustine Colohan, 3¾ months

Christopher Martin Begley, 18 days

Catherine Ann Meehan, 4 months

Martin McLynskey, 5½ months

Mary Josephine Crehan, 3 months

Mary Ann McDonagh, 2 months

Joseph Folan, 22 days

Evelyn Barrett, 4 months

Paul Morris, 4 months

Peter Morris, 4¾ months

Mary Martyna Joyce, 1½ years

Mary Margaret Lane, 7 months

John Noone, 4 months

Anne Josephine McDonnell, 5½ months

Joseph Anthony Burke, 5½ months

Patrick Hardiman, 5½ months

Patrick Naughton, 12 days

Josephine Teresa Staunton, 2 days

John Joseph Mills, 4 months 3 weeks

Unknown (boy) Hastings, 3 hours

Mary Donlon, 4 months

Nora Connolly, 15 months

Anne Heneghan, 3 months

Mary Keville, 9 months

Martin Murphy, 5 months

Mary Barbara McDonagh, 5 months

Mary Philomena Logue, 5 months

Margaret Elizabeth Cooke, 6 months

Mary Ann Broderick, 1 year 2 months

Anne Marian Fahy, 3¾ months

Anne Dillon, 3½ months

Imelda Halloran, 2 years

Joseph Gavin, 10 months

Marian Brigid Mulryan, 10 months

Mary Christina Rafferty, 3 months

Nora Mary Howard, 3½ months

Francis Martin Heaney, 2 years 10 months

Joseph Dempsey, 3 months

Patrick Walsh, 3 weeks

Dermot Gavin, 2 weeks

Mary Christina Burke, 3½ years

Patrick Burke, 1 year 11 days

Gerard Connaughton, 11 months

Rose Marie Murphy, 2 9/12 years

Paul Henry Nee, 4½ months

Margaret Connaire, 3½ months

Stephen Noel Browne, 2 years

Oliver Reilly, 4 months

Peter Folan, 4 months

Baby (boy) Fallon, 4 days

Geraldine O'Malley, 6 months

Dolores Conneely, 7 months

Mary Maloney, 3½ months

Mary Carty, 4½ months